FAR-AWAY STORIES
by
WILLIAM J. LOCKE

JOHN LANE
THE BODLEY HEAD LTD

The Works of
William J. Locke

THE WORKS OF
WILLIAM J. LOCKE
AUTOGRAPH EDITION
Vol. XVII

BIBLIOGRAPHICAL NOTE

First Published	*1916*
Reprinted	*1916*
Reprinted	*1920*
Cheap Edition	*1922*
Reprinted	*1922*
Popular Cr. 8vo Edition	*1924*
Autograph Edition	*1926*

To the Reader

DEAR SIR OR MADAM,—

Good wine needs no bush, but a collection of mixed vintages does. And this book is just such a collection. Some of the stories I do not want to remain buried for ever in the museum files of dead magazine-numbers—an author's not unpardonable vanity; others I have resuscitated from the same vaults in the hope that they still may please you.

The title of a volume of short stories is always a difficult matter. It ought to indicate frankly the nature of the book, so that the unwary purchaser shall have no grievance (except on the score of merit, which is a different affair altogether) against either author or publisher. In my title I have tried to solve the problem. But why "Far-away"? Well, the stories cover a long stretch of years, and all were written in calm days far-away from the present convulsion of the world.

Anyhow, no one will buy the book under the impression that it is a novel, and, finding that it isn't, revile me as a cheat. And so I have the pleasure of offering it for your perusal with a clear conscience.

You, Dear Sir or Madam, have given me, this many a year, an indulgence beyond my deserts. Till now, I have had no opportunity of thanking you. I do so now with a grateful heart, and to you I dedicate the two stories that I love the best, hoping that they may excuse those for which you may not so much care, and that they may win continuance of that which is to me, both as a writer and as a human being, my most cherished possession, namely, your favourable regard for

Your most humble and obedient Servant to command,

W. J. LOCKE

February, 1916.

CONTENTS

FAR-AWAY STORIES

FAR-AWAY STORIES

THE SONG OF LIFE

NON cuivis homini contingit adire Corinthum. It is not everybody's good fortune to go to Corinth. It is also not everybody's good fortune to go to Peckham—still less to live there. But if you were one of the favoured few, and were wont to haunt the Peckham Road and High Street, the bent figure of Angelo Fardetti would have been as familiar to you as the vast frontage of the great Emporium which, in the drapery world, makes Peckham illustrious among London suburbs. You would have seen him humbly threading his way through the female swarms that clustered at the plate-glass windows—the mere drones of the hive were fooling their frivolous lives away over ledgers in the City—the inquiry of a lost dog in his patient eyes, and an unconscious challenge to Philistia in the wiry bush of white hair that protruded beneath his perky soft felt hat. If he had been short, he might have passed unregarded ; but he was very tall—in his heyday he had been six foot two—and very thin. You smile as you recall to mind the black frock-coat, somewhat white at the seams, which, tightly buttoned, had the fit of a garment of corrugated iron. Although he was so tall one never noticed the inconsiderable stretch of trouser below the long skirt. He always appeared to be wearing a truncated cassock. You

I

were inclined to laugh at this queer exotic of the Peckham Road until you looked more keenly at the man himself. Then you saw an old, old face, very swarthy, very lined, very beautiful still in its regularity of feature, maintaining in a little white moustache with waxed ends a pathetic braggadocio of youth ; a face in which the sorrows of the world seemed to have their dwelling, but sorrows that on their way thither had passed through the crucible of a simple soul.

Twice a day it was his habit to walk there ; shops and faces a meaningless confusion to his eyes, but his ears alert to the many harmonies of the orchestra of the great thoroughfare. For Angelo Fardetti was a musician. Such had he been born ; such had he lived. Those aspects of life which could not be interpreted in terms of music were to him unintelligible. During his seventy years empires had crumbled, mighty kingdoms had arisen, bloody wars had been fought, magic conquests been made by man over nature. But none of these convulsive facts had ever stirred Angelo Fardetti's imagination. Even his country he had well-nigh forgotten ; it was so many years since he had left it, so much music had passed since then through his being. Yet he had never learned to speak English correctly ; and, not having an adequate language (save music) in which to clothe his thoughts, he spoke very little. When addressed he smiled at you sweetly like a pleasant, inarticulate old child.

Though his figure was so familiar to the inhabitants of Peckham, few knew how and where he lived. As a matter of fact, he lived a few hundred yards away from the busy High Street, in Formosa Terrace, at the house of one Anton Kirilov, a musician. He had lodged with the Kirilovs for over twenty years—but

2

not always in the roomy splendour of Formosa Terrace.
Once Angelo was first violin in an important orchestra, a man of mark, while Anton fiddled away in
the obscurity of a fifth-rate music-hall. Then the
famous violinist rented the drawing-room floor of the
Kirilovs' little house in Clapham, while the Kirilovs,
humble folk, got on as best they could. Now things
had changed. Anton Kirilov was musical director of
a London theatre, but Angelo, through age and rheu-
matism and other infirmities, could fiddle in public
no more ; and so it came to pass that Anton Kirilov
and Olga, his wife, and Sonia, their daughter (to whom
Angelo had stood godfather twenty years ago), rioted
in spaciousness, while the old man lodged in tiny rooms
at the top of the house, paying an infinitesimal rent
and otherwise living on his scanty savings and such
few shillings as he could earn by copying out parts
and giving lessons to here and there a snub-nosed little
girl in a tradesman's back parlour. Often he might
have gone without sufficient nourishment had not Mrs.
Kirilov seen to it ; and whenever an extra good dish,
succulent and strong, appeared at her table, either
Sonia or the servant carried a plateful upstairs with
homely compliments.

"You are making of me a spoiled child, Olga," he
would say sometimes, "and I ought not to eat of the
food for which Anton works so hard."

And she would reply with a laugh :

"If we did not keep you alive, Signor Fardetti,
how should we have our quatuors on Sunday after-
noons ? "

You see, Mrs. Kirilov, like the good Anton, had
lived all her life in music too—she was a pianist ; and
Sonia also was a musician—she played the 'cello in a

3

ladies' orchestra. So they had famous Sunday quatuors at Formosa Terrace, in which Fardetti was well content to play second fiddle to Anton's first.

You see, also, that but for these honest souls to whom a musician like Fardetti was a sort of blood-brother, the evening of the old man's days might have been one of tragic sadness. But even their affection and his glad pride in the brilliant success of his old pupil, Geoffrey Chase, could not mitigate the one great sorrow of his life. The violin, yes ; he had played it well ; he had not aimed at a great soloist's fame, for want of early training, and he had never dreamed such unrealizable dreams ; but other dreams had he dreamed with passionate intensity. He had dreamed of being a great composer, and he had beaten his heart out against the bars that shut him from the great mystery. A waltz or two, a few songs, a catchy march, had been published and performed, and had brought him unprized money and a little hateful repute ; but the compositions into which he had poured his soul remained in dusty manuscript, despised and rejected of musical men. For many years the artist's imperious craving to create and hope and will kept him serene. Then, in the prime of his days, a tremendous inspiration shook him. He had a divine message to proclaim to the world, a song of life itself, a revelation. It was life, indestructible, eternal. It was the seed that grew into the tree ; the tree that flourished lustily, and then grew bare and stark and perished ; the seed, again, of the tree that rose unconquerable into the laughing leaf of spring. It was the kiss of lovers that, when they were dead and gone, lived immortal on the lips of grandchildren. It was the endless roll of the seasons, the majestic, triumphant rhythm of existence. It was a

4

cosmic chant, telling of things as only music could tell of them, and as no musician had ever told of them before.

He attempted the impossible, you will say. He did. That was the pity of it. He spent the last drop of his heart's blood over his sonata. He wrote it and re-wrote it, wasting years, but never could he imprison within those remorseless ruled lines the elusive sounds that shook his being. An approximation to his dream reached the stage of a completed score. But he knew that it was thin and lifeless. The themes that were to be developed into magic harmonies tinkled into commonplace. The shell of this vast conception was there, but the shell alone. The thing could not live without the unseizable, and that he had not seized. Angelo Fardetti, broken down by toil and misery, fell very sick. Doctors recommended Brighton. Docile as a child, he went to Brighton, and there a pretty lady who admired his playing at the Monday Popular Concerts at St. James's Hall, got hold of him and married him. When she ran away, a year later, with a dashing young stockbroker, he took the score of the sonata that was to be the whole interpretation of life from its half-forgotten hiding-place, played it through on the piano, burst into a passion of tears, in the uncontrollable Italian way, sold up his house, and went to lodge with Anton Kirilov. To no son or daughter of man did he ever show a note or play a bar of the sonata. And never again did he write a line of music. Bravely and humbly he faced life, though the tragedy of failure made him prematurely old. And all through the years the sublime message reverberated in his soul and haunted his dreams ; and his was the bitter sorrow of knowing that never should that message be delivered for the comforting of the world.

5

The loss of his position as first violin forced him, at sixty, to take more obscure engagements. That was when he followed the Kirilovs to Peckham. And then he met the joy of his old age—his one pupil of genius, Geoffrey Chase, an untrained lad of fourteen, the son of a well-to-do seed merchant in the High Street.

"His father thinks it waste of time," said Mrs. Chase, a gentle, mild-eyed woman, when she brought the boy to him, "but Geoffrey is so set on it—and so I've persuaded his father to let him have lessons."

"Do you, too, love music?" he asked.

Her eyes grew moist, and she nodded.

"Poor lady! He should not let you starve. Never mind," he said, patting her shoulder. "Take comfort. I will teach your boy to play for you."

And he did. He taught him for three years. He taught him passionately all he knew, for Geoffrey, with music in his blood, had the great gift of the composer. He poured upon the boy all the love of his lonely old heart, and dreamed glorious dreams of his future. The Kirilovs, too, regarded Geoffrey as a prodigy, and welcomed him into their circle, and made much of him. And little Sonia fell in love with him, and he, in his boyish way, fell in love with the dark-haired maiden who played on a 'cello so much bigger than herself. At last the time came when Angelo said:

"My son, I can teach you no more. You must go to Milan."

"My father will never consent," said Geoffrey.

"We will try to arrange that," said Angelo.

So, in their simple ways, Angelo and Mrs. Chase intrigued together until they prevailed upon Mr. Chase to attend one of the Kirilovs' Sunday concerts. He came in church-going clothes, and sat with irrecon-cilable stiffness on a straight-backed chair. His wife sat close by, much agitated. The others played a concerto arranged as a quintette ; Geoffrey first violin, Angelo second, Sonia 'cello, Anton bass, and Mrs. Kirilov at the piano. It was a piece of exquisite tenderness and beauty.

"Very pretty," said Mr. Chase.

"It's beautiful," cried his wife, with tears in her eyes.

"I said so," remarked Mr. Chase.

"And what do you think of my pupil ? " Angelo asked excitedly.

"I think he plays very nicely," Mr. Chase admitted.

"But, dear heavens ! " cried Angelo. "It is not his playing ! One could pick up fifty better violinists in the street. It is the concerto—the composition."

Mr. Chase rose slowly to his feet. "Do you mean to tell me that Geoffrey made up all that himself ? "

"Of course. Didn't you know ? "

"Will you play it again ? "

Gladly they assented. When it was over he took Angelo out into the passage.

"I'm not one of those narrow-minded people who don't believe in art, Mr. Fardetti," said he. "And Geoff has already shown me that he can't sell seeds for toffee. But if he takes up music, will he be able to earn his living at it ? "

"Beyond doubt," replied Angelo, with a wide gesture.

"But a good living ? You'll forgive me being personal, Mr. Fardetti, but you yourself——"

"I," said the old man humbly, "am only a poor fiddler—but your son is a great musical genius."

"I'll think over it," said Mr. Chase.

7

Mr. Chase thought over it, and Geoffrey went to Milan, and Angelo Fardetti was once more left desolate. On the day of the lad's departure he and Sonia wept a little in each other's arms, and late that night he once more unearthed the completed score of his sonata, and scanned it through in vain hope of comfort. But as the months passed comfort came. His beloved swan was not a goose, but a wonder among swans. He was a wonder at the Milan Conservatoire, and won prize after prize and medal after medal, and every time he came home he bore his blushing honours thicker upon him. And he remained the same frank, simple youth, always filled with gratitude and reverence for his old master, and though on familiar student terms with all conditions of cosmopolitan damsels, never faithless to the little Anglo-Russian maiden whom he had left at home.

In the course of time his studies were over, and he returned to England. A professorship at the Royal School of Music very soon rendered him financially independent. He began to create. Here and there a piece of his was played at concerts. He wrote incidental music for solemn productions at great London theatres. Critics discovered him, and wrote much about him in the newspapers. Mr. Chase, the seed merchant, though professing to his wife a man-of-the-world's indifference to notoriety, used surreptitiously to cut out the notices and carry them about in his fat pocket-book, and whenever he had a new one he would lie in wait for the lean figure of Angelo Fardetti, and hale him into the shop and make him drink Geoffrey's health in sloe gin, which Angelo abhorred, but gulped down in honour of the prodigy.

One fine October morning Angelo Fardetti missed

his walk. He sat instead by his window, and looked unseeingly at the prim row of houses on the opposite side of Formosa Terrace. He had not the heart to go out—and, indeed, he had not the money; for these walks, twice daily, along the High Street and the Peckham Road, took him to and from a queer little Italian restaurant, which, with him apparently as its only client, had eked out for years a mysterious and precarious existence. He felt very old—he was seventy-two—very useless, very poor. He had lost his last pupil, a fat, unintelligent girl of thirteen, the daughter of a local chemist, and no one had sent him any copying work for a week. He had nothing to do. He could not even walk to his usual sparrow's meal. It is sad when you are so old that you cannot earn the right to live in a world which wants you no longer.

Looking at unseen bricks through a small window-pane was little consolation. Mechanically he rose and went to a grand piano, his one possession of price, which, with an old horsehair sofa, an oval table covered with a maroon cloth, and a chair or two, congested the tiny room, and, sitting down, began to play one of Stephen Heller's *Nuits Blanches*. You see, Angelo Fardetti was an old-fashioned musician. Suddenly a phrase arrested him. He stopped dead, and remained staring out over the polished plane of the piano. For a few moments he was lost in the chain of associated musical ideas. Then suddenly his swarthy, lined face lit up, and he twirled his little white moustache and began to improvise, striking great majestic chords. Presently he rose, and from a pile of loose music in a corner drew a sheet of ruled paper. He returned to the piano, and began feverishly to pencil down his inspiration. His pulses throbbed. At last he had got

9

the great *andante* movement of his sonata. For an hour he worked intensely; then came the inevitable check. Nothing more would come. He rose and walked about the room, his head swimming. After a quarter of an hour he played over what he had written, and then, with a groan of despair, fell forward, his arms on the keys, his bushy white head on his arms.

The door opened, and Sonia, comely and shapely, entered the room, carrying a tray with food and drink set out on a white cloth. Seeing him bowed over the piano, she put the tray on the table and advanced.

" Dear godfather," she said gently, her hand on his shoulder.

He raised his head and smiled.

" I did not hear you, my little Sonia."

" You have been composing ? "

He sat upright, and tore the pencilled sheets into fragments which he dropped in a handful on the floor.

" Once, long ago, I had a dream. I lost it. To-day I thought that I had found it. But do you know what I did really find ? "

" No, godfather," replied Sonia, stooping, with housewifely tidiness, to pick up the litter.

" That I am a poor old fool," said he.

Sonia threw the paper into the grate and again came up behind him.

" It is better to have lost a dream than never to have had one at all. What was your dream ? "

" I thought I could write the Song of Life as I heard it—as I hear it still." He smote his forehead lightly. " But no ! God has not considered me worthy to sing it. I bow my head to His—to His "—he sought for the word with thin fingers—" to His decree."

10

She said, with the indulgent wisdom of youth speaking to age :

"He has given you the power to love and to win love."

The old man swung round on the music-stool and put his arm round her waist and smiled into her young face.

"Geoffrey is a very fortunate fellow."

"Because he's a successful composer ? "

He looked at her and shook his head, and Sonia, knowing what he meant, blushed very prettily. Then she laughed and broke away.

"Mother has had seventeen partridges sent her as presents this week, and she wants you to help her eat them, and father's offered a bargain in some good Beaujolais, and won't decide until you tell him what you think of it."

Deftly she set out the meal, and drew a chair to the table. Angelo Fardetti rose.

"That I should love you all," said he simply, "is only human, but that you should so much love me is more than I can understand."

You see, he knew that watchful ears had missed his usual outgoing footsteps, and that watchful hearts had divined the reason. To refuse, to hesitate, would be to reject love. So there was no more to be said. He sat down meekly, and Sonia ministered to his wants. As soon as she saw that he was making headway with the partridge and the burgundy, she too sat by the table.

"Godfather," she said, "I've had splendid news this morning."

"Geoffrey ? "

"Of course. What other news could be splendid ?

His Symphony in E flat is going to be given at the Queen's Hall."

"That is indeed beautiful news," said the old man, laying down knife and fork, "but I did not know that he had written a Symphony in E flat."

"That was why he went and buried himself for months in Cornwall—to finish it," she explained.

"I knew nothing about it. Aie! aie!" he sighed. "It is to you, and no longer to me, that he tells things."

"You silly, jealous old dear!" she laughed. "He *had* to account for deserting me all the summer. But as to what it's all about, I'm as ignorant as you are. I've not heard a note of it. Sometimes Geoff is like that, you know. If he's dead certain sure of himself, he won't have any criticism or opinions while the work's in progress. It's only when he's doubtful that he brings one in. And the doubtful things are never anything like the certain ones. You must have noticed it."

"That is true," said Angelo Fardetti, taking up knife and fork again. "He was like that since he was a boy."

"It is going to be given on Saturday fortnight. He'll conduct himself. They've got a splendid programme to send him off. Lembrich's going to play, and Carli's going to sing—just for his sake. Isn't it gorgeous?"

"It is grand. But what does Geoffrey say about it? Come, come, after all, he is not the sphinx." He drummed his fingers impatiently on the table.

"Would you really like to know?"

"I am waiting."

"He says it's going to knock 'em!" she laughed.

"Knock 'em?"

"Those were his words."

"But——"

12

She interpreted into purer English. Geoffrey was confident that his symphony would achieve a sensational success.

" In the meanwhile," said she, " if you don't finish your partridge you'll break mother's heart."

She poured out a glass of burgundy, which the old man drank ; but he refused the food.

" No, no," he said, " I cannot eat more. I have a lump there—in my throat. I am too excited. I feel that he is marching to his great triumph. My little Geoffrey." He rose, knocking his chair over, and strode about the confined space. " *Sacramento !* But I am a wicked old man. I was sorrowful because I was so dull, so stupid that I could not write a sonata. I blamed the good God. *Mea maxima culpa.* And at once he sends me a partridge in a halo of love, and the news of my dear son's glory——"

Sonia stopped him, her plump hands on the front of his old corrugated frock-coat.

" And your glory, too, dear godfather. If it hadn't been for you, where would Geoffrey be ? And who realizes it more than Geoffrey ? Would you like to see a bit of his letter ? Only a little bit—for there's a lot of rubbish in it that I would be ashamed of anybody who thinks well of him to read—but just a little bit."

Her hand was at the broad belt joining blouse and skirt. Angelo, towering above her, smiled with an old man's tenderness at the laughing love in her dark eyes, and at the happiness in her young, comely face. Her features were generous, and her mouth frankly large, but her lips were fresh and her teeth white and even, and to the old fellow she looked all that man could dream of the virginal mother-to-be of great sons. She fished the letter from her belt, scanned and folded it carefully.

" There ! Read."

And Angelo Fardetti read :

" I've learned my theory and technique, and God knows what—things that only they could teach me— from professors with world-famous names. But for real inspiration, for the fount of music itself, I come back all the time to our dear old *maestro*, Angelo Fardetti. I can't for the life of me define what it is, but he opened for me a secret chamber behind whose concealed door all these illustrious chaps have walked unsuspectingly. It seems silly to say it because, beyond a few odds and ends, the dear old man has composed nothing, but I am convinced that I owe the *essentials* of everything I do in music to his teaching and influence."

Angelo gave her back the folded letter without a word, and turned and stood again by the window, staring unseeingly at the prim, semi-detached villas opposite. Sonia, having re-hidden her treasure, stole up to him. Feeling her near, he stretched out a hand and laid it on her head.

" God is very wonderful," said he—" very mysterious. Oh, and so good ! "

He fumbled, absently and foolishly, with her well-ordered hair, saying nothing more. After a while she freed herself gently and led him back to his partridge.

A day or two afterwards Geoffrey came to Peckham, and mounted with Sonia to Fardetti's rooms, where the old man embraced him tenderly, and expressed his joy in the exuberant foreign way. Geoffrey received the welcome with an Englishman's laughing embarrassment. Perhaps the only fault that Angelo Fardetti

14

could find in the beloved pupil was his uncompromising English manner and appearance. His well-set figure and crisp, short fair hair and fair moustache did not sufficiently express him as a great musician. Angelo had to content himself with the lad's eyes—musician's eyes, as he said, very bright, arresting, dark blue, with depths like sapphires, in which lay strange thoughts and human laughter.

" I've only run in, dear old *maestro*, to pass the time of day with you, and to give you a ticket for my Queen's Hall show. You'll come, won't you ? "

" He asks if I will come ! I would get out of my coffin and walk through the streets ! "

" I think you'll be pleased," said Geoffrey. " I've been goodness knows how long over it, and I've put into it all I know. If it doesn't come off, I'll——"

He paused.

" You will commit no rashness," cried the old man in alarm.

" I will. I'll marry Sonia the very next day ! "

There was laughing talk, and the three spent a happy little quarter of an hour. But Geoffrey went away without giving either of the others an inkling of the nature of his famous symphony. It was Geoffrey's way.

The fateful afternoon arrived. Angelo Fardetti, sitting in the stalls of the Queen's Hall with Sonia and her parents, looked round the great auditorium, and thrilled with pleasure at seeing it full. London had thronged to hear the first performance of his beloved's symphony. As a matter of fact, London had also come to hear the wonderful orchestra give Tchaikowsky's Fourth Symphony, and to hear Lembrich play the violin and Carli sing, which they did once in a blue moon at a symphony concert. But in the old man's eyes these ineffectual fires paled before Geoffrey's genius. So great was his suspense and agitation that he could pay but scant attention to the first two items on the programme. It seemed almost like unmeaning music, far away.

During the interval before the Symphony in E flat his thin hand found Sonia's, and held it tight, and she returned the pressure. She, too, was sick with anxiety. The great orchestra, tier upon tier, was a-flutter with the performers scrambling into their places, and with leaves of scores being turned over, and with a myriad moving bows. Then all having settled into the order of a vast machine, Geoffrey appeared at the conductor's stand. Comforting applause greeted him. Was he not the rising hope of English music? Many others beside those four to whom he was dear, and the mother and father who sat a little way in front of them, felt the same nervous apprehension. The future of English music was at stake. Would it be yet one more disappointment and disillusion, or would it rank the young English composer with the immortals? Geoffrey bowed smilingly at the audience, turned and with his baton gave the signal to begin.

Although only a few years have passed since that memorable first performance, the modestly named Symphony in E flat is now famous and Geoffrey Chase is a great man the wide world over. To every lover of music the symphony is familiar. But only those who were present at the Queen's Hall on that late October afternoon can realize the wild rapture of enthusiasm with which the symphony was greeted. It answered all longings, solved all mysteries. It interpreted, for all who had ears to hear, the fairy dew of love, the burning depths of passion, sorrow and death, and the eternal Triumph of Life. Intensely modern and faultless in technique, it was new, unexpected, individual, unrelated to any school.

The scene was one of raging tumult ; but there was one human being who did not applaud, and that was the old musician, forgotten of the world, Angelo Fardetti. He had fainted.

All through the piece he had sat, bolt upright, his nerves strung to breaking-point, his dark cheeks growing greyer and greyer, and the stare in his eyes growing more and more strange, and the grip on the girl's hand growing more and more vice-like, until she, for sheer agony, had to free herself. And none concerned themselves about him ; not even Sonia, for she was enwrapped in the soul of her lover's music. And even between the movements her heart was too full for speech or thought, and when she looked at the old man, she saw him smile wanly and nod his head as one who, like herself, was speechless with emotion. At the end the storm burst. She rose with the shouting, clapping, hand- and handkerchief-waving house, and suddenly, missing him from her side, glanced round and saw him huddled up unconscious in his stall.

The noise and movement were so great that few noticed the long lean old figure being carried out of the hall by one of the side doors fortunately near. In the vestibule, attended by the good Anton and his wife and Sonia, and a commissionaire, he recovered. When he could speak, he looked round and said :

" I am a silly old fellow. I am sorry I have spoiled your happiness. I think I must be too old for happiness, for this is how it has treated me."

There was much discussion between his friends as

17

to what should be done, but good Mrs. Kirilov, once
girlishly plump, when Angelo had first known her, now
florid and fat and motherly, had her way, and, leaving
Anton and Sonia to see the hero of the afternoon, if
they could, drove off in a cab to Peckham with the over-
wrought old man and put him to bed and gave him
homely remedies, invalid food and drink, and com-
manded him to sleep till morning.

But Angelo Fardetti disobeyed her. For Sonia,
although she had found him meekly between the sheets
when she went up to see him that evening, heard him
later, as she was getting to bed—his sitting-room was
immediately above her—playing over, on muted
strings, various themes of Geoffrey's symphony. At
last she went up to his room and put her head in at the
door, and saw him, a lank, dilapidated figure in an
old, old dressing-gown, fiddle and bow in hand.

"Oh! oh!" she rated. "You are a naughty,
naughty old dear. Go to bed at once."

He smiled like a guilty but spoiled child. "I will
go," said he.

In the morning she herself took up his simple breakfast and all the newspapers, folded at the page on
which the notices of the concert were printed. The
Press was unanimous in acclamation of the great
genius that had raised English music to the spheres.
She sat at the foot of the bed and read to him while
he sipped his coffee and munched his roll, and, absorbed
in her own tremendous happiness, was content to feel
the glow of the old man's sympathy. There was little
to be said save exclamatory pæans, so overwhelming was the triumph. Tears streamed down his
lined cheeks, and between the tears there shone the
light of a strange gladness in his eyes. Presently Sonia

left him and went about her household duties. An hour or so afterwards she caught the sound of his piano ; again he was recalling bits of the great symphony, and she marvelled at his musical memory. Then about half-past eleven she saw him leave the house and stride away, his head in the air, his bent shoulders curiously erect.

Soon came the clatter of a cab stopping at the front door, and Geoffrey Chase, for whom she had been watching from her window, leaped out upon the pavement. She ran down and admitted him. He caught her in his arms and they stood clinging in a long embrace.

" It's too wonderful to talk about," she whispered.

" Then don't let us talk about it," he laughed.

" As if we could help it! I can think of nothing else."

" I can—you," said he, and kissed her again.

Now, in spite of the spaciousness of the house in Formosa Terrace, it had only two reception-rooms, as the house-agents grandiloquently term them, and these, dining-room and drawing-room, were respectively occupied by Anton and Mrs. Kirilov engaged in their morning lessons. The passage where the young people stood was no fit place for lovers' meetings.

" Let us go up to the *maestro's*. He's out," said Sonia.

They did as they had often done in like circumstances. Indeed, the old man, before now, had given up his sitting-room to them, feigning an unconquerable desire to walk abroad. Were they not his children, dearer to him than anyone else in the world ? So it was natural that they should make themselves at home in his tiny den. They sat and talked of the great victory, of the playing of the orchestra, of passages that he might take slower or quicker next time, of the ovation, of the mountain of congratulatory telegrams and letters that blocked up his rooms. They talked of Angelo Fardetti and his deep emotion and his pride. And they talked of the future, of their marriage which was to take place very soon. She suggested postponement.

"I want you to be quite sure. This must make a difference."

"Difference!" he cried indignantly.

She waved him off and sat on the music-stool by the piano.

"I must speak sensibly. You are one of the great ones of the musical world, one of the great ones of the world itself. You will go on and on. You will have all sorts of honours heaped on you. You will go about among lords and ladies, what is called Society—oh, I know, you'll not be able to help it. And all the time I remain what I am, just a poor little common girl, a member of a twopenny-halfpenny ladies' band. I'd rather you regretted having taken up with me before than after. So we ought to put it off."

He answered her as a good man who loves deeply can only answer. Her heart was convinced; but she turned her head aside and thought of further argument. Her eye fell on some music open on the rest, and mechanically, with a musician's instinct, she fingered a few bars. The strange familiarity of the theme startled her out of preoccupation. She continued the treble, and suddenly, with a cold shiver of wonder, crashed down both hands and played on.

Geoffrey strode up to her.

"What's that you're playing?"

She pointed hastily to the score. He bent over and stared at the faded manuscript.

20

" Why, good God ! " he cried, " it's my symphony."

She stopped, swung round and faced him with fear in her eyes.

" Yes. It's your symphony."

He took the thick manuscript from the rest and looked at the brown-paper cover. On it was written :

" The Song of Life. A Sonata by Angelo Fardetti. September, 1878."

There was an amazed silence. Then, in a queer accusing voice, Sonia cried out :

" Geoffrey, what have you done ? "

" Heaven knows ; but I've never known of this before. My God ! Open the thing somewhere else and see."

So Sonia opened the manuscript at random and played, and again it was an echo of Geoffrey's symphony. He sank on a chair like a man crushed by an overwhelming fatality, and held his head in his hands.

" I oughtn't to have done it," he groaned. " But it was more than me. The thing overmastered me, it haunted me so that I couldn't sleep, and the more it haunted me the more it became my own, my very own. It was too big to lose."

Sonia held him with scared eyes.

" What are you talking of ? " she asked.

" The way I came to write the Symphony. It's like a nightmare." He rose. " A couple of years ago," said he, " I bought a bundle of old music at a second-hand shop. It contained a collection of eighteenth-century stuff which I wanted. I took the whole lot, and on going through it, found a clump of old, discoloured manuscript partly in faded brown ink, partly in pencil. It was mostly rough notes. I tried it out

21   B

of curiosity. The composition was feeble and the orchestration childish—I thought it the work of some dead and forgotten amateur—but it was crammed full of ideas, crammed full of beauty. I began tinkering it about, to amuse myself. The more I worked on it the more it fascinated me. It became an obsession. Then I pitched the old score away and started it on my own."

"The *maestro* sold a lot of old music about that time," said Sonia.

The young man threw up his hands. "It's a fatality, an awful fatality. My God," he cried, " to think that I of all men should have stolen Angelo Fardetti's music !"

"No wonder he fainted yesterday," said Sonia.

It was catastrophe. Both regarded it in remorseful silence. Sonia said at last :

" You'll have to explain."

" Of course, of course. But what must the dear old fellow be thinking of me ? What else but that I've got hold of this surreptitiously, while he was out of the room ? What else but that I'm a mean thief ? "

" He loves you, dear, enough to forgive you anything."

" It's the Unforgivable Sin. I'm wiped out. I cease to exist as an honest man. But I had no idea," he cried, with the instinct of self-defence, " that I had come so near him. I thought I had just got a theme here and there. I thought I had recast all the odds and ends according to my own scheme." He ran his eye over a page or two of the score. " Yes, this is practically the same as the old rough notes. But there was a lot, of course, I couldn't use. Look at that, for instance." He indicated a passage.

"I can't read it like you," said Sonia. "I must play it."

She turned again to the piano, and played the thin, uninspired music that had no relation to the Symphony in E flat, and her eyes filled with tears as she remembered poignantly what the old man had told her of his Song of Life. She went on and on until the music quickened into one of the familiar themes; and the tears fell, for she knew how poorly it was treated.

And then the door burst open. Sonia stopped dead in the middle of a bar, and they both turned round to find Angelo Fardetti standing on the threshold.

"Ah, no!" he cried, waving his thin hands. "Put that away. I did not know I had left it out. You must not play that. Ah, my son! my son!"

He rushed forward and clasped Geoffrey in his arms, and kissed him on the cheeks, and murmured foolish, broken words.

"You have seen it. You have seen the miracle. The miracle of the good God. Oh, I am happy! My son, my son! I am the happiest of old men. Ah!" He shook him tremulously by both shoulders, and looked at him with a magical light in his old eyes. "You are really what our dear Anton calls a prodigy. I have thought and you have executed. Santa Maria!" he cried, raising hands and eyes to heaven. "I thank you for this miracle that has been done!"

He turned away. Geoffrey, in blank bewilderment, made a step forward.

"*Maestro*, I never knew——"

But Sonia, knowledge dawning in her face, clapped her hand over his mouth—and he read her conjecture in her eyes, and drew a great breath. The old man came again and laughed and cried and wrung his hand,

and poured out his joy and wonder into the amazed ears of the conscience-stricken young musician. The floodgates of speech were loosened.

"You see what you have done, *figlio mio*. You see the miracle. This—this poor rubbish is of me, Angelo Fardetti. On it I spent my life, my blood, my tears, and it is a thing of nothing, nothing. It is wind and noise ; but by the miracle of God I breathed it into your spirit and it grew—and it grew into all that I dreamed—all that I dreamed and could not express. It is my Song of Life sung as I could have sung it if I had been a great genius like you. And you have taken my song from my soul, from my heart, and all the sublime harmonies that could get no farther than this dull head you have put down in immortal music."

He went on exalted, and Sonia and Geoffrey stood pale and silent. To undeceive him was impossible.

"You see it is a miracle ? " he asked.

"Yes," replied Geoffrey in a low voice.

"You never saw this before. Ha ! ha ! " he laughed delightedly. "Not a human soul has seen it or heard it. I kept it locked up there, in my little strong-box. And it was there all the time I was teaching you. And you never suspected."

"No, *maestro*, I did not," said the young man truthfully.

"Now, when did you begin to think of it ? How did it come to you—my Song of Life ? Did it sing in your brain while you were here and my brain was guiding yours, and then gather form and shape all through the long years ? "

"Yes," said Geoffrey. "That was how it came about."

Angelo took Sonia's plump cheeks between his

24

hands and smiled. "Now you understand, my little Sonia, why I was so foolish yesterday. It was emotion, such emotion as a man has never felt before in the world. And now you know why I could not speak this morning. I thought of the letter you showed me. He confessed that old Angelo Fardetti had inspired him, but he did not know how. I know. The little spark flew from the soul of Angelo Fardetti into his soul, and it became a Divine Fire. And my Song of Life is true. The symphony was born in me—it died in me—it is re-born so gloriously in him. The seed is imperishable. It is eternal."

He broke away, laughing through a little sob, and stood by the window, once more gazing unseeingly at the opposite villas of Formosa Terrace. Geoffrey went up to him and fell on his knees—it was a most un-English thing to do—and took the old hand very reverently.

"*Padre mio*," said he.

"Yes, it is true. I am your father," said the old man in Italian, "and we are bound together by more than human ties." He laid his hand on the young man's head. "May all the blessings of God be upon you."

Geoffrey rose, the humblest man in England. Angelo passed his hand across his forehead, but his face bore a beautiful smile.

"I feel so happy," said he. "So happy that it is terrible. And I feel so strange. And my heart is full. If you will forgive me, I will lie down for a little." He sank on the horsehair sofa and smiled up in the face of the young man. "And my head is full of the *andante* movement that I could never write, and you have made it like the harmonies before the Throne of

God. Sit down at the piano and play it for me, my son."

So Geoffrey took his seat at the piano, and played, and as he played, he lost himself in his music. And Sonia crept near and stood by him in a dream while the wonderful story of the passing of human things was told. When the sound of the last chords had died away she put her arms around Geoffrey's neck and laid her cheek against his. For a while Time stood still. Then they turned and saw the old man sleeping peacefully. She whispered a word, he rose, and they began to tiptoe out of the room. But suddenly instinct caused Sonia to turn her head again. She stopped and gripped Geoffrey's hand. She caught a choking breath.

" Is he asleep ? "

They went back and bent over him. He was dead.

Angelo Fardetti had died of a happiness too great for mortal man. For to which one of us in a hundred million is it given to behold the utter realization of his life's dream ?

LADIES IN LAVENDER

I

AS soon as the sun rose out of the sea its light streamed through a white-curtained casement window into the whitest and most spotless room you can imagine. It shone upon two little white beds, separated by the width of the floor covered with straw-coloured matting; on white garments neatly folded which lay on white chairs by the side of each bed; on a white enamelled bedroom suite; on the one picture (over the mantelpiece) which adorned the white walls, the enlarged photograph of a white-whiskered, elderly gentleman in naval uniform; and on the white, placid faces of the sleepers.

It awakened Miss Ursula Widdington, who sat up in bed, greeted it with a smile, and forthwith aroused her sister.

"Janet, here's the sun."

Miss Widdington awoke and smiled too.

Now to awake at daybreak with a smile and a child-like delight at the sun when you are over forty-five is a sign of an unruffled conscience and a sweet disposition.

"The first glimpse of it for a week," said Miss Widdington.

"Isn't it strange," said Miss Ursula, "that when we went to sleep the storm was still raging?"

"And now—the sea hasn't gone down yet. Listen."

"The tide's coming in. Let us go out and look at it," cried Miss Ursula, delicately getting out of bed.

"You're so impulsive, Ursula," said Miss Widdington.

She was forty-eight, and three years older than her
sister. She could therefore smile indulgently at the
impetuosity of youth. But she rose and dressed, and
presently the two ladies stole out of the silent house.

They had lived there for many years, perched away
on top of a projecting cliff on the Cornish coast, midway
between sea and sky, like two fairy princesses in an
enchanted bit of the world's end, who had grown grey
with waiting for the prince who never came. Theirs
was the only house on the wind-swept height. Below
in the bay on the right of their small headland nestled
the tiny fishing village of Trevannic; below, sheer
down to the left, lay a little sandy cove, accessible
farther on by a narrow gorge that split the majestic
stretch of bastioned cliffs. To that little stone weather-
beaten house their father, the white-whiskered gentleman of the portrait, had brought them quite young
when he had retired from the Navy with a pension
and a grievance—an ungrateful country had not made
him an admiral—and there, after his death, they had
continued to lead their remote and gentle lives, untouched by the happenings of the great world.

The salt-laden wind buffeted them, dashed strands
of hair stingingly across their faces and swirled their
skirts around them as they leaned over the stout stone
parapet their father had built along the edge of the
cliff, and drank in the beauty of the morning. The
eastern sky was clear of clouds and the eastern sea
tossed a fierce silver under the sun and gradually deepened into frosted green, which changed in the west
into the deep ocean blue; and the Atlantic heaved
and sobbed after its turmoil of the day before. Miss

Ursula pointed to the gilt-edged clouds in the west and likened them to angels' thrones, which was a pretty conceit. Miss Widdington derived a suggestion of Pentecostal flames from the golden flashes of the sea-gulls' wings. Then she referred to the appetite they would have for breakfast. To this last observation Miss Ursula did not reply, as she was leaning over the parapet intent on something in the cove below. Presently she clutched her sister's arm.

"Janet, look down there—that black thing—what is it?"

Miss Widdington's gaze followed the pointing finger.

At the foot of the rocks that edged the gorge sprawled a thing checkered black and white.

"I do believe it's a man!"

"A drowned man! Oh, poor fellow! Oh, Janet, how dreadful!"

She turned brown, compassionate eyes on her sister, who continued to peer keenly at the helpless figure below.

"Do you think he's dead, Janet?"

"The sensible thing would be to go down and see," replied Miss Widdington.

It was by no means the first dead man cast up by the waves that they had stumbled upon during their long sojourn on this wild coast, where wrecks and founderings and loss of men's lives at sea were commonplace happenings. They were dealing with the sadly familiar; and though their gentle hearts throbbed hard as they made for the gorge and sped quickly down the ragged, rocky path, they set about their task as a matter of course.

Miss Ursula reached the sand first, and walked over to the body which lay on a low shelf of rock. Then she turned with a glad cry.

"Janet. He's alive. He's moaning. Come quickly." And, as Janet joined her : "Did you ever see such a beautiful face in your life?"

"We should have brought some brandy," said Miss Widdington.

But, as she bent over the unconscious form, a foolish moisture gathered in her eyes which had nothing to do with forgetfulness of alcohol. For indeed there lay sprawling anyhow in catlike grace beneath them the most romantic figure of a youth that the sight of maiden ladies ever rested on. He had long black hair, a perfectly chiselled face, a preposterously feminine mouth which, partly open, showed white young teeth, and the most delicate, long-fingered hands in the world. Miss Ursula murmured that he was like a young Greek god. Miss Widdington sighed. The fellow was ridiculous. He was also dank with sea water, and moaned as if he were in pain. But as gazing wrapt in wonder and admiration at young Greek gods is not much good to them when they are half drowned, Miss Widdington despatched her sister in search of help.

"The tide is still low enough for you to get round the cliff to the village. Mrs. Pendered will give you some brandy, and her husband and Luke will bring a stretcher. You might also send Joe Gullow on his bicycle for Dr. Mead."

Miss Widdington, as behoved one who has the charge of an orphaned younger sister, did not allow the sentimental to weaken the practical. Miss Ursula, though she would have preferred to stay by the side of the beautiful youth, was docile, and went forthwith on her errand. Miss Widdington, left alone with him, rolled up her jacket and pillowed his head on it, brought his limbs into an attitude suggestive of comfort, and tried

30

by chafing to restore him to animation. Being unsuccessful in this, she at last desisted, and sat on the
rocks near by and wondered who on earth he was and
where in the world he came from. His garments consisted in a nondescript pair of trousers and a flannel
shirt with a collar, which was fastened at the neck,
not by button or stud, but by a tasselled cord ; and he
was barefoot. Miss Widdington glanced modestly at
his feet, which were shapely ; and the soles were soft
and pink like the palms of his hands. Now, had he
been the coarsest and most callosity-stricken shell-
back half-alive, Janet Widdington would have tended
him with the same devotion ; but the lingering though
unoffending Eve in her rejoiced that hands and feet
betokened gentler avocations than that of sailor or
fisherman. And why ? Heaven knows, save that the
stranded creature had a pretty face and that his long
black hair was flung over his forehead in a most interesting manner. She wished he would open his eyes.
But as he kept them shut and gave no sign of returning
consciousness, she sat there waiting patiently ; in front
of her the rough, sun-kissed Atlantic, at her feet
the semicircular patch of golden sand, behind her the
sheer white cliffs, and by her side on the slab of rock
this good-looking piece of jetsam.

At length Miss Ursula appeared round the corner of
the headland, followed by Jan Pendered and his son
Luke carrying a stretcher. While Miss Widdington
administered brandy without any obvious result, the
men looked at the castaway, scratched their heads, and
guessed him to be a foreigner ; but how he managed
to be there alone with never a bit of wreckage to supply
a clue surpassed their powers of imagination. In lifting him the right foot hung down through the trouser-

31

leg, and his ankle was seen to be horribly black and swollen.   Old Jan examined it carefully.

"Broken," said he.

"Oh, poor boy, that's why he's moaning so," cried the compassionate Miss Ursula.

The men grasped the handles of the stretcher.

"I'd better take him home to my old woman," said Jan Pendered thoughtfully.

"He can have my bed, father," said Luke.

Miss Widdington looked at Miss Ursula and Miss Ursula looked at Miss Widdington, and the eyes of each lady were wistful.   Then Miss Widdington spoke.

"You can carry him up to the house, Pendered. We have a comfortable spare room, and Dorcas will help us to look after him."

The men obeyed, for in Trevannic Miss Widdington's gentle word was law.

II

It was early afternoon.   Miss Widdington had retired to take her customary after-luncheon siesta, an indulgence permitted to her seniority, but not granted, except on rare occasions, to the young.   Miss Ursula, therefore, kept watch in the sick chamber, just such a little white spotless room as their own, but containing only one little white bed in which the youth lay dry and warm and comfortably asleep.   He was exhausted from cold and exposure, said the doctor who had driven in from St. Madoc, eight miles off, and his ankle was broken.   The doctor had done what was necessary, had swathed him in one of old Dorcas's flannel nightgowns, and had departed.   Miss Ursula had the patient all to herself.   A bright fire burned in the grate, and the strong Atlantic breeze came in through the open window where she sat, her knitting in her hand. Now and then she glanced at the sleeper, longing, in a most feminine manner, for him to awake and render an account of himself. Miss Ursula's heart fluttered mildly. For beautiful youths, baffling curiosity, are not washed up alive by the sea at an old maid's feet every day in the week. It was indeed an adventure, a bit of a fairy-tale suddenly gleaming and dancing in the grey atmosphere of an eventless life. She glanced at him again, and wondered whether he had a mother. Presently Dorcas came in, stout and matronly, and cast a maternal eye on the boy and smoothed his pillow. She had sons herself, and two of them had been claimed by the pitiless sea.

" It's lucky I had a sensible nightgown to give him," she remarked. " If we had had only the flimsy things that you and Miss Janet wear——"

" Sh ! " said Miss Ursula, colouring faintly ; " he might hear you."

Dorcas laughed and went out. Miss Ursula's needles clicked rapidly. When she glanced at the bed again she became conscious of two great dark eyes regarding her in utter wonder She rose quickly and went over to the bed.

" Don't be afraid," she said, though what there was to terrify him in her mild demeanour and the spotless room she could not have explained ; " don't be afraid, you're among friends."

He murmured some words which she did not catch.

" What do you say ? " she asked sweetly.

He repeated them in a stronger voice. Then she realized that he spoke in a foreign tongue. A queer dismay filled her.

" Don't you speak English ? "

He looked at her for a moment, puzzled. Then the

33

echo of the last word seemed to reach his intelligence. He shook his head. A memory rose from schoolgirl days.

"*Parlez-vous français?*" she faltered ; and when he shook his head again she almost felt relieved. Then he began to talk, regarding her earnestly, as if seeking by his mere intentness to make her understand. But it was a strange language which she had not heard before.

In one mighty effort Miss Ursula gathered together her whole stock of German.

"*Sprechen sie Deutsch?*"

"*Ach ja! Einige Worte,*" he replied, and his face lit up with a smile so radiant that Miss Ursula wondered how Providence could have neglected to inspire a being so beautiful with a knowledge of the English language. "*Ich kann mich auf deutsch verständlich machen, aber ich bin polnisch.*"

But not a word of the halting sentence could Miss Ursula make out ; even the last was swallowed up in guttural unintelligibility. She only recognized the speech as German and different from that which he used at first, and which seemed to be his native tongue.

"Oh, dear, I must give it up," she sighed.

The patient moved slightly and uttered a sudden cry of pain. It occurred to Miss Ursula that he had not had time to realize the fractured ankle. That he realized it now was obvious, for he lay back with closed eyes and white lips until the spasm had passed. After that Miss Ursula did her best to explain in pantomime what had happened. She made a gesture of swimming, then laid her cheek on her hand and simulated fainting, acted her discovery of his body on the beach, broke a wooden match in two and pointed to his ankle, exhibited the medicine bottles by the bedside, smoothed his pillow, and smiled so as to assure him of kind treat-

ment. He understood, more or less, murmured thanks
in his own language, took her hand, and, to her Englishwoman's astonishment, pressed it to his lips. Miss
Widdington, entering softly, found the pair in this
romantic situation.

When it dawned on him a while later that he owed
his deliverance equally to both of the gentle ladies, he
kissed Miss Widdington's hand too. Whereupon Miss
Ursula coloured and turned away. She did not like to
see him kiss her sister's hand. Why, she could not tell,
but she felt as if she had received a tiny stab in the heart.

III

Providence has showered many blessings on Trevannic, but among them is not the gift of tongues.
Dr. Mead, who came over every day from St. Madoc,
knew less German than the ladies. It was impossible
to communicate with the boy except by signs. Old
Jan Pendered, who had served in the Navy in the
China seas, felt confident that he could make him
understand, and tried him with pidgin-English. But
the youth only smiled sweetly and shook hands with
him, whereupon old Jan scratched his head and acknowledged himself jiggered. To Miss Widdington, at
last, came the inspiration that the oft-repeated word
" *Polnisch* " meant Polish.

" You come from Poland ? "

" *Aus Polen, ja,*" laughed the boy.

" Kosciusko," murmured Miss Ursula.

He laughed again, delighted, and looked at her
eagerly for more ; but there Miss Ursula's conversation about Poland ended. If the discovery of his
nationality lay to the credit of her sister, she it was
who found out his name, Andrea Marowski, and taught

35

him to say : " Miss Ursula." She also taught him the
English names of the various objects around him.
And here the innocent rivalry of the two ladies began
to take definite form.   Miss Widdington, without taking counsel of Miss Ursula, borrowed an old Otto's
German grammar from the girls' school at St. Madoc,
and, by means of patient research, put to him such
questions as : " Have you a mother ? " " How old
are you ? " and, collating his written replies with the
information vouchsafed by the grammar, succeeded in
discovering, among other biographical facts, that he was
alone in the world, save for an old uncle who lived in
Cracow, and that he was twenty years of age.   So that
when Miss Ursula boasted that she had taught him
to say : " Good morning.   How do you do ? " Miss
Widdington could cry with an air of triumph : " He
told me that he doesn't suffer from toothache."

It was one of the curious features of the ministra-
tions which they afforded Mr. Andrea Marowski alter-
nately, that Miss Ursula would have nothing whatever
to do with Otto's German grammar and Miss Widdington scorned the use of English and made as little use
of sign language as possible.

" I don't think it becoming, Ursula," she said, " to
indicate hunger by opening your mouth and rubbing
the front of your waist, like a cannibal."

Miss Ursula accepted the rebuke meekly, for she
never returned a pert answer to her senior ; but re-
flecting that Janet's disapproval might possibly arise
from her want of skill in the art of pantomime, she went
away comforted and continued her unbecoming prac-
tices.   The conversations, however, that the ladies,
each in her own way, managed to have with the invalid,
were sadly limited in scope.   No means that they could

devise could bring them enlightenment on many interesting points. Who he was, whether noble or peasant, how he came to be lying like a jellyfish on the slab of rock in their cove, coatless and barefoot, remained as great a puzzle as ever. Of course he informed them, especially the grammar-equipped Miss Widdington, over and over again in his execrable German; but they grew no wiser, and at last they abandoned in despair their attempts to solve these mysteries. They contented themselves with the actual, which indeed was enough to absorb their simple minds. There he was cast up by the sea or fallen from the moon, young, gay, and helpless, a veritable gift of the gods. The very mystery of his adventure invested him with a curious charm; and then the prodigious appetite with which he began to devour fish and eggs and chickens formed of itself a joy hitherto undreamed of in their philosophy.

"When he gets up he must have some clothes," said Miss Widdington.

Miss Ursula agreed; but did not say that she was knitting him socks in secret. Andrea's interest in the progress of these garments was one of her chief delights.

"There's the trunk upstairs with our dear father's things," said Miss Widdington with more diffidence than usual. "They are so sacred to us that I was wondering——"

"Our dear father would be the first to wish it," said Miss Ursula.

"It's a Christian's duty to clothe the naked," said Miss Widdington.

"And so we must clothe him in what we've got," said Miss Ursula. Then with a slight flush she added: "It's so many years since our great

37

loss that I've almost forgotten what a man wears."

"I haven't," said Miss Widdington. "I think I ought to tell you, Ursula," she continued, after pausing to put sugar and milk into the cup of tea which she handed to her sister—they were at the breakfast-table, at the head of which she formally presided, as she had done since her emancipation from the schoolroom—"I think I ought to tell you that I have decided to devote my twenty-five pounds to buying him an outfit. Our dear father's things can only be a makeshift—and the poor boy hasn't a penny in the pockets he came ashore in."

Now, some three years before, an aunt had bequeathed Miss Widdington a tiny legacy, the disposal of which had been a continuous subject of grave discussion between the sisters. She always alluded to it as "my twenty-five pounds."

"Is that quite fair, dear?" said Miss Ursula impulsively.

"Fair? Do you mind explaining?"

Miss Ursula regretted her impetuosity. "Don't you think, dear Janet," she said with some nervousness, "that it would lay him under too great an obligation to you personally? I should prefer to take the money out of our joint income. We both are responsible for him, and," she added with a timid smile, "I found him first."

"I don't see what that has to do with it," Miss Widdington retorted with a quite unusual touch of acidity. "But if you feel strongly about it, I am willing to withdraw my five-and-twenty pounds."

"You're not angry with me, Janet?"

"Angry? Of course not," Miss Widdington replied freezingly. "Don't be silly. And why aren't you eating your bacon?"

38

This was the first shadow of dissension that had arisen between them since their childhood. On the way to the sick-room, Miss Ursula shed a few tears over Janet's hectoring ways, and Miss Widdington, in pursuit of her housekeeping duties, made Dorcas the scapegoat for Ursula's unreasonableness. Before luncheon time they kissed with mutual apologies; but the spirit of rivalry was by no means quenched.

IV

One afternoon Miss Janet had an inspiration.

"If I played the piano in the drawing-room with the windows open you could hear it in the spare room quite plainly."

"If you think it would disturb Mr. Andrea," said Miss Ursula, "you might shut the windows."

"I was proposing to offer him a distraction, dear," said Miss Widdington. "These foreign gentlemen are generally fond of music."

Miss Ursula could raise no objection, but her heart sank. She could not play the piano.

She took her seat cheerfully, however, by the bed, which had been wheeled up to the window so that the patient could look out on the glory of sky and sea, took her knitting from a drawer and began to turn the heel of one of the sacred socks. Andrea watched her lazily and contentedly. Perhaps he had never seen two such soft-treaded, soft-fingered ladies in lavender in his life. He often tried to give some expression to his gratitude, and the hand-kissing had become a thrice daily custom. For Miss Widdington he had written the word "Engel," which the vocabulary at the end of Otto's German grammar rendered as "Angel"; whereat she had blushed quite prettily.

39

For Miss Ursula he had drawn, very badly, but still unmistakably, the picture of a winged denizen of Paradise, and she, too, had treasured the compliment; she also treasured the drawing. Now, Miss Ursula held up the knitting, which began distinctly to indicate the shape of a sock, and smiled. Andrea smiled, too, and blew her a kiss with his fingers. He had many graceful foreign gestures. The doctor, who was a plain, bullet-headed Briton, disapproved of Andrea, and expressed to Dorcas his opinion that the next things to be washed ashore would be the young man's monkey and organ. This was sheer prejudice, for Andrea's manners were unexceptionable, and his smile, in the eyes of his hostesses, the most attractive thing in the world.

"Heel," said Miss Ursula.

"'Eel," repeated Andrea.

"Wool," said Miss Ursula.

"Vool," said Andrea.

"No—wo-o," said Miss Ursula, puffing out her lips so as to accentuate the " w."

"Wo-o," said Andrea, doing the same. And then they both burst out laughing. They were enjoying themselves mightily.

Then, from the drawing-room below, came the tinkling sound of the old untuned piano which had remained unopened for many years. It was the " Spring Song " of Mendelssohn, played, schoolgirl fashion, with uncertain fingers that now and then struck false notes. The light died away from Andrea's face, and he looked inquiringly, if not wonderingly, at Miss Ursula. She smiled encouragement, pointed first at the floor, and then at him, thereby indicating that the music was for his benefit. For a while he remained quite patient.

At last he clapped his hands on his ears, and, his features distorted with pain, cried out :

"*Nein, nein, nein, das lieb' ich nicht ! Es ist hässlich !*"

In eager pantomime he besought her to stop the entertainment. Miss Ursula went downstairs, halting to hurt her sister's feelings, yet unable to crush a wicked, unregenerate feeling of pleasure.

"I am so sorry, dear Janet," she said, laying her hand on her sister's arm, "but he doesn't like music. It's astonishing, his dislike. It makes him quite violent."

Miss Widdington ceased playing and accompanied her sister upstairs. Andrea, with an expressive shrug of the shoulders, reached out his two hands to the musician and, taking hers, kissed her finger-tips. Miss Widdington consulted Otto.

"*Lieben Sie nicht Musik ?*"

"*Ja wohl,*" he cried, and, laughing, played an imaginary fiddle.

"He *does* like music," cried Miss Widdington. "How can you make such silly mistakes, Ursula ? Only he prefers the violin."

Miss Ursula grew downcast for a moment ; then she brightened. A brilliant idea occurred to her.

"Adam Penruddocke. He has a fiddle. We can ask him to come up after tea and play to us."

She reassured Andrea in her queer sign-language, and later in the afternoon Adam Penruddocke, a sheepish giant of a fisherman, was shown into the room. He bowed to the ladies, shook the long white hand proffered him by the beautiful youth, tuned up, and played *The Carnival of Venice* from start to finish. Andrea regarded him with mischievous, laughing eyes, and at the end he applauded vigorously.

Miss Widdington turned to her sister.

"I knew he liked music," she said.

"Shall I play something else, sir?" asked Penruddocke.

Andrea, guessing his meaning, beckoned him to approach the bed, and took the violin and bow from his hands. He looked at the instrument critically, smiled to himself, tuned it afresh, and with an air of intense happiness drew the bow across the strings.

"Why, he can play it!" cried Miss Ursula.

Andrea laughed and nodded, and played a bit of *The Carnival of Venice* as it ought to be played, with gaiety and mischief. Then he broke off, and after two or three tearing chords that made his hearers start, plunged into a wild czardas. The ladies looked at him in open-mouthed astonishment as the mad music such as they had never heard in their lives before filled the little room with its riot and devilry. Penruddocke stood and panted, his eyes staring out of his head. When Andrea had finished there was a bewildered silence. He nodded pleasantly at his audience, delighted at the effect he had produced. Then, with an artist's malice, he went to the other extreme of emotion. He played a sobbing folk-song, rending the heart with cries of woe and desolation and broken hopes. It clutched at the heart-strings, turning them into vibrating chords; it pierced the soul with its poignant despair; it ended in a long-drawn-out note high up in the treble, whose pain became intolerable; and the end was greeted with a sharp gasp of relief. The white lips of the ruddy giant quivered. Tears streamed down the cheeks of Miss Widdington and Miss Ursula. Again there was silence, but this time it was broken by a clear, shrill voice outside.

"Encore! Encore!"

The sisters looked at one another. Who had dared

intrude at such a moment ? Miss Widdington went to the window to see.

In the garden stood a young woman of independent bearing, with a palette and brushes in her hand. An easel was pitched a few yards beyond the gate. Miss Widdington regarded this young woman with marked disfavour. The girl calmly raised her eyes.

"I apologize for trespassing like this," she said, "but I simply couldn't resist coming nearer to this marvellous violin-playing—and my exclamation came out almost unconsciously."

"You are quite welcome to listen," said Miss Widdington stiffly.

"May I ask who is playing it ?"

Miss Widdington almost gasped at the girl's impertinence. The latter laughed frankly.

"I ask because it seems as if it could only be one of the big, well-known people."

"It's a young friend who is staying with us," said Miss Widdington.

"I beg your pardon," said the girl. "But, you see, my brother is Boris Danilof, the violinist, so I've that excuse for being interested."

"I don't think Mr. Andrea can play any more to-day," said Miss Ursula from her seat by the bed. "He's tired."

Miss Widdington repeated this information to Miss Danilof, who bade her good afternoon and withdrew to her easel.

"A most forward, objectionable girl," exclaimed Miss Widdington. "And who is Boris Danilof, I should like to know ?"

If she had but understood German, Andrea could have told her. He caught at the name of the world-famous violinist and bent eagerly forward in great excitement.

" Doris Danilof? *Ist er unten?* "

" *Nicht*—I mean *Nein*," replied Miss Widdington, proud at not having to consult Otto.

Andrea sank back disappointed on his pillow.

V

However much Miss Widdington disapproved of the young woman, and however little the sisters knew of Boris Danilof, it was obvious that they were harbouring a remarkable violinist. That even the bullet-headed doctor, who had played the double bass in his Hospital Orchestral Society, and was, therefore, an authority, freely admitted. It gave the romantic youth a new and somewhat awe-inspiring value in the eyes of the ladies. He was a genius, said Miss Ursula—and her imagination became touched by the magic of the word. As he grew stronger he played more. His fame spread through the village and he gave recitals to crowded audiences—as many fisher-folk as could be squeezed into the little bedroom, and more standing in the garden below. Miss Danilof did not come again. The ladies learned that she was staying in the next village, Polwern, two or three miles off. In their joy at Andrea's recovery they forgot her existence.

Happy days came when he could rise from bed and hobble about on a crutch, attired in the quaint garments of Captain Widdington, R.N., who had died twenty years before, at the age of seventy-three. They added to his romantic appearance, giving him the air of the *jeune premier* in costume drama. There was a blue waistcoat with gilt buttons, calculated to win any feminine approval. The ladies admired him vastly. Conversation was still difficult, as Miss Ursula had succeeded in teaching him very little English, and Miss Widdington, after a desperate grapple with Otto on her own account, had given up the German language in despair. But what matters the tongue when the heart speaks? And the hearts of Miss Widdington and Miss Ursula spoke; delicately, timidly, tremulously, in the whisper of an evening breeze, in undertones, it is true—yet they spoke all the same. The first walks on the heather of their cliff in the pure spring sunshine were rare joys. As they had done with their watches by his bedside, they took it in turns to walk with him; and each in her turn of solitude felt little pricklings of jealousy. But as each had instituted with him her own particular dainty relations and confidences—Miss Widdington more maternal, Miss Ursula more sisterly—to which his artistic nature responded involuntarily, each felt sure that she was the one who had gained his especial affection.

Thus they wove their gossamer webs of romance in the secret recess of their souls. What they hoped for was as dim and vague as their concept of heaven, and as pure. They looked only at the near future—a circle of light encompassed by mists; but in the circle stood ever the beloved figure. They could not imagine him out of it. He would stay with them, irradiating their lives with his youth and his gaiety, playing to them his divine music, kissing their hands, until he grew quite strong and well again. And that was a long, long way off. Meanwhile life was a perpetual spring. Why should it ever end?

One afternoon they sat in the sunny garden, the ladies busy with needlework, and Andrea playing snatches of dreamy things on the violin. The dainty remains of tea stood on a table, and the young man's crutch rested against it. Presently he began to play Tschaikowsky's *Chanson Triste*. Miss Ursula, look-

45

ing up, saw a girl of plain face and independent bearing
standing by the gate.

"Who is that, Janet'?" she whispered.

Miss Janet glanced round. "It is the impertinent
young woman who was listening the other day."

Andrea followed their glances, and, perceiving a
third listener, half consciously played to her. When
the piece was finished the girl slowly walked away.

"I know it's wrong and unchristianlike," said Miss
Widdington, "but I dislike that girl intensely."

"So do I," said Miss Ursula. Then she laughed.
"She looks like the wicked fairy in a story-book."

VI

The time came when he threw aside his crutch and
flew, laughing, away beyond their control. This they
did not mind, for he always came back and accompanied them on their wild rambles. He now resembled
the ordinary young man of the day as nearly as the
St. Madoc tailors and hosiers could contrive; and the
astonishing fellow, with his cameo face and his hyacin-
thine locks, still looked picturesque.

One morning he took Penruddocke's fiddle and went
off, in high spirits, and when he returned in the late
afternoon his face was flushed and a new light burned
in his eyes. He explained his adventures volubly.
They had a vague impression that, Orion-like, he had
been playing his stringed instrument to dolphins and
waves and things some miles off along the coast. To
please him they said "*Ja*" at every pause in his
narration, and he thought they understood. Finally
he kissed their hands.

Two mornings later he started, without his fiddle,
immediately after breakfast. To Miss Ursula, who

46

accompanied him down the road to the village, he announced Polwern as his destination. Unsuspecting and happy, she bade him good-bye and lovingly watched his lithe young figure disappear behind the bounding cliff of the little bay.

Miss Olga Danilof sat reading a novel by the door of the cottage where she lodged when the beautiful youth came up. He raised his hat—she nodded.

" Well," said she in German, " have you told the funny old maids ? "

" *Ach*," said he, " they are dear, gracious ladies—but I have told them."

" I've heard from my brother," she remarked, taking a letter from the book. " He trusts my judgment implicitly, as I said he would—and you are to come with me to London at once."

" To-day ? "

" By the midday train."

He looked at her in amazement. " But the dear ladies———"

" You can write and explain. My brother's time is valuable—he has already put off his journey to Paris one day in order to see you."

" But I have no money," he objected weakly.

" What does that matter ? I have enough for the railway ticket, and when you see Boris he will give you an advance. Oh, don't be grateful," she added in her independent way. " In the first place, we're brother artists, and in the second it's a pure matter of business. It's much better to put yourself in the hands of Boris Danilof and make a fortune in Europe than to play in a restaurant orchestra in New York ; don't you think so ? "

Andrea did think so, and he blessed the storm that

drove the ship out of its course from Hamburg and
terrified him out of his wits in his steerage quarters, so
that he rushed on deck in shirt and trousers, grasping
a life-belt, only be to cursed one moment by a sailor
and the next to be swept by a wave clean over the
taffrail into the sea. He blessed the storm and he
blessed the wave and he blessed the life-belt which he
lost just before consciousness left him ; and he blessed
the jag of rock on the sandy cove against which he
must have broken his ankle ; and he blessed the ladies
and the sun and the sea and sky and Olga Danilof
and the whole of this beautiful world that had suddenly laid itself at his feet.

The village cart drew up by the door, and Miss
Danilof's luggage that lay ready in the hall was lifted in.

"Come," she said. "You can ask the old maids
to send on your things."

He laughed. "I have no things. I am as free as
the wind."

At St. Madoc, whence he intended to send a telegram to the dear, gracious ladies, they only had just
time to catch the train. He sent no telegram ; and
as they approached London he thought less and less
about it, his mind, after the manner of youth, full of
the wonder that was to be.

VII

The ladies sat down to tea. Eggs were ready to be
boiled as soon as he returned. Not having lunched, he
would be hungry. But he did not come. By dinner-
time they grew anxious. They postponed the meal.
Dorcas came into the drawing-room periodically to
report deterioration of cooked viands. But they
could not eat the meal alone. At last they grew

48

terrified lest some evil should have befallen him, and
Miss Widdington went into the village and despatched
Jan Pendered and Joe Gullow on his bicycle in search.
When she returned she found Miss Ursula looking as
if she had seen a ghost.

"Janet, that girl is living there."

"Where?"

"Polwern. He went there this morning."

Miss Widdington felt as if a cold hand had touched
her heart, but she knew that it behoved her as the
elder to dismiss her sister's fears.

"You're talking nonsense, Ursula; he has never
met her."

"How do we know?" urged Miss Ursula.

"I don't consider it delicate," replied Miss Widdington, "to discuss the possibility."

They said no more, and went out and stood by the
gate, waiting for their messengers. The moon rose
and silvered the sea, and the sea-breeze sprang up; the
surf broke in a melancholy rhythm on the sands beneath.

"It sounds like the *Chanson Triste*," said Miss Ursula. And before them both rose the picture of the girl
standing there like an Evil Fairy while Andrea played.

At last Jan Pendered appeared on the cliff. The
ladies went out to meet him.

Then they learned what had happened.

In a dignified way they thanked Jan Pendered and
gave him a shilling for Joe Gullow, who had brought
the news. They bade him good-night in clear, brave
voices, and walked back very silent and upright through
the garden into the house. In the drawing-room they
turned to each other, and, their arms about each other's
necks, they broke down utterly.

The stranger woman had come and had taken him

49

away from them. Youth had flown magnetically to
youth. They were left alone unheeded in the dry
lavender of their lives.

The moonlight streamed through the white-curtained casement window into the white, spotless room.
It shone on the two little white beds, on the white garments, neatly folded on white chairs, on the white-
whiskered gentleman over the mantelpiece, and on the
white faces of the sisters. They slept little that night
Once Miss Widdington spoke.

"Ursula, we must go to sleep and forget it all.
We've been two old fools."

Miss Ursula sobbed for answer. With the dawn
came a certain quietude of spirit. She rose, put on
her dressing-gown, and, leaving her sister asleep, stole
out on tiptoe. The window was open and the curtains
were undrawn in the boy's empty room. She leaned
on the sill and looked out over the sea. Sooner or
later, she knew, would come a letter of explanation.
She hoped Janet would not force her to read it. She
no longer wanted to know whence he came, whither
he was going. It were better for her, she thought,
not to know. It were better for her to cherish the most
beautiful thing that had ever entered her life. For all
those years she had waited for the prince who never
came ; and he had come at last out of fairyland, cast
up by the sea. She had had with him her brief season
of tremulous happiness. If he had been carried off,
against his will, by the strange woman into the unknown whence he had emerged, it was only the inevitable ending of such a fairy-tale.

Thus wisdom came to her from sea and sky, and
made her strong. She smiled through her tears, and
she, the weaker, went forth for the first time in her
life to comfort and direct her sister.

I

An Old-World Episode

1

I HAVE often thought of editing the diary (which is in my possession) of one Jeremy Wendover, of Bullingford, in the county of Berkshire, England, Gent., who departed this life in the year of grace 1758, and giving to the world a document as human as the record of Pepys and as deeply imbued with the piety of a devout Christian as the Confessions of Saint Augustine. A little emendation of an occasional ungrammatical and disjointed text—though in the main the diary is written in the scholarly, florid style of the eighteenth century ; a little intelligent conjecture as to certain dates ; a footnote now and then elucidating an obscure reference—and the thing would be done. It has been a great temptation, but I have resisted it. The truth is that to the casual reader the human side would seem to be so meagre, the pietistic so full: One has to seek so carefully for a few flowers of fact among a wilderness of religious and philosophical fancy—nay, more : to be so much in sympathy with the diarist as to translate the pious rhetoric into terms of mundane incident, that only to the curious student can the real life history of the man be revealed. And who in these hurrying days would give weeks of patient toil to a task so barren of immediate profit? I myself certainly would not do it; and it is a good working philosophy of life (though it has its drawbacks) not to expect others to do what you would not do yourself. It is only because the study of these yellow pages, covered with the brown, almost microscopic, pointed handwriting, has amused the odd moments of years that I have arrived at something like a comprehension of the things that mattered so much to Jeremy Wendover, and so pathetically little to any other of the sons and daughters of Adam.

How did the diary, you ask, come into my possession? I picked it up, years ago, for a franc, at a second-hand bookseller's in Geneva. It had the bookplate of a long-forgotten Bishop of Sodor and Man, and an inscription on the flyleaf: "John Henderson, Calcutta, 1835." How it came into the hands of the Bishop, into those of John Henderson, how it passed thence and eventually found its way to Geneva, Heaven alone knows.

I have said that Jeremy Wendover departed this life in 1758. My authority for the statement is a lichen-covered gravestone in the churchyard of Bullingford, whither I have made many pious pilgrimages in the hope of finding more records of my obscure hero. But I have been unsuccessful. The house, however, in which he lived, described at some length in his diary, is still standing—an Early Tudor building, the residence of the maltster who owned the adjoining long, gabled malthouse, and from whom he rented it for a considerable term of years. It is situated on the river fringe of the little town, at the end of a lane running at right angles to the main street just before this loses itself in the market square.

I have stood at the front gate of the house and

watched the Thames, some thirty yards away, flow between its alder-grown banks ; the wide, lush meadows and cornfields beyond dotted here and there with the red roofs of farms and spreading amid the quiet greenery of oaks and chestnuts to the low-lying Oxfordshire hills ; I have breathed in the peace of the evening air and I have found myself very near in spirit to Jeremy Wendover, who stood, as he notes, many and many a summer afternoon at that selfsame gate, watching the selfsame scene, far away from the fever and the fret of life.

I have thought, therefore, that instead of publishing his diary I might with some degree of sympathy set forth in brief the one dramatic episode in his inglorious career.

II

The overwhelming factor in Jeremy Wendover's life was the appalling, inconceivable hideousness of his face. The refined, cultivated, pious gentleman was cursed with a visage which it would have pleased Dante to ascribe to a White Guelph whom he particularly disliked, and would have made Orcagna shudder in the midst of his dreams of shapes of hell. As a child of six, in a successful effort to rescue a baby sister, he had fallen headforemost into a great wood fire, and when they picked him up his face " was like unto a charred log that had long smouldered." Almost the semblance of humanity had been wiped from him, and to all beholders he became a thing of horror. Men turned their heads away, women shivered and children screamed at his approach. He was a pariah, condemned from early boyhood to an awful loneliness. His parents, a certain Sir Julius Wendover, Baronet,

c

and his wife, his elder brother and his sisters—they must have been a compassionless family—turned from him as from an evil and pestilential thing. Love never touched him with its consoling feather, and for love the poor wretch pined his whole youth long. Human companionship, even, was denied him. He seems to have lived alone in a wing of a great house, seldom straying beyond the bounds of the park, under the tutorship of a reverend but scholarly sot who was too drunken and obese and unbuttoned to be admitted into the family circle. This fellow, one Doctor Tubbs, of St. Catherine's College, Cambridge, seems to have shown Jeremy some semblance of affection, but chiefly while in his cups, " when," as Jeremy puts it bitterly, " he was too much like unto the beasts that perish to distinguish between me and a human being." When sober he railed at the boy for a monster, and frequently chastised him for his lack of beauty. But, in some strange way, in alternate fits of slobbering and castigating, he managed to lay the groundwork of a fine education, teaching Jeremy the classics, Italian and French, some mathematics, and the elements of philosophy and theology ; he also discoursed much to him on the great world, of which, till his misfortunes came upon him, he boasted of having been a distinguished ornament ; and when he had three bottles of wine inside him he told his charge very curious and instructive things indeed.

So Jeremy grew to man's estate, sensitive, shy, living in the world of books and knowing little, save at second-hand, of the ways of men and women. But with all the secrets of the birds and beasts in the far-stretching Warwickshire park he was intimately acquainted. He became part of the woodland life.

Squirrels would come to him and munch their acorns on his shoulder.

"So intimate was I in this innocent community," says he, not without quiet humour, "that I have been a wet-nurse to weasels and called in as physician to a family of moles."

When Sir Julius died, Jeremy received his younger son's portion (fortunately, it was a goodly one) and was turned neck and crop out of the house by his ill-conditioned brother. Tubbs, having also suffered ignominious expulsion, persuaded him to go on the grand tour. They started. But they only got as far as Abbeville on the road to Paris, where Tubbs was struck down by an apoplexy of which he died. Up to that point the sot's company had enabled Jeremy to endure the insult, ribaldry and terror that attended his unspeakable deformity; but, left alone, he lost heart; mankind rejected him as a pack of wolves reject a maimed cub. Stricken with shame and humiliation, he crept back to England and established himself in the maltster's house at Bullingford, guided thither by no other consideration than that it had been the birth-place of the dissolute Tubbs. He took up his lonely abode there as a boy of three-and-twenty, and there he spent the long remainder of his life.

III

The great event happened in his thirty-fourth year. You may picture him as a solitary, scholarly figure living in the little Tudor house, with its mullioned windows, set in the midst of an old-world garden bright with stocks and phlox and hollyhocks and great pink roses, its southern wall generously glowing with purple plums. Indoors, the house was somewhat dark.

The casement window of the main living-room was small and overshadowed by the heavy ivy outside. The furniture, of plain dark oak, mainly consisted of bookcases, in which were ranged the solemn, leather-covered volumes that were Jeremy's world. A great table in front of the window contained the books of the moment, the latest news-sheets from London, and the great brass-clasped volume in which he wrote his diary. In front of it stood a great straight-backed chair.

You may picture him on a late August afternoon, sitting in this chair, writing his diary by the fading light. His wig lay on the table, for the weather was close. He paused, pen in hand, and looked wistfully at the mellow eastern sky, lost in thought. Then he wrote these words :

O Lord Jesus, fill me plentifully with Thy love, which passeth the love of woman ; for love of woman never will be mine, and therefore, O Lord, I require Thy love bountifully : I yearn for love even as a weaned child. Even as a weaned child yearns for the breast of its mother, so yearn I for love.

He closed and clasped the book with a sigh, put on his wig, rose and, going into the tiny hall, opened the kitchen door and announced to his household, one ancient and incompetent crone, his intention of taking the air. Then he clapped on his old three-cornered hat and, stick in hand, went out of the front gate into the light of the sunset. He stood for a while watching the deep reflections of the alders and willows in the river and the golden peace of the meadows beyond, and his heart was uplifted in thankfulness for the beauty of the earth. He was a tall, thin man, with the stoop of the scholar and, despite his rough, country-made clothes, the unmistakable air of the eighteenth-century gentleman. The setting sun shone full on the piteous medley of marred features that served him for a face.

A woman, sickle on arm, leading a toddling child, passed by with averted head. But she curtsied and said respectfully : "Good evening, your honour." The child looked at him and with a cry of fear shrank into the mother's skirts. Jeremy touched his hat.

"Good evening, Mistress Blackacre. I trust your husband is recovered from his fever."

"Thanks to your honour's kindness," said the woman, her eyes always turned from him, "he is well-nigh recovered. For shame of yourself ! " she added, shaking the child.

"Nay, nay," said Jeremy kindly. "'Tis not the urchin's fault that he met a bogey in broad daylight."

He strolled along the river bank, pleased at his encounter. In that little backwater of the world where he had lived secluded for ten years folks had learned to suffer him—nay, more, to respect him ; and though they seldom looked him in the face their words were gentle and friendly. He could even jest at his own misfortune.

"God is good," he murmured as he walked with head bent down and hands behind his back, "and the earth is full of His goodness. Yet if He in His mercy could only give me a companion in my loneliness, as He gives to every peasant, bird and beast——"

A sigh ended the sentence. He was young and not always able to control the squabble between sex and piety. The words had scarcely passed his lips, however, when he discerned a female figure seated on the bank, some fifty yards away. His first impulse—an

57

impulse which the habit of years would, on ordinary occasions, have rendered imperative—was to make a wide detour round the meadows ; but this evening the spirit of mild revolt took possession of him and guided his steps in the direction of the lady—for lady he perceived her to be when he drew a little nearer.

She wore a flowered muslin dress cut open at the neck, and her arms, bare to the elbows, were white and shapely. A peach-blossom of a face appeared below the mob-cap bound by a cherry-coloured ribbon, and as Jeremy came within speaking distance her dark-blue eyes were fixed on him fearlessly. Jeremy halted and looked at her, while she looked at Jeremy. His heart beat wildly. The miracle of miracles had happened—the hopeless, impossible thing that he had prayed for in rebellious hours for so many years, ever since he had realized that the world held such a thing as the joy and the blessing of woman's love. A girl looked at him smilingly, frankly in the face, without a quiver of repulsion—and a girl more dainty and beautiful than any he had seen before. Then, as he stared, transfixed like a person in a beatitude, into her eyes, something magical occurred to Jeremy. The air was filled with the sound of fairy harps of which his own tingling nerves from head to foot were the vibrating strings. Jeremy fell instantaneously in love.

" Will you tell me, sir," she said in a musical voice—the music of the spheres to Jeremy—" will you tell me how I can reach the house of Mistress Wotherspoon ? "

Jeremy took off his three-cornered hat and made a sweeping bow.

" Why, surely, madam," said he, pointing with his stick ; " 'tis yonder red roof peeping through the trees only three hundred yards distant."

58

"You are a gentleman," said the girl quickly.

"My name is Jeremy Wendover, younger son of the late Sir Julius Wendover, Baronet, and now and always, madam, your very humble servant."

She smiled. Her rosy lips and pearly teeth (Jeremy's own description) filled Jeremy's head with lunatic imaginings.

"And I, sir," said she, "am Mistress Barbara Seaforth, and I came but yesterday to stay with my aunt, Mistress Wotherspoon. If I could trespass so far on your courtesy as to pray you to conduct me thither I should be vastly beholden to you."

His sudden delight at the proposition was mingled with some astonishment. She only had to walk across the open meadow to the clump of trees. He assisted her to rise and with elaborate politeness offered his arm. She made no motion, however, to take it.

"I thought I was walking in my aunt's little railed enclosure," she remarked ; "but I must have passed through the gate into the open fields, and when I came to the river I was frightened and sat down and waited for some one to pass."

"Pray pardon me, madam," said Jeremy, "but I don't quite understand——"

"La, sir ! how very thoughtless of me," she laughed. "I never told you. I am blind."

"Blind !" he echoed. The leaden weight of a piteous dismay fell upon him. That was why she had gazed at him so fearlessly. She had not seen him. The miracle had not happened. For a moment he lost count of the girl's sad affliction in the stress of his own bitterness. But the lifelong habit of resignation prevailed.

"Madam, I crave your pardon for not having noticed it," he said in an unsteady voice. "And I admire

59

the fortitude wherewith you bear so grievous a burden."

"Just because I can't see is no reason for my drowning the world in my tears. We must make the best of things. And there are compensations, too," she added lightly, allowing her hand to be placed on his arm and led away. "I refer to an adventure with a young gentleman which, were I not blind, my Aunt Wotherspoon would esteem mightily unbecoming."

"Alas, madam," said he with a sigh, "there you are wrong. I am not young. I am thirty-three."

He thought it was a great age. Mistress Barbara turned up her face saucily and laughed. Evidently, she did not share his opinion. Jeremy bent a wistful gaze into the beautiful, sightless eyes, and then saw what had hitherto escaped his notice : a thin, grey film over the pupils.

"How did you know," he asked, "that I was a man, when I came up to you ? "

"First by your aged, tottering footsteps, sir," she said with a pretty air of mockery, "which were not those of a young girl. And then you were standing 'twixt me and the sun, and one of my poor eyes can still distinguish light from shadow."

"How long have you suffered from this great affliction ? " he asked.

"I have been going blind for two years. It is now two months since I have lost sight altogether. But please don't talk of it," she added hastily. "If you pity me I shall cry, which I hate, for I want to laugh as much as I can. I can also walk faster, sir, if it would not tire your aged limbs."

Jeremy started guiltily. She had divined his evil purpose. But who will blame him for not wishing to

60

relinquish oversoon the delicious pressure of her little hand on his arm and to give over this blind flower of womanhood into another's charge ? He replied disingenuously, without quickening his pace :

" 'Tis for your sake, madam, I am walking slowly. The afternoon is warm."

" I am vastly sensible of your gallantry, sir," she retorted. " But I fear you must have practised it much on others to have arrived at this perfection."

" By heavens, madam," he cried, cut to the heart by her innocent raillery, " 'tis not so. Could you but see me you would know it was not. I am a recluse, a student, a poor creature set apart from the ways of men. You are the first woman that has walked arm-in-arm with me in all my life—except in dreams. And now my dream has come true."

His voice vibrated, and when she answered hers was responsive.

" You, too, have your burden ? "

" Could you but know how your touch lightens it ! " said he.

She blushed to the brown hair that was visible beneath the mob-cap.

" Are we very far now from my Aunt Wotherspoon's ? " she asked. Whereupon Jeremy, abashed, took refuge in the commonplace.

The open gate through which she had strayed was reached all too quickly. When she had passed through she made him a curtsy and held out her hand. He touched it with his lips as if it were sacramental bread. She avowed herself much beholden to his kindness.

" Shall I ever see you again, Mistress Barbara ? " he asked in a low voice, for an old servant was hobbling down from the house to meet her.

"My Aunt Wotherspoon is bedridden and receives no visitors."

"But could I be of no further service to you?" pleaded Jeremy.

She hesitated and then she said demurely:

"It would be a humane action, sir, to see sometimes that this gate is shut, lest I stray through it again and drown myself in the river."

Jeremy could scarce believe his ears.

IV

This was the beginning of Jeremy's love-story. He guarded the gate like Cerberus or Saint Peter. Sometimes at dawn he would creep out of his house and tramp through the dew-filled meadows to see that it was safely shut. During the day he would do sentry-go within sight of the sacred portal, and when the flutter of a mob-cap and a flowered muslin met his eye he would advance merely to report that the owner ran no danger. And then, one day, she bade him open it, and she came forth and they walked arm-in-arm in the meadows; and this grew to be a daily custom, to the no small scandal of the neighbourhood. Very soon, Jeremy learned her simple history. She was an orphan, with a small competence of her own. Till recently she had lived in Somersetshire with her guardian; but now he was dead, and the only home she could turn to was that of her bedridden Aunt Wotherspoon, her sole surviving relative.

Jeremy, with a lamentable lack of universality, thanked God on his knees for His great mercy. If Mistress Wotherspoon had not been confined to her bed she would not have allowed her niece to wander at will with a notorious scarecrow over the Bullingford

meadows, and if Barbara had not been blind she could
not have walked happily in his company and hung
trustfully on his arm.   For days she was but a wonder
and a wild desire.   Her beauty, her laughter, her wit,
her simplicity, her bravery, bewildered him.   It was
enough to hear the music of her voice, to feel the
fragrance of her presence, to thrill at her light touch.
He, Jeremy Wendover, from whose distortion all
human beings, his life long, had turned shuddering
away, to have this ineffable companionship !   It tran-
scended thought.   At last—it was one night, as he lay
awake, remembering how they had walked that afternoon, not arm-in-arm, but hand-in-hand—the amazing,
dazzling glory of a possibility enveloped him.   She was
blind.   She could never see his deformity.   Had God
listened · to his prayer and delivered this fair and
beloved woman into his keeping ? He shivered all night
long in an ecstasy of happiness, rose at dawn and
mounted guard at Barbara's gate.   But as he waited,
foodless, for the thrilling sight of her, depression came
and sat heavy on his shoulders until he felt that in
daring to think of her in the way of marriage he was
committing an abominable crime.

When she came, fresh as the morning, bareheaded,
her beautiful hair done up in a club behind, into the
little field, and he tried to call to her, his tongue was
dry and he could utter no sound.   Accidentally he
dropped his stick, which clattered down the bars of the
gate.   She laughed.   He entered the enclosure.

"I knew I should find you there," she cried, and
sped towards him.

"How did you know ? " he asked.

" 'By the pricking of my thumbs,' " she quoted
gaily ; and then, as he took both her outstretched

63

hands, she drew near him and whispered : " and by the beating of my heart."

His arms folded around her and he held her tight against him, stupefied, dazed, throbbing, vainly trying to find words. At last he said huskily :

" God has sent you to be the joy and comfort of a sorely stricken man. I accept it because it is His will. I will cherish you as no man has ever cherished woman before. My love for you, my dear, is as infinite—as infinite—oh, God ! "

Speech failed him. He tore his arms away from her and fell sobbing at her feet and kissed the skirts of her gown.

v

The Divine Mercy, as Jeremy puts it, thought fit to remove Aunt Wotherspoon to a happier world before the week was out ; and so, within a month, Jeremy led his blind bride into the little Tudor house. And then began for him a happiness so exquisite that sometimes he was afraid to breathe lest he should disturb the enchanted air. Every germ of love and tenderness that had lain undeveloped in his nature sprang into flower. Sometimes he grew afraid lest, in loving her, he was forgetting God. But he reassured himself by a pretty sophistry. " O Lord," says he, " it is Thou only that I worship—through Thine own great gift." And indeed what more could be desired by a reasonable Deity ?

Barbara, responsive, gave him her love in full. From the first she would hear nothing of his maimed visage.

" My dear," she said as they wandered one golden autumn day by the riverside, " I have made a picture of you out of your voice, the plash of water, the sunset and the summer air. 'Twas thus that my heart saw you the first evening we met. And that is more than sufficing for a poor, blind creature whom a gallant gentleman married out of charity."

" Charity ! " His voice rose in indignant repudiation.

She laughed and laid her head on his shoulder.

" Ah, dear, I did but jest. I know you fell in love with my pretty doll's face. And also with a little mocking spirit of my own."

" But what made you fall in love with me ? "

" Faith, Mr. Wendover," she replied, " a woman with eyes in her head has but to go whither she is driven. And so much the more a blind female like me. You led me plump into the middle of the morass ; and when you came and rescued me I was silly enough to ·be grateful."

Under Jeremy's love her rich nature expanded day by day. She set her joyous courage and her wit to work to laugh at blindness, and to make her the practical, serviceable housewife as well as the gay companion. The ancient crone was replaced by a brisk servant and a gardener, and Jeremy enjoyed creature comforts undreamed of. And the months sped happily by. Autumn darkened into winter and winter cleared into spring, and daffodils and crocuses and primroses began to show themselves in corners of the old-world garden, and tiny gossamer garments in corners of the dark old house. Then a newer, deeper happiness enfolded them.

But there came a twilight hour when, whispering of the wonder that was to come, she suddenly began to cry softly.

" But why, why, dear ? " he asked in tender astonishment.

"Only—only to think, Jeremy, that I shall never see it."

VI

One evening in April, while Jeremy was reading and Barbara sewing in the little candle-lit parlour, almost simultaneously with a sudden downpour of rain came a knock at the front door. Jeremy, startled by this unwonted occurrence, went himself to answer the summons, and, opening the door, was confronted by a stout, youngish man dressed in black with elegant ruffles and a gold-headed cane.

"Your pardon, sir," said the new-comer, "but may I crave a moment's shelter during this shower? I am scarce equipped for the elements."

"Pray enter," said Jeremy hospitably.

"I am from London, and lodging at the 'White Hart' at Bullingford for the night," the stranger explained, shaking the raindrops from his hat. "During a stroll before supper I lost my way, and this storm has surprised me at your gate. I make a thousand apologies for deranging you."

"If you are wet the parlour fire will dry you. I beg you, sir, to follow me," said Jeremy. He led the way through the dark passage and, pausing with his hand on the door-knob, turned to the stranger and said with his grave courtesy :

"I think it right to warn you, sir, that I am afflicted with a certain personal disfigurement which not all persons can look upon with equanimity."

"Sir," replied the other, "my name is John Hattaway, surgeon at St. Thomas's Hospital in London, and I am used to regard with equanimity all forms of human affliction."

66

Mr. Hattaway was shown into the parlour and introduced in due form to Barbara. A chair was set for him near the fire. In the talk that followed he showed himself to be a man of parts and education. He was on his way, he said, to Oxford to perform an operation on the Warden of Merton College.

"What kind of operation?" asked Barbara.

His quick, keen eyes swept her like a searchlight.

"Madam," said he, not committing himself, "'tis but a slight one."

But when Barbara had left the room to mull some claret for her guest, Mr. Hattaway turned to Jeremy.

"'Tis a cataract," said he, "I am about to remove from the eye of the Warden of Merton by the new operation invented by my revered master, Mr. William Cheselden, my immediate predecessor at St. Thomas's. I did not tell your wife, for certain reasons; but I noticed that she is blinded by the same disease."

Jeremy rose from his chair.

"Do you mean that you will restore the Warden's sight?"

"I have every hope of doing so."

"But if his sight can be restored—then my wife's——"

"Can be restored also," said the surgeon complacently.

Jeremy sat down feeling faint and dizzy.

"Did you not know that cataract was curable?"

"I am scholar enough," answered Jeremy, "to have read that King John of Aragon was so cured by the Jew, Abiathar of Lerida, by means of a needle thrust through the eyeball——"

"Barbarous, my dear sir, barbarous!" cried the surgeon, raising a white, protesting hand. "One in a million may be so cured. There is even now a pestilential fellow of a quack, calling himself the Chevalier Taylor, who is prodding folks' eyes with a six-inch skewer. Have you never heard of him?"

"Alas, sir," said Jeremy, "I live so out of the world, and my daily converse is limited to my dear wife and the parson hard by, who is as recluse a scholar as I am myself."

"If you wish your wife to regain her sight," said Mr. Hattaway, "avoid this Chevalier Taylor like the very devil. But if you will intrust her to my care, Mr. Hattaway, surgeon of St. Thomas's Hospital, London, pupil of the great Cheselden——"

He waved his hand by way of completing the unfinished sentence.

"When?" asked Jeremy, greatly agitated.

"After her child is born."

"Shall I tell her?" Jeremy trembled.

"As you will. No—perhaps you had better wait a while."

Then Barbara entered, bearing a silver tray, with the mulled claret and glasses, proud of her blind surety of movement. Mr. Hattaway sprang to assist her and, unknown to her, took the opportunity of scrutinizing her eyes. Then he nodded confidently at Jeremy.

VII

From that evening Jeremy's martyrdom began. Hitherto he had regarded the blindness of his wife as a special dispensation of Divine Providence. She had not seen him save on that first afternoon as a shadowy mass, and had formed no conception of his disfigurement beyond the vague impression conveyed to her by loving fingers touching his face. She had made her own mental picture of him, as she had said, and whatever it was, so far from repelling her, it pleased her mightily. Her ignorance indeed was bliss—for both of them. And now, thought poor Jeremy, knowledge would come with the restored vision, and, like our too-wise first parents, they would be driven out of Eden. Sometimes the devil entered his heart and prompted cowardly concealment. Why tell Barbara of Mr. Hattaway's proposal? Why disturb a happiness already so perfect? All her other senses were eyes to her. She had grown almost unconscious of her affliction. She was happier loving him with blinded eyes than recoiling from him in horror with seeing ones. It was, in sooth, for her own dear happiness, that she should remain in darkness. But then Jeremy remembered the only cry her brave soul had ever uttered, and after wrestling long in prayer he knew that the Evil One had spoken, and in the good, old-fashioned way he bade Satan get behind him. " *Retro me, Satanas.*" The words are in his diary, printed in capital letters.

But one day, when she repeated her cry, his heart ached for her and he comforted her with the golden hope. She wept tears of joy and flung her arms around his neck and kissed him, and from that day forth filled the house with song and laughter and the mirth of unbounded happiness. But Jeremy, though he bespoke her tenderly and hopefully, felt that he had signed his death-warrant. Now and then, when her gay spirit danced through the glowing future, he was tempted to say : " When you see me as I am your love will turn to loathing and our heaven to hell." But he could not find it in his heart to dash her joy. And she never spoke of seeing him—only of seeing the child and the sun and the flowers and the buttons of his shirts, which she vowed must seem to be sewed on by a drunken cobbler.

VIII

The child was born, a boy, strong and lusty—to Jeremy the incarnation of miraculous wonder. That the thing was alive, with legs and arms and feet and hands, and could utter sounds, which it did with much vigour, made demands almost too great on his credulity.

"What is he like?" asked Barbara.

This was a poser for Jeremy. For the pink brat was like nothing on earth—save any other newborn infant.

"I think," he said hesitatingly, "I think he may be said to resemble Cupid. He has a mouth like Cupid's bow."

"And Cupid's wings?" she laughed. "Fie, Jeremy, I thought we had born to us a Christian child."

"But that he has a body," said Jeremy, "I should say he was a cherub. He has eyes of a celestial blue, and his nose——"

"Yes, yes, his nose?" came breathlessly from Barbara.

"I'm afraid, my dear, there is so little of it to judge by," said Jeremy.

"Before the summer's out I shall be able to judge for myself," said Barbara, and terror gripped the man's heart.

The days passed, and Barbara rose from her bed and again sang and laughed.

"See, I am strong enough to withstand any operation," she declared one day, holding out the babe at arm's length.

"Not yet," said Jeremy, "not yet. The child needs you."

The child was asleep. She felt with her foot for its cradle, and with marvellous certainty deposited him gently in the nest and covered him with the tiny coverlet. Then she turned to Jeremy.

"My husband, don't you wish me to have my sight restored?"

"How can you doubt it?" he cried. "I would have you undergo this operation were my life the fee."

She came close to him and put her hands about his maimed face. "Dear," she said, "do you think anything could change my love for you?"

It was the first hint that she had divined his fears; but he remained silent, every fibre of his being shrinking from the monstrous argument. For answer, he kissed her hands as she withdrew them.

At last the time came for the great adventure. Letters passed between Jeremy and Mr. Hattaway of St. Thomas's Hospital, who engaged lodgings in Cork Street, so that they should be near his own residence in Bond Street hard by. A great travelling chariot and post-horses were hired from Bullingford, two great horse-pistols, which Jeremy had never fired off in his life, were loaded and primed and put in the holsters, and one morning in early August Jeremy and Barbara and the nurse and the baby started on their perilous journey. They lay at Reading that night and arrived without misadventure at Cork Street on the following afternoon. Mr. Hattaway called in the evening with two lean and solemn young men, his apprentices—for even the great Mr. Hattaway was but a barber-surgeon practising a trade under the control of a City Guild— and made his preparations for the morrow.

In these days of anæsthetics and cocaine, sterilized instruments, trained nurses and scientific ventilation it is almost impossible to realize the conditions under which surgical operations were conducted in the first half of the eighteenth century. Yet they occasionally were successful, and patients sometimes did survive, and nobody complained, thinking, like Barbara Wendover, that all was for the best in this best of all possible worlds. For, as she lay in the close, darkened room the next day, after the operation was over, tended by a chattering beldame of a midwife, she took the burning pain in her bandaged eyes—after the dare-devil fashion of the time Mr. Hattaway had operated on both at once—as part of the cure, and thanked God she was born into so marvellous an epoch. Then Jeremy came and sat by her bed and held her hand, and she was very happy.

But Jeremy then, and in the slow, torturing days that followed, went about shrunken like a man doomed to worse than death. London increased his agony. At first a natural curiosity (for he had passed through the town but twice before, once as he set out for the grand tour with Doctor Tubbs, and once on his return thence) and a countryman's craving for air took him out into the busy streets. But he found the behaviour of the populace far different from that of the inhabitants of Bullingford, who passed him by respectfully, though with averted faces. Porters and lackeys openly jeered at him, ragged children summoned their congeners and followed hooting in his train ; it was a cruel age, and elegant gentlemen in flowered silk coats and lace ruffles had no compunction in holding their cambric handkerchiefs before their eyes and vowing within his hearing that, stab their vitals, such a fellow should wear a mask or be put into the Royal Society's Museum ; and in St. James's Street one fine lady, stepping out of her sedan-chair almost into his arms, fell back shrieking that she had seen a monster, and pretended to faint as the obsequious staymaker ran out of his shop to her assistance.

He ceased to go abroad in daylight and only crept about the streets at night, even then nervously avoiding the glare of a chance-met linkboy's torch. Desperate thoughts came to him during these gloomy rambles. Fear of God alone, as is evident from the diary, prevented him from taking his life. And the poor wretch prayed for he knew not what.

IX

One morning Mr. Hattaway, after his examination of the patient, entered the parlour where Jeremy was reading *Tillotson's Sermons* (there were the fourteen volumes of them in the room's unlively bookcase) and closed the door behind him with an air of importance.

"Sir," said he, "I bring you good news."

Jeremy closed his book.

"She sees?"

"On removing the bandages just now," replied Mr. Hattaway, "I perceived to my great regret that with the left eye my skill has been unavailing. The failure is due, I believe, to an injury to the retina which I have been unable to discover." He paused and took snuff. "But I rejoice to inform you that sight is restored to the right eye. I admitted light into the room, and though the vision is diffused, which a lens will rectify, she saw me distinctly."

"Thank God she has the blessing of sight," said Jeremy reverently.

"Amen," said the surgeon. He took another pinch.

"Also, perhaps, thank your humble servant for restoring it."

"I owe you an unpayable debt," replied Jeremy.

"She is crying out for the baby," said Mr. Hattaway. "If you will kindly send it in to her I can allow her a fleeting glimpse of it before I complete the rebandaging for the day."

Jeremy rang the bell and gave the order. "And I ?" he inquired bravely.

The surgeon hesitated and scratched his plump cheek.

"You know that my wife has never seen me."

"To-morrow, then," said Hattaway.

The nurse and child appeared at the doorway, and the surgeon followed them into Barbara's room.

When the surgeon had left the house Jeremy went to Barbara and found her crooning over the babe, which lay in her arms.

"I've seen him, dear, I've seen him !" she cried joyously. "He is the most wonderfully beautiful thing on the earth. His eyes are light blue, and mine are dark, so he must have yours. And his mouth is made for kisses, and his expression is that of a babe born in Paradise."

Jeremy bent over and looked at the boy, who sniggered at him in a most unparadisaical fashion and they talked parentwise over his perfections.

"Before we go back to Bullingford you will let me take a coach, Jeremy, and drive about the streets and show him to the town ? I will hold him up and cry : ' Ladies and gentlemen, look ! 'Tis the tenth wonder of the world. You only have this one chance of seeing him.' "

She rattled on in the gayest of moods, making him

laugh in spite of the terror. The failure of the operation in the left eye she put aside as of no account. One eye was a necessity, but two were a mere luxury.

"And it is the little rogue that will reap the benefit," she cried, cuddling the child. "For, when he is naughty mammy will turn the blind side of her face to him."

"And will you turn the blind side of your face to me?" asked Jeremy with a quiver of the lips.

She took his hand and pressed it against her cheek.

"You have no faults, my beloved husband, for me to be blind to," she said, wilfully or not misunderstanding him.

Such rapture had the sight of the child given her that she insisted on its lying with her that night, a truckle-bed being placed in the room for the child's nurse. When Jeremy took leave of her before going to his own room he bent over her and whispered:

"To-morrow."

Her sweet lips—pathetically sweet below the bandage—parted in a smile—and they never seemed sweeter to the anguished man—and she also whispered, "To-morrow!" and kissed him.

He went away, and as he closed the door he felt that it was the gate of Paradise shut against him for ever.

He did not sleep that night, but spent it as a brave man spends the night before his execution. For, after all, Jeremy Wendover was a gallant gentleman.

In the morning he went into Barbara's room before breakfast, as his custom was, and found her still gay and bubbling over with the joy of life. And when he was leaving her she stretched out her hands and clasped his maimed face, as she had done once before, and said the same reassuring words. Nothing could

75

shake her immense, her steadfast love. But Jeremy, entering the parlour and catching sight of himself in the Queen Anne mirror over the mantelpiece, shuddered to the inmost roots of his being. She had no conception of what she vowed.

He was scarce through breakfast when Mr. Hattaway entered, a full hour before his usual time.

"I am in a prodigious hurry," said he, "for I must go post-haste into Norfolk, to operate on my Lord Winteringham for the stone. I have not a moment to lose, so I pray you to accompany me to your wife's bedchamber."

The awful moment had come. Jeremy courteously opened doors for the surgeon to pass through, and followed with death in his heart. When they entered the room he noticed that Barbara had caused the nurse's truckle-bed to be removed and that she was lying, demure as a nun, in a newly-made bed. The surgeon flung the black curtains from the window and let the summer light filter through the linen blinds.

"We will have a longer exposure this morning," said he, "and to-morrow a little longer still, and so on until we can face the daylight altogether. Now, madam, if you please."

He busied himself with the bandages. Jeremy, on the other side of the bed, stood clasping Barbara's hand : stood stock-still, with thumping heart, holding his breath, setting his teeth, nerving himself for the sharp, instinctive gasp, the reflex recoil, that he knew would be the death sentence of their love. And at that supreme moment he cursed himself bitterly for a fool for not having told her of his terror, for not having sufficiently prepared her for the devastating revelation. But now it was too late.

The bandages were removed. The surgeon bent down and peered into the eyes. He started back in dismay. Before her right eye he rapidly waved his finger.

"Do you see that?"

"No," said Barbara.

"My God, madam!" cried he, with a stricken look on his plump face, "what in the devil's name have you been doing with yourself?"

Great drops of sweat stood on Jeremy's brow.

"What do you mean?" he asked.

"She can't see. The eye is injured. Yesterday, save for the crystalline lens which I extracted, it was as sound as mine or yours."

"I was afraid something had happened," said Barbara in a matter-of-fact tone. "Baby was restive in the night and pushed his little fist into my eye."

"Good heavens, madam!" exclaimed the angry surgeon, "you don't mean to say that you took a young baby to sleep with you in your condition?"

Barbara nodded, as if found out in a trifling peccadillo. "I suppose I'm blind for ever?" she asked casually.

He examined the eye again. There was a moment's dead silence. Jeremy, white-lipped and haggard, hung on the verdict. Then Hattaway rose, extended his arms and let them drop helplessly against his sides.

"Yes," said he. "The sight is gone."

Jeremy put his hands to his head, staggered, and, overcome by the reaction from the terror and the shock of the unlooked-for calamity, fell in a faint on the floor.

After he had recovered and the surgeon had gone, promising to send his apprentice the next day to dress

77

the eyes, which, for fear of inflammation, still needed tending, Jeremy sat by his wife's bedside with an aching heart.

"'Tis the will of God," said he gloomily. "We must not rebel against His decrees."

"But, you dear, foolish husband," she cried, half laughing, "who wants to rebel against them? Not I, of a certainty. I am the happiest woman in the world."

"'Tis but to comfort me that you say it," said Jeremy.

"'Tis the truth. Listen." She sought for his hand and continued with sweet seriousness: "I was selfish to want to regain my sight; but my soul hungered to see my babe. And now that I have seen him I care not. Just that one little peep into the heaven of his face was all I wanted. And 'twas the darling wretch himself who settled that I should not have more." After a little she said, "Come nearer to me," and she drew his ear to her lips and whispered:

"Although I have not regained my sight, on the other hand I have not lost a thing far dearer—the face that I love which I made up of your voice and the plash of water and the sunset and the summer air." She kissed him. "My poor husband, how you must have suffered!"

And then Jeremy knew the great, brave soul of the woman whom the Almighty had given him to wife, and, as he puts it in his diary, he did glorify God exceedingly.

So when Barbara was able to travel again Jeremy sent for the great, roomy chariot and the horse-pistols and the post-horses, and they went back to Bulling-ford, where they spent the remainder of their lives in unclouded felicity.

II

The Conqueror

MISS WINIFRED GOODE sat in her garden in the shade of a clipped yew, an unopened novel on her lap, and looked at the gabled front of the Tudor house that was hers and had been her family's for many generations. In that house, Duns Hall, in that room beneath the southernmost gable, she had been born. From that house, save for casual absences rarely exceeding a month in duration, she had never stirred. All the drama, such as it was, of her life had been played in that house, in that garden. Up and down the parapeted stone terrace walked the ghosts of all those who had been dear to her—her father, a vague but cherished memory; a brother and a sister who had died during her childhood; her mother, dead three years since, to whose invalid and somewhat selfish needs she had devoted all her full young womanhood. Another ghost walked there, too; but that was the ghost of the living—a young man who had kissed and ridden away, twenty years ago. He had kissed her over there, under the old wistaria arbour at the end of the terrace. What particular meaning he had put into the kiss, loverly, brotherly, cousinly, friendly—for they had played together all their young lives, and were distantly connected—she had never been able to determine. In

79

spite of his joy at leaving the lethargic country town of Dunsfield for America, their parting had been sad and sentimental. The kiss, at any rate, had been, on his side, one of sincere affection—an affection proven afterwards by a correspondence of twenty years. To her the kiss had been—well, the one and only kiss of her life, and she had treasured it in a neat little sacred casket in her heart. Since that far-off day no man had ever showed an inclination to kiss her, which, in one way, was strange, as she had been pretty and gentle and laughter-loving, qualities attractive to youths in search of a mate. But in another way it was not strange, as mate-seeking youths are rare as angels in Dunsfield, beyond whose limits Miss Goode had seldom strayed. Her romance had been one kiss, the girlish dreams of one man. At first, when he had gone fortune-hunting in America, she had fancied herself broken-hearted ; but Time had soon touched her with healing fingers. Of late, freed from the slavery of a querulous bedside, she had grown in love with her unruffled and delicately ordered existence, in which the only irregular things were her herbaceous borders, between which she walked like a prim schoolmistress among a crowd of bright but unruly children. She had asked nothing more from life than what she had— her little duties in the parish, her little pleasures in the neighbourhood, her good health, her old house, her trim lawns, her old-fashioned garden, her black cocker spaniels. As it was at forty, she thought, so should it be till the day of her death.

But a month ago had come turmoil. Roger Orme announced his return. Fortune-making in America had tired him. He was coming home to settle down for good in Dunsfield, in the house of his fathers. This was Duns Lodge, whose forty acres marched with the two hundred acres of Duns Hall. The two places were known in the district as "The Lodge" and "The Hall." About a century since, a younger son of The Hall had married a daughter of The Lodge, whence the remote tie of consanguinity between Winifred Goode and Roger Orme. The Lodge had been let on lease for many years, but now the lease had fallen in and the tenants gone. Roger had arrived in England yesterday. A telegram had bidden her expect him that afternoon. She sat in the garden expecting him, and stared wistfully at the old grey house, a curious fear in her eyes.

Perhaps, if freakish chance had not brought Mrs. Donovan to Dunsfield on a visit to the Rector, a day or two after Roger's letter, fear—foolish, shameful, sickening fear—might not have had so dominant a place in her anticipation of his home-coming. Mrs. Donovan was a contemporary, a Dunsfield girl, who had married at nineteen and gone out with her husband to India. Winifred Goode remembered a gipsy beauty riotous in the bloom of youth. In the Rector's drawing-room she met a grey-haired, yellow-skinned, shrivelled caricature, and she looked in the woman's face as in a mirror of awful truth in which she herself was reflected. From that moment she had known no peace. Gone was her placid acceptance of the footprints of the years, gone her old-maidish pride in dainty, old-maidish dress. She had mixed little with the modern world, and held to old-fashioned prejudices which prescribed the outward demeanour appropriate to each decade. One of her earliest memories was a homely saying of her father's—which had puzzled her childish mind considerably—as to the absurdity of

81

sheep being dressed lamb fashion. Later she understood and cordially agreed with the dictum. The
Countess of Ingleswood, the personage of those lati-
tudes, at the age of fifty showed the fluffy golden hair
and peach-bloom cheeks and supple figure of twenty ;
she wore bright colours and dashing hats, and danced
and flirted and kept a tame-cattery of adoring young
men. Winifred visited with Lady Ingleswood because
she believed that, in these democratic days, it was the
duty of county families to outmatch the proletariat in
solidarity ; but, with every protest of her gentle-
woman's soul, she disapproved of Lady Ingleswood.
Yet now, to her appalling dismay, she saw that, with
the aid of paint, powder, and peroxide, Lady Ingleswood had managed to keep young. For thirty years
to Winifred's certain knowledge, she had not altered.
The blasting hand that had swept over Madge Donovan's face had passed her by.

Winifred envied the woman's power of attraction.
She read, with a curious interest, hitherto disregarded
advertisements. They were so alluring, they seemed
so convincing. Such a cosmetic used by queens of
song and beauty restored the roses of girlhood ; under
such a treatment, wrinkles disappeared within a week
—there were the photographs to prove it. All over
London bubbled fountains of youth, at a mere guinea
or so a dip. She sent for a little battery of washes and
powders, and, when it arrived, she locked herself in
her bedroom. But the sight of the first unaccustomed
—and unskilfully applied—dab of rouge on her cheek
terrified her. She realized what she was doing. No !
Ten thousand times no ! Her old-maidishness, her
puritanism revolted. She flew to her hand-basin and
vigorously washed the offending bloom away with

soap and water. She would appear before the man she loved just as she was—if need be, in the withered truth of a Madge Donovan. . . . And, after all, had her beauty faded so utterly ? Her glass said " No." But her glass mocked her, for how could she conjure up the young face of twenty which Roger Orme carried in his mind, and compare it with the present image ?

She sat in the garden, this blazing July afternoon, waiting for him, her heart beating with the love of years ago, and the shrinking fear in her eyes. Presently she heard the sound of wheels, and she saw the open fly of " The Red Lion "—Dunsfield's chief hotel —crawling up the drive, and in it was a man wearing a straw hat. She fluttered a timid handkerchief, but the man, not looking in her direction, did not respond. She crossed the lawn to the terrace, feeling hurt, and entered the drawing-room by the open French window and stood there, her back to the light. Soon he was announced. She went forward to meet him.

" My dear Roger, welcome home."

He laughed and shook her hand in a hearty grip.

" It's you, Winifred ? How good ! Are you glad to see me back ? "

" Very glad."

" And I."

" Do you find things changed ? "

" Nothing," he declared with a smile ; " the house is just the same." He ran his fingers over the corner of a Louis XVI table near which he was standing. " I remember this table, in this exact spot, twenty years ago."

" And you have scarcely altered. I should have known you anywhere."

" I should just hope so," said he.

She realized, with a queer little pang, that time had improved the appearance of the man of forty-five. He was tall, strong, erect; few accusing lines marked his clean-shaven, florid, clear-cut face; in his curly brown hair she could not detect a touch of grey. He had a new air of mastery and success which expressed itself in the corners of his firm lips and the steady, humorous gleam in his eyes.

"You must be tired after your hot train journey," she said.

He laughed again. "Tired? After a couple of hours? Now, if it had been a couple of days, as we are accustomed to on the other side—— But go on talking, just to let me keep on hearing your voice. It's yours—I could have recognized it over a long-distance telephone—and it's English. You've no idea how delicious it is. And the smell of the room "—he drew in a deep breath—" is you and the English country. I tell you, it's good to be back!"

She flushed, his pleasure was so sincere, and she smiled.

"But why should we stand? Let me take your hat and stick."

"Why shouldn't we sit in the garden—after my hot and tiring journey?" They both laughed. "Is the old wistaria still there, at the end of the terrace?"

She turned her face away. "Yes, still there. Do you remember it?" she asked in a low voice.

"Do you think I could forget it? I remember every turn of the house."

"Let us go outside, then."

She led the way, and he followed, to the trellis arbour, a few steps from the drawing-room door. The long lilac blooms had gone with the spring, but the

84

luxuriant summer leafage cast a grateful shade. Roger Orme sat in a wicker chair and fanned himself with his straw hat.

"Delightful!" he said. "And I smell stocks! It does carry me back. I wonder if I have been away at all."

"I'm afraid you have," said Winifred—"for twenty years."

"Well, I'm not going away again. I've had my share of work. And what's the good of work just to make money? I've made enough. I sold out before I left."

"But in your letters you always said you liked America."

"So I did. It's the only country in the world for the young and eager. If I had been born there, I should have no use for Dunsfield. But a man born and bred among old, sleepy things has the nostalgia of old, sleepy things in his blood. Now tell me about the sleepy old things. I want to hear."

"I think I have written to you about everything that ever happened in Dunsfield," she said.

But still there were gaps to be bridged in the tale of births and marriages and deaths, the main chronicles of the neighbourhood. He had a surprising memory, and plucked obscure creatures from the past whom even Winifred had forgotten.

"It's almost miraculous how you remember."

"It's a faculty I've had to cultivate," said he.

They talked about his immediate plans. He was going to put The Lodge into thorough repair, bring everything up-to-date, lay in electric light and a central heating installation, fix bathrooms wherever bathrooms would go, and find a place somewhere for a billiard-room. His surveyor had already made his report, and was to meet him at the house the following morning. As for decorations, curtaining, carpeting, and such-like æsthetic aspects, he was counting on Winifred's assistance. He thought that blues and browns would harmonize with the oak-panelling in the dining-room. Until the house was ready, his headquarters would be " The Red Lion."

" You see, I'm going to begin right now," said he.

She admired his vitality, his certainty of accomplishment. The Hall was still lit by lamps and candles ; and although, on her return from a visit, she had often deplored the absence of electric light, she had shrunk from the strain and worry of an innovation. And here was Roger turning the whole house inside out more cheerfully than she would turn out a drawer.

" You'll help me, won't you ? " he asked. " I want a home with a touch of the woman in it ; I've lived so long in masculine stiffness."

" You know that I should love to do anything I could, Roger," she replied happily.

He remarked again that it was good to be back. No more letters—they were unsatisfactory, after all. He hoped she had not resented his business man's habit of typewriting. This was in the year of grace eighteen hundred and ninety-two, and, save for Roger's letters, typewritten documents came as seldom as judgment summonses to Duns Hall.

" We go ahead in America," said he.

" ' The old order changeth, yielding place to new.' I accept it," she said with a smile.

" What I've longed for in Dunsfield," he said, " is

the old order that doesn't change. I don't believe anything has changed."

She plucked up her courage. Now she would challenge him—get it over at once. She would watch his lips as he answered.

"I'm afraid I must have changed, Roger."

"In what way?"

"I am no longer twenty."

"Your voice is just the same."

Shocked, she put up her delicate hands. "Don't— it hurts!"

"What?"

"You needn't have put it that way—you might have told a polite lie."

He rose, turned aside, holding the back of the wicker chair.

"I've got something to tell you," he said abruptly. "You would have to find out soon, so you may as well know now. But don't be alarmed or concerned. I can't see your face."

"What do you mean?"

"I've been stone blind for fifteen years."

"Blind?"

She sat for some moments paralysed. It was inconceivable. This man was so strong, so alive, so masterful, with the bright face and keen, humorous eyes— and blind! A trivial undercurrent of thought ran subconsciously beneath her horror. She had wondered why he had insisted on sounds and scents, why he had kept his stick in his hand, why he had touched things —tables, window jambs, chairs—now she knew. Roger went on talking, and she heard him in a dream. He had not informed her when he was stricken, because he had wished to spare her unnecessary anxiety.

Also, he was proud, perhaps hard, and resented sympathy. He had made up his mind to win through in spite of his affliction. For some years it had been the absorbing passion of his life. He had won through like many another, and, as the irreparable detachment of the retina had not disfigured his eyes, it was his joy to go through the world like a seeing man, hiding his blindness from the casual observer. By dictated letter he could never have made her understand how trifling a matter it was.

"And I've deceived even you!" he laughed.

Tears had been rolling down her cheeks. At his laugh she gave way. An answering choke, hysterical, filled her throat, and she burst into a fit of sobbing. He laid his hand tenderly on her head.

"My dear, don't. I am the happiest man alive. And, as for eyes, I'm rich enough to buy a hundred pairs. I'm a perfect Argus!"

But Winifred Goode wept uncontrollably. There was deep pity for him in her heart, but—never to be revealed to mortal—there was also horrible, terrifying joy. She gripped her hands and sobbed frantically to keep herself from laughter. A woman's sense of humour is often cruel, only to be awakened by tragic incongruities. She had passed through her month's agony and shame for a blind man.

At last she mastered herself. "Forgive me, dear Roger. It was a dreadful shock. Blindness has always been to me too awful for thought—like being buried alive."

"Not a bit of it," he said cheerily. " I've run a successful business in the dark—real estate—buying and selling and developing land, you know—a thing which requires a man to keep a sharp look-out, and which he couldn't do if he were buried alive. It's a confounded nuisance, I admit, but so is gout. Not half as irritating as the position of a man I once knew who had both hands cut off."

She shivered. " That's horrible."

" It is," said he, " but blindness isn't."

The maid appeared with the tea-tray, which she put on a rustic table. It was then that Winifred noticed the little proud awkwardnesses of the blind man. There was pathos in his insistent disregard of his affliction. The imperfectly cut lower half of a water-cress sandwich fell on his coat and stayed there. She longed to pick it off but did not dare, for fear of hurting him. He began to talk again of the house—the scheme of decoration.

" Oh, it all seems so sad ! " she cried.

" What ? "

" You'll not be able to see the beautiful things."

" Good Heavens," he retorted, " do you think I am quite devoid of imagination ? And do you suppose no one will enter the house but myself ? "

" I never thought of that," she admitted.

" As for the interior, I've got the plan in my head, and could walk about it now blindfold, only that's unnecessary ; and when it's all fixed up, I'll have a ground model made of every room, showing every piece of furniture, so that, when I get in, I'll know the size, shape, colour, quality of every blessed thing in the house. You see if I don't."

" These gifts are a merciful dispensation of Providence."

" Maybe," said he dryly. " Only they were about the size of bacteria when I started, and it took me years of incessant toil to develop them."

He asked to be shown around the garden. She took him up the gravelled walks beside her gay borders and her roses, telling him the names and varieties of the flowers. Once he stopped and frowned.

"I've lost my bearings. We ought to be passing under the shade of the old walnut tree."

"You are quite right," she said, marvelling at his accuracy. "It stood a few steps back, but it was blown clean down three years ago. It had been dead for a long time."

He chuckled as he strolled on. "There's nothing makes me so mad as to be mistaken."

Some time later, on their return to the terrace, he held out his hand.

"But you'll stay for dinner, Roger," she exclaimed. "I can't bear to think of you spending your first evening at home in that awful 'Red Lion.'"

"That's very dear of you, Winnie," he said, evidently touched by the softness in her voice. "I'll dine with pleasure, but I must get off some letters first. I'll come back. You've no objection to my bringing my man with me?"

"Why, of course not." She laid her hand lightly on his arm. "Oh, Roger dear, I wish I could tell you how sorry I am, how my heart aches for you!"

"Don't worry," he said—"don't worry a little bit, and, if you really want to help me, never let me feel that you notice I'm blind. Forget it, as I do."

"I'll try," she said.

"That's right." He held her hand for a second or two, kissed it, and dropped it, abruptly. "God bless you!" said he. "It's good to be with you again."

When he was gone, Winifred Goode returned to her seat by the clipped yew and cried a little, after

90

the manner of women. And, after the manner of women, she dreamed dreams oblivious of the flight of time till her maid came out and hurried her indoors.

She dressed with elaborate care, in her best and costliest, and wore more jewels than she would have done had her guest been of normal sight, feeling oddly shaken by the thought of his intense imaginative vision. In trying to fasten the diamond clasp of a velvet band round her neck, her fingers trembled so much that the maid came to her assistance. Her mind was in a whirl. Roger had left her a headstrong, dissatisfied boy. He had returned, the romantic figure of a conqueror, all the more romantic and conquering by reason of his triumph over the powers of darkness. In his deep affection she knew her place was secure. The few hours she had passed with him had shown her that he was a man trained in the significance not only of words, but also of his attitude towards individual men and women. He would not have said " God bless you ! " unless he meant it. She appreciated to the full his masculine strength ; she took to her heart his masculine tenderness ; she had a woman's pity for his affliction ; she felt unregenerate exultancy at the undetected crime of lost beauty, and yet she feared him on account of the vanished sense. She loved him with a passionate recrudescence of girlish sentiment ; but the very thing that might have, that ought to have, that she felt it indecent not to have, inflamed all her woman's soul and thrown her reckless into his arms, raised between them an impalpable barrier against which she dreaded lest she might be dashed and bruised.

At dinner this feeling was intensified. Roger made

91

little or no allusion to his blindness ; he talked with the ease of the cultivated man of the world. He had humour, gaiety, charm. As a mere companion, she had rarely met, during her long seclusion, a man so instinctive in sympathy, so quick in diverting talk into a channel of interest. In a few flashing yet subtle questions, he learned what she wore. The diamond clasp to the black velvet band he recognized as having been her mother's. He complimented her delicately on her appearance, as though he saw her clearly, in the adorable twilight beauty that was really hers. There were moments when it seemed impossible that he should be blind. But behind his chair, silent, impassive, arresting, freezing, hovered his Chinese body-servant, capped, pig-tailed, loosely clad in white, a creature as unreal in Dunsfield as gnome or merman, who, with the unobtrusiveness of a shadow from another world, served, in the mechanics of the meal, as an accepted, disregarded, and unnoticed pair of eyes for his master. The noble Tudor dining-room, with its great carved oak chimney-piece, its stately gilt-framed portraits, its Jacobean sideboards and presses, all in the gloom of the spent illumination of the candles on the daintily-set table, familiar to her from her earliest childhood, part of her conception of the cosmos, part of her very self, seemed metamorphosed into the unreal, the phantasmagoric, by the presence of this white-clad, exotic figure—not a man, but an eerie embodiment of the sense of sight.

Her reason told her that the Chinese servant was but an ordinary serving-man, performing minutely specified duties for a generous wage. But the duties were performed magically, like conjuror's tricks. It was practically impossible to say who cut up Roger's meat, who helped him to salt or to vegetables, who guided his hand unerringly to the wine-glass. So abnormally exquisite was the co-ordination between the two, that Roger seemed to have the man under mesmeric control. The idea bordered on the monstrous. Winifred shivered through the dinner, in spite of Roger's bright talk, and gratefully welcomed the change of the drawing-room, whither the white-vestured automaton did not follow.

"Will you do me a favour, Winnie?" he asked during the evening. "Meet me at The Lodge to-morrow at eleven, and help me interview these building people. Then you can have a finger in the pie from the very start."

She said somewhat tremulously: "Why do you want me to have a finger in the pie?"

"Good Heavens," he cried, "aren't you the only human creature in this country I care a straw about?"

"Is that true, Roger?"

"Sure," said he. After a little span of silence he laughed. "People on this side don't say 'sure.' That's sheer American."

"I like it," said Winifred.

When he parted from her, he again kissed her hand and again said: "God bless you!" She accompanied him to the hall, where the Chinaman, ghostly in the dimness, was awaiting him with hat and coat. Suddenly she felt that she abhorred the Chinaman.

That night she slept but little, striving to analyse her feelings. Of one fact only did the dawn bring certainty—that, for all her love of him, for all his charm, for all his tenderness towards her, during dinner she had feared him horribly.

She saw him the next morning in a new and yet

oddly familiar phase. He was attended by his secretary, a pallid man with a pencil, note-book, and documents, for ever at his elbow, ghostly, automatic, during their wanderings with the surveyor through the bare and desolate old house.

She saw the master of men at work, accurate in every detail of a comprehensive scheme, abrupt, imperious, denying difficulties with harsh impatience. He leaned over his secretary and pointed to portions of the report just as though he could read them, and ordered their modification.

" Mr. Withers," he said once to the surveyor, who was raising objections, " I always get what I want because I make dead sure that what I want is attainable. I'm not an idealist. If I say a thing is to be done, it has got to be done, and it's up to you or to some one else to do it."

They went through the house from furnace to garret, the pallid secretary ever at Roger's elbow, ever rendering him imperceptible services, ever identifying himself with the sightless man, mysteriously following his thoughts, co-ordinating his individuality with that of his master. He was less a man than a trained faculty, like the Chinese servant. And again Winifred shivered and felt afraid.

More and more during the weeks that followed, did she realize the iron will and irresistible force of the man she loved. He seemed to lay a relentless grip on all those with whom he came in contact and compel them to the expression of himself. Only towards her was he gentle and considerate. Many times she accompanied him to London to the great shops, the self-effacing secretary shadow-like at his elbow, and discussed with him colours and materials, and he listened to her with affectionate deference. She often noticed that the secretary translated into other terms her description of things. This irritated her, and once she suggested leaving the secretary behind. Surely, she urged, she could do all that was necessary. He shook his head.

"No, my dear," he said very kindly. "Jukes sees for me. I shouldn't like you to see for me in the way Jukes does."

She was the only person from whom he would take advice or suggestion, and she rendered him great service in the tasteful equipment of the house and in the engagement of a staff of servants. So free a hand did he allow her in certain directions, so obviously and deliberately did he withdraw from her sphere of operations, that she was puzzled. It was not until later, when she knew him better, that the picture vaguely occurred to her of him caressing her tenderly with one hand, and holding the rest of the world by the throat with the other.

On the day when he took up his residence in the new home, they walked together through the rooms. In high spirits, boyishly elated, he gave her an exhibition of his marvellous gifts of memory, minutely describing each bit of furniture and its position in every room, the colour-scheme, the texture of curtains, the pictures on the walls, the knick-knacks on mantelpieces and tables. And when he had done, he put his arm round her shoulders.

"But for you, Winnie," said he, "this would be the dreariest possible kind of place; but the spirit of you pervades it and makes it a fragrant paradise."

The words and tone were lover-like, and so was his clasp. She felt very near him, very happy, and her heart throbbed quickly. She was ready to give her life to him.

"You are making me a proud woman," she murmured.

He patted her shoulder and laughed as he released her.

"I only say what's true, my dear," he replied, and then abruptly skipped from sentiment to practical talk.

Winifred had a touch of dismay and disappointment. Tears started, which she wiped away furtively. She had made up her mind to accept him, in spite of Wang Fu and Mr. Jukes, if he should make her a proposal of marriage. She had been certain that the moment had come. But he made no proposal.

She waited. She waited a long time. In the meanwhile, she continued to be Roger's intimate friend and eagerly-sought companion. One day his highly-paid and efficient housekeeper came to consult her. The woman desired to give notice. Her place was too difficult. She could scarcely believe the master was blind. He saw too much, he demanded too much. She could say nothing explicit, save that she was frightened. She wept, after the nature of upset housekeepers. Winifred soothed her and advised her not to throw up so lucrative a post, and, as soon as she had an opportunity, she spoke to Roger. He laughed his usual careless laugh.

"They all begin that way with me, but after a while they're broken in. You did quite right to tell Mrs. Strode to stay."

And after a few months Winifred saw a change in Mrs. Strode, and not only in Mrs. Strode, but in all the servants whom she had engaged. They worked the household like parts of a flawless machine. They

96

grew to be imperceptible, shadowy, automatic, like Wang Fu and Mr. Jukes.

*   *   *   *   *

The months passed and melted into years. Roger Orme became a great personage in the neighbourhood. He interested himself in local affairs, served on the urban district council and on boards innumerable. They made him Mayor of Dunsfield. He subscribed largely to charities and entertained on a sumptuous scale. He ruled the little world, setting a ruthless heel on proud necks and making the humble his instruments. Mr. Jukes died, and other secretaries came, and those who were not instantly dismissed grew to be like Mr. Jukes. In the course of time Roger entered Parliament as member for the division. He became a force in politics, in public affairs. In the appointment of Royal Commissions, committees of inquiry, his name was the first to occur to ministers, and he was invariably respected, dreaded, and hated by his colleagues.

"Why do you work so hard, Roger?" Winifred would ask.

He would say, with one of his laughs : " Because there's a dynamo in me that I can't stop."

And all these years Miss Winifred Goode stayed at Duns Hall, leading her secluded, lavender-scented life when Roger was in London, and playing hostess for him, with diffident graciousness, when he entertained at The Lodge. His attitude towards her never varied, his need of her never lessened.

He never asked her to be his wife. At first she wondered, pined a little, and then, like a brave, proud woman, put the matter behind her. But she knew that she counted for much in his strange existence, and the knowledge comforted her. And as the years went on, and all the lingering shreds of youth left her, and she grew gracefully into the old lady, she came to regard her association with him as a spiritual marriage.

Then, after twenty years, the dynamo wore out the fragile tenement of flesh. Roger Orme, at sixty-five, broke down and lay on his death-bed. One day he sent for Miss Winifred Goode.

She entered the sick-room, a woman of sixty, white-haired, wrinkled, with only the beauty of a serene step across the threshold of old age. He bade the nurse leave them alone, and put out his hand and held hers as she sat beside the bed.

"What kind of a day is it, Winnie?"

"As if you didn't know! You've been told, I'm sure, twenty times."

"What does it matter what other people say? I want to get at the day through you."

"It's bright and sunny—a perfect day of early summer."

"What things are out?"

"The may and the laburnum and the lilac——"

"And the wistaria?"

"Yes, the wistaria."

"It's forty years ago, dear, and your voice is just the same. And to me you have always been the same. I can see you as you sit there, with your dear, sensitive face, the creamy cheek, in which the blood comes and goes—oh, Heavens, so different from the blowsy, hard-featured girls nowadays, who could not blush if—well—well—— I know 'em, although I'm blind—I'm Argus, you know, dear. Yes, I can see you, with your soft, brown eyes and pale brown hair waved over your

98

pure brow. There is a fascinating little kink on the left-hand side. Let me feel it."

She drew her head away, frightened. Then suddenly she remembered, with a pang of thankfulness, that the queer little kink had defied the years, though the pale brown hair was white. She guided his hand and he felt the kink, and he laughed in his old, exultant way.

" Don't you think I'm a miracle, Winnie ? "

" You're the most wonderful man living," she said.

" I shan't be living long. No, my dear, don't talk platitudes. I know. I'm busted. And I'm glad I'm going before I begin to dodder. A seeing dodderer is bad enough, but a blind dodderer's only fit for the grave. I've lived my life. I've proved to this stupendous clot of ignorance that is humanity that a blind man can guide them wherever he likes. You know I refused a knighthood. Any tradesman can buy a knighthood—the only knighthoods that count are those that are given to artists and writers and men of science—and, if I could live, I'd raise hell over the matter, and make a differentiation in the titles of honour between the great man and the rascally cheese-monger——"

" My dear," said Miss Winifred Goode, " don't get so excited."

" I'm only saying, Winnie, that I refused a knighthood. But—what I haven't told you, what I'm supposed to keep a dead secret—if I could live a few weeks longer, and I shan't, I should be a Privy Councillor—a thing worth being. I've had the official intimation—a thing that can't be bought. Heavens, if I were a younger man, and there were the life in me, I should be the Prime Minister of this country—the first great

99

blind ruler that ever was in the world. Think of it! But I don't want anything now. I'm done. I'm glad. The whole caboodle is but leather and prunella. There is only one thing in the world that is of any importance."

"What is that, dear?" she asked quite innocently, accustomed to, but never familiar with, his vehement paradox.

"Love," said he.

He gripped her hand hard. There passed a few seconds of tense silence.

"Winnie dear," he said at last, "will you kiss me?"

She bent forward, and he put his arm round her neck and drew her to him. They kissed each other on the lips.

"It's forty years since I kissed you, dear—that day under the wistaria. And, now I'm dying, I can tell you. I've loved you all the time, Winnie. I'm a tough nut, as you know, and whatever I do I do intensely. I've loved you intensely, furiously."

She turned her head away, unable to bear the living look in the sightless eyes.

"Why did you never tell me?" she asked in a low voice.

"Would you have married me?"

"You know I would, Roger."

"At first I vowed I would say nothing," he said, after a pause, "until I had a fit home to offer you. Then the blindness came, and I vowed I wouldn't speak until I had conquered the helplessness of my affliction. Do you understand?"

"Yes, but when you came home a conqueror——"

"I loved you too much to marry you. You were far too dear and precious to come into the intimacy of my life. Haven't you seen what happened to all those who did ? " He raised his old knotted hands, clenched tightly. " I squeezed them dry. I couldn't help it. My blindness made me a coward. It has been hell. The darkness never ceased to frighten me ; I lied when I said it didn't matter. I stretched out my hands like tentacles and gripped every one within reach in a kind of madness of self-preservation. I made them give up their souls and senses to me. It was some ghastly hypnotic power I seemed to have. When I had got them, they lost volition, individuality. They were about as much living creatures to me as my arm or my foot. Don't you see ? "

The white-haired woman looked at the old face working passionately, and she felt once more the deadly fear of him.

" But with me it would have been different," she faltered. " You say you loved me."

" That's the devil of it, my sweet, beautiful Winnie —it wouldn't have been different. I should have squeezed you, too, reduced you to the helpless thing that did my bidding, sucked your life's blood from you. I couldn't have resisted. So I kept you away. Have I ever asked you to use your eyes for me ? "

Her memory travelled down the years, and she was amazed. She remembered Mr. Jukes at the great shops and many similar incidents that had puzzled her.

" No," she said.

There was a short silence. The muscles of his face relaxed, and the old, sweet smile came over it. He reached again for her hand and caressed it tenderly.

" By putting you out of my life, I kept you, dear. I kept you as the one beautiful human thing I had.

Every hour of happiness I have had for the last twenty years has come through you."

She said tearfully : "You have been very good to me, Roger."

"It's a queer mix-up, isn't it?" he said, after a pause. "Most people would say that I've ruined your life. If it hadn't been for me, you might have married."

"No, dear," she replied. "I've had a very full and happy life."

The nurse came into the room to signify the end of the visit, and found them hand in hand like lovers. He laughed.

"Nurse," said he, "you see a dying but a jolly happy old man !"

Two days afterwards Roger Orme died. On the afternoon of the funeral, Miss Winifred Goode sat in the old garden in the shade of the clipped yew, and looked at the house in which she had been born and in which she had passed her sixty years of life, and at the old wistaria beneath which he had kissed her forty years ago. She smiled and murmured aloud :

"No, I would not have had a single thing different."

III

A Lover's Dilemma

"HOW are you feeling now?"
Words could not express the music of
these six liquid syllables that fell through the stillness
and the blackness on my ears.

"Not very bright, I'm afraid, nurse," said I.

Think of something to do with streams and moonlight, and you may have an idea of the mellow ripple
of the laugh I heard.

"I'm not the nurse. Can't you tell the difference?
I'm Miss Deane—Dr. Deane's daughter."

"Deane?" I echoed.

"Don't you know where you are?"

"Everything is still confused," said I.

I had an idea that they had carried me somewhere
by train and put me into a bed, and that soft-fingered
people had tended my eyes; but where I was I neither
knew nor cared. Torture and blindness had been
quite enough to occupy my mind.

"You are at Dr. Deane's house," said the voice,
"and Dr. Deane is the twin brother of Mr. Deane, the
great oculist of Grandchester, who was summoned to
Shepton-Marling when you met with your accident.
Perhaps you know you had a gun accident?"

"I suppose it was only that after all," said I,

"but it felt like the disruption of the solar system."

"Are you still in great pain?" my unseen hostess asked sympathetically.

"Not since you have been in the room I mean," I added, chilled by a span of silence, "I mean—I am just stating what happens to be a fact."

"Oh!" she said shortly. "Well my uncle found that you couldn't be properly treated at your friend's little place at Shepton-Marling, so he brought you to Grandchester—and here you are."

"But I don't understand," said I, "why I should be a guest in your house."

"You are not a guest," she laughed. "You are here on the most sordid and commercial footing. Your friend—I forget his name——"

"Mobray," said I.

"Mr. Mobray settled it with my uncle. You see the house is large and father's practice small, so we keep a nursing home for my uncle's patients. Of course we have trained nurses."

"Are you one?" I asked.

"Not exactly. I do the housekeeping. But I can settle those uncomfortable pillows."

I felt her dexterous cool hands about my head and neck. For a moment or two my eyes ceased to ache, and I wished I could see her. In tendering my thanks, I expressed the wish. She laughed her delicious laugh.

"If you could see you wouldn't be here, and therefore you couldn't see me anyhow."

"Shall I ever see you?" I asked dismally.

"Why, of course! Don't you know that Henry Deane is one of the greatest oculists in England?"

We discussed my case and the miraculous skill of Henry Deane. Presently she left me, promising to return. The tones of her voice seemed to linger, as perfume would, in the darkness.

That was the beginning of it. It was love, not at first sight, but at first sound. Pain and anxiety stood like abashed goblins at the back of my mind. Valerie Deane's voice danced in front like a triumphant fairy. When she came and talked sick-room platitudes I had sooner listened to her than to the music of the spheres. At that early stage what she said mattered so little. I would have given rapturous heed to her reading of logarithmic tables. I asked her silly questions merely to elicit the witchery of her voice. When Melba sings, do you take count of the idiot words ? You close eyes and intellect and just let the divine notes melt into your soul. And when you are lying on your back, blind and helpless, as I was, your soul is a very sponge for anything beautiful that can reach it. After a while she gave me glimpses of herself, sweet and womanly ; and we drifted from commonplace into deeper things. She was the perfect companion. We discussed all topics, from chiffons to Schopenhauer. Like most women, she execrated Schopenhauer. She must have devoted much of her time to me ; yet I ungratefully complained of the long intervals between her visits. But oh ! those interminable idle hours of darkness, in which all the thoughts that had ever been thought were rethought over and over again until the mind became a worn-out rag-bag ! Only those who have been through the valley of this shadow can know its desolation. Only they can understand the magic of the unbeheld Valerie Deane.

"What is the meaning of this ? " she asked one morning. "Nurse says you are fretful and fractious."

"She insisted on soaping the soles of my feet and tickling me into torments, which made me fractious, and I'm dying to see your face, which makes me fretful."

"Since when have you been dying?" she asked.

"From the first moment I heard your voice saying, 'How are you feeling now?' It's irritating to have a friend and not in the least know what she is like. Besides," I added, "your voice is so beautiful that your face must be the same."

She laughed.

"Your face is like your laugh," I declared.

"If my face were my fortune I should come off badly," she said in a light tone. I think she was leaning over the foot-rail, and I longed for her nearer presence.

"Nurse has tied this bandage a little too tightly," I said mendaciously.

I heard her move, and in a moment her fingers were busy about my eyes. I put up my hand and touched them. She patted my hand away.

"Please don't be foolish," she remarked. "When you recover your sight and find what an exceedingly plain girl I am, you'll go away like the others, and never want to see me again."

"What others?" I exclaimed.

"Do you suppose you're the only patient I have had to manage?"

I loathed "the others" with a horrible detestation; but I said, after reflection:

"Tell me about yourself. I know you are called Valerie from Dr. Deane. How old are you?"

She pinned the bandage in front of my forehead.

"Oh, I'm young enough," she answered with a

laugh. "Three-and-twenty. And I'm five-foot-four, and I haven't a bad figure. But I haven't any good looks at all, at all."

"Tell me," said I impatiently, "exactly how you do look. I must know."

"I have a sallow complexion. Not very good skin. And a low forehead."

"An excellent thing," said I.

"But my eyebrows and hair run in straight parallel lines, so it isn't," she retorted. "It is very ugly. I have thin black hair."

"Let me feel."

"Certainly not. And my eyes are a sort of watery china blue and much too small. And my nose isn't a bad nose altogether, but it's fleshy. One of those nondescript, unaristocratic noses that always looks as if it has got a cold. My mouth is large—I am looking at myself in the glass—and my teeth are white. Yes, they are nice and white. But they are large and protrude—you know the French caricature of an Englishwoman's teeth. Really, now I consider the question, I am the image of the English *mees* in a French comic paper."

"I don't believe it," I declared.

"It is true. I know I have a pretty voice—but that is all. It deceives blind people. They think I must be pretty too, and when they see me—*bon soir, la compagnie !* And I've such a thin, miserable face, coming to the chin in a point, like a kite. There ! Have you a clear idea of me now ?"

"No," said I, "for I believe you are wilfully misrepresenting yourself. Besides, beauty does not depend upon features regular in themselves, but the way those features are put together."

"Oh, mine are arranged in an amiable sort of way. I don't look cross."

"You must look sweetness itself," said I.

She sighed and said meditatively :

"It is a great misfortune for a girl to be so desperately plain. The consciousness of it comes upon her like a cold shower-bath when she is out with other girls. Now there is my cousin——"

"Which cousin ? "

"My Uncle Henry's daughter. Shall I tell you about her ? "

"I am not in the least interested in your cousin," I replied.

She laughed, and the entrance of the nurse put an end to the conversation.

Now I must make confession. I was grievously disappointed. Her detailed description of herself as a sallow, ill-featured young woman awoke me with a shock from my dreams of a radiant goddess. It arrested my infatuation in mid-course. My dismay was painful. I began to pity her for being so unattractive. For the next day or two even her beautiful voice failed in its seduction.

But soon a face began to dawn before me, elusive at first, and then gradually gaining in definition. At last the picture flashed upon my mental vision with sudden vividness, and it has never left me to this day. Its steadfastness convinced me of its accuracy. It was so real that I could see its expression vary, as she spoke, according to her mood. The plainness, almost ugliness, of the face repelled me. I thought ruefully of having dreamed of kisses from the lips that barely closed in front of the great white teeth. Yet, after a while, its higher qualities exercised a peculiar

108

attraction. A brave, tender spirit shone through. An intellectual alertness redeemed the heavy features—the low ugly brow, the coarse nose, the large mouth ; and as I lay thinking and picturing there was revealed in an illuminating flash the secret of the harmony between face and voice. Thenceforward Valerie Deane was invested with a beauty all her own. I loved the dear plain face as I loved the beautiful voice, and the touch of her fingers, and the tender, laughing womanliness, and all that went with the concept of Valerie Deane.

Had I possessed the daring of Young Lochinvar, I should, on several occasions, have declared my passion. But by temperament I am a diffident procrastinator. I habitually lose golden moments as some people habitually lose umbrellas. Alas ! There is no Lost Property Office for golden moments !

Still I vow, although nothing definite was said, that when the unanticipated end drew near, our intercourse was arrant love-making.

All pain had gone from my eyes. I was up and dressed and permitted to grope my way about the blackness. To-morrow I was to have my first brief glimpse of things for three weeks, in the darkened room. I was in high spirits. Valerie, paying her morning visit, seemed depressed.

" But think of it ! " I cried in pardonable egotism. " To-morrow I shall be able to see you. I've longed for it as much as for the sight of the blue sky."

" There isn't any blue sky," said Valerie. " It's an inverted tureen that has held pea-soup."

Her voice had all the melancholy notes of the woodwind in the unseen shepherd's lament in *Tristan und Isolde.*

"I don't know how to tell you," she exclaimed tragically, after a pause. "I shan't be here to-morrow. It's a bitter disappointment. My aunt in Wales is dying. I have been telegraphed for, and I must go."

She sat on the end of the couch where I was lounging, and took my hands.

"It isn't my fault."

My spirits fell headlong.

"I would just as soon keep blind," said I blankly.

"I thought you would say that."

A tear dropped on my hand. I felt that it was brutal of her aunt to make Valerie cry. Why could she not postpone her demise to a more suitable opportunity? I murmured, however, a few decent words of condolence.

"Thank you, Mr. Winter," said Valerie. "I am fond of my aunt; but I had set my heart on your seeing me. And she may not die for weeks and weeks! She was dying for ever so long last year, and got round again."

I ventured an arm about her shoulders, and spoke consolingly. The day would come when our eyes would meet. I called her Valerie and bade her address me as Harold.

I have come to the conclusion that the man who strikes out a new line in love-making is a genius.

"If I don't hurry I shall miss my train," she sighed at last.

She rose; I felt her bend over me. Her hands closed on my cheeks, and a kiss fluttered on my lips. I heard the light swish of her skirts and the quick opening and shutting of the door, and she was gone.

Valerie's aunt, like King Charles II, was an unconscionable time a-dying. When a note from Valerie announced her return to Grandchester, I had already gone blue-spectacled away. For some time I was not allowed to read or write, and during this period of probation urgent affairs summoned me to Vienna. Such letters as I wrote to Valerie had to be of the most elementary nature. If you have a heart of any capacity worth troubling about, you cannot empty it on one side of a sheet of notepaper. For mine reams would have been inadequate. I also longed to empty it in her presence, my eyes meeting hers for the first time. Thus, ever haunted by the beloved plain face and the memorable voice, I remained inarticulate.

As soon as my busniness was so far adjusted that I could leave Vienna, I started on a flying visit, post-haste, to England. The morning after my arrival beheld me in a railway carriage at Euston waiting for the train to carry me to Grandchester. I had telegraphed to Valerie ; also to Mr. Deane, the oculist, for an appointment which might give colour to my visit. I was alone in the compartment. My thoughts, far away from the long platform, leaped the four hours that separated me from Grandchester. For the thousandth time I pictured our meeting. I foreshadowed speeches of burning eloquence. I saw the homely features transfigured. I closed my eyes the better to retain the beatific vision. The train began to move. Suddenly the door was opened, a girlish figure sprang into the compartment, and a porter running by the side of the train threw in a bag and a bundle of wraps, and slammed the door violently. The young lady stood with her back to me, panting for breath. The luggage lay on the floor. I stooped to pick up the bag ; so did the young lady. Our hands met as I lifted it to the rack.

"Oh, please, don't trouble !" she cried in a voice whose familiarity made my heart beat.

I caught sight of her face, for the first time, and my heart beat faster than ever. It was *her* face—the face that had dawned upon my blindness—the face I had grown to worship. I looked at her, transfixed with wonder. She settled herself unconcerned in the farther corner of the carriage. I took the opposite seat and leaned forward.

"You are Miss Deane ?" I asked tremulously.

She drew herself up, on the defensive.

"That is my name," she said.

"Valerie !" I cried in exultation.

She half rose. "What right have you to address me ?"

"I am Harold Winter," said I, taken aback by her outraged demeanour. "Is it possible that you don't recognize me ?"

"I have never seen or heard of you before in my life," replied the young lady tartly, "and I hope you won't force me to take measures to protect myself against your impertinence."

I lay back against the cushions, gasping with dismay.

"I beg your pardon," said I, recovering ; "I am neither going to molest you nor be intentionally impertinent. But, as your face has never been out of my mind for three months, and as I am travelling straight through from Vienna to Grandchester to see it for the first time, I may be excused for addressing you."

She glanced hurriedly at the communication-cord and then back at me, as if I were a lunatic.

"You are Miss Deane of Grandchester—daughter of Dr. Deane?" I asked.

"Yes."

"Valerie Deane, then?"

"I have told you so."

"Then all I can say is," I cried, losing my temper at her stony heartlessness, "that your conduct in turning an honest, decent man into a besotted fool, and then disclaiming all knowledge of him, is outrageous. It's damnable. The language hasn't a word to express it!"

She stood with her hand on the cord.

"I shall really have to call the guard," she said, regarding me coolly.

"You are quite free to do so," I answered. "But if you do, I shall have to show your letters, in sheer self-defence. I am not going to spend the day in a police-station."

She let go the cord and sat down again.

"What on earth do you mean?" she asked.

I took a bundle of letters from my pocket and tossed one over to her. She glanced at it quickly, started, as if in great surprise, and handed it back with a smile.

"I did not write that."

I thought I had never seen her equal for unblushing impudence. Her mellow tones made the mockery appear all the more diabolical.

"If you didn't write it," said I, "I should like to know who did."

"My Cousin Valerie."

"I don't understand," said I.

"My name is Valerie Deane and my cousin's name is Valerie Deane, and this is her handwriting."

Bewildered, I passed my hand over my eyes. What

feline trick was she playing ?   Her treachery was incomprehensible.

"I suppose it was your Cousin Valerie who tended me during my blindness at your father's house, who shed tears because she had to leave me, who——"

"Quite possibly," she interrupted.   "Only it would have been at *her* father's house and not mine.   She does tend blind people, my father's patients."

I looked at her open-mouthed.   "In the name of Heaven," I exclaimed, "who are you, if not the daughter of Dr. Deane of Stavaton Street ?"

"My father is Mr. Henry Deane, the oculist.   You asked if I were the daughter of Dr. Deane.   So many people give him the wrong title that I didn't trouble to correct you."

It took me a few moments to recover.   I had been making a pretty fool of myself.   I stammered out pleas for a thousand pardons.   I confused myself, and her, in explanation.   Then I remembered that the fathers were twin brothers and bore a strong resemblance one to the other.   What more natural than that the daughters should also be alike ?

"What I can't understand," said Miss Deane, "is how you mistook me for my cousin."

"Your voices are identical."

"But our outer semblances——"

"I have never seen your cousin—she left me before I recovered my sight."

"How then could you say you had my face before you for three months ?"

"I am afraid, Miss Deane, I was wrong in that as in everything else.   It was her face.   It had a mental picture of it."

She put on a puzzled expression.   "And you used

the mental picture for the purpose of recognition ? "

" Yes," said I.

" I give it up," said Miss Deane.

She did not press me further. Her Cousin Valerie's love affairs were grounds too delicate for her to tread upon. She turned the conversation by politely asking me how I had come to consult her father. I mentioned my friend Mobray and the gun accident. She remembered the case and claimed a slight acquaintance with Mobray, whom she had met at various houses in Grandchester. My credit as a sane and reputable person being established, we began to chat most amicably. I found Miss Deane an accomplished woman. We talked books, art, travel. She had the swift wit which delights in bridging the trivial and the great. She had a playful fancy. Never have I found a personality so immediately sympathetic. I told her a sad little Viennese story in which I happened to have played a minor part, and her tenderness was as spontaneous as Valerie's—my Valerie's. She had Valerie's woodland laugh. Were it not that her personal note, her touch on the strings of life differed essentially from my beloved's, I should have held it grotesquely impossible for any human being but Valerie to be sitting in the opposite corner of that railway carriage. Indeed there were moments when she *was* Valerie, when the girl waiting for me at Grandchester faded into the limbo of unreal things. A kiss from those lips had fluttered on mine. It were lunacy to doubt it.

During intervals of non-illusion I examined her face critically. There was no question of its unattractiveness to the casual observer. The nose was too large and fleshy, the teeth too prominent, the eyes too small. But my love had pierced to its underlying spirituality, and it was the face above all others that I desired.

Towards the end of a remarkably short four hours' journey, Miss Deane graciously expressed the hope that we might meet again.

"I shall ask Valerie," said I, "to present me in due form."

She smiled maliciously. "Are you quite sure you will be able to distinguish one from the other when my cousin and I are together?"

"Are you, then, so identically alike?"

"That's a woman's way of answering a question—by another question," she laughed.

"Well, but are you?" I persisted.

"How otherwise could you have mistaken me for her?" She had drawn off her gloves, so as to give a tidying touch to her hair. I noticed her hands, small, long, and deft. I wondered whether they resembled Valerie's.

"Would you do me the great favour of letting me touch your hand while I shut my eyes, as if I were blind?"

She held out her hand frankly. My fingers ran over it for a few seconds, as they had done many times over Valerie's. "Well?" she asked.

"Not the same," said I.

She flushed, it seemed angrily, and glanced down at her hand, on which she immediately proceeded to draw a glove.

"Yours are stronger. And finer," I added, when I saw that the tribute of strength did not please.

"It's the one little personal thing I am proud of," she remarked.

"You have made my four hours pass like four

minutes," said I. "A service to a fellow-creature which you might take some pride in having performed."

"When I was a child I could have said the same of performing elephants."

"I am no longer a child, Miss Deane," said I with a bow.

What there was in this to make the blood rush to her pale cheeks I do not know. The ways of women have often surprised me. I have heard other men make a similar confession.

"I think most men are children," she said shortly.

"In what way?"

"Their sweet irresponsibility," said Miss Deane.

And then the train entered Grandchester Station.

I deposited my bag at the station hotel and drove straight to Stavaton Street. I forgot Miss Deane. My thoughts and longings centred in her beloved counterpart, with her tender, caressing ways, and just a subtle inflection in the voice that made it more exquisite than the voice to which I had been listening.

The servant who opened the door recognized me and smiled a welcome. Miss Valerie was in the drawing-room.

"I know the way," said I.

Impetuous, I ran up the stairs, burst into the drawing-room, and stopped short on the threshold in presence of a strange and exceedingly beautiful young woman. She was stately and slender. She had masses of bright brown hair waving over a beautiful brow. She had deep sapphire eyes, like stars. She had the complexion of a Greuze child. She had that air of fairy diaphaneity combined with the glow of superb health which makes the typical loveliness of the

Englishwoman. I gaped for a second or two at this gracious apparition.

"I beg your pardon," said I ; "I was told——"

The apparition who was standing by the fireplace smiled and came forward with extended hands.

"Why, Harold ! Of course you were told. It is all right. I am Valerie."

I blinked ; the world seemed upside down ; the enchanting voice rang in my ears, but it harmonized in no way with the equally enchanting face. I put out my hand. "How do you do ? " I said stupidly.

"But aren't you glad to see me ? " asked the lovely young woman.

"Of course," said I ; "I came from Vienna to see you."

"But you look disappointed."

"The fact is," I stammered, " I expected to see some one different—quite different. The face you described has been haunting me for three months."

She had the effrontery to laugh. Her eyes danced mischief.

"Did you really think me such a hideous fright ? "

"You were not a fright at all," said I, remembering my late travelling companion.

And then in a flash I realized what she had done.

"Why on earth did you describe your cousin instead of yourself ? "

"My cousin ! How do you know that ? "

"Never mind," I answered. "You did. During your description you had her face vividly before your mind. The picture was in some telepathic way transferred from your brain to mine, and there it remained. The proof is that when I saw a certain lady to-day I recognized her at once and greeted her effusively as

Valerie. Her name did happen to be Valerie, and Valerie Deane too, and I ran the risk of a police-station—and I don't think it was fair of you. What prompted you to deceive me?"

I was hurt and angry, and I spoke with some acerbity. Valerie drew herself up with dignity.

"If you claim an explanation, I will give it to you. We have had young men patients in the house before, and, as they had nothing to do, they have amused themselves and annoyed me by falling in love with me. I was tired of it, and decided that it shouldn't happen in your case. So I gave a false description of myself. To make it consistent, I took a real person for a model."

"So you were fooling me all the time?" said I, gathering hat and stick.

Her face softened adorably. Her voice had the tones of the wood-wind.

"Not all the time, Harold," she said.

I laid down hat and stick.

"Then why did you not undeceive me afterward?"

"I thought," she said, blushing and giving me a fleeting glance, "well, I thought you—you wouldn't be sorry to find I wasn't—bad-looking."

"I *am* sorry, Valerie," said I, "and that's the mischief of it."

"I was so looking forward to your seeing me," she said tearfully. And then, with sudden petulance, she stamped her small foot. "It is horrid of you—perfectly horrid—and I never want to speak to you again." The last word ended in a sob. She rushed to the door, pushed me aside, as I endeavoured to stop her, and fled in a passion of tears. *Spretæ injuria formæ!*

119

Women have remained much the same since the days of Juno.

A miserable, remorseful being, I wandered through the Grandchester streets, to keep my appointment with Mr. Henry Deane. After a short interview he dismissed me with a good report of my eyes. Miss Deane, dressed for walking, met me in the hall as the servant was showing me out, and we went together into the street.

"Well," she said with a touch of irony, "have you seen my cousin?"

"Yes," said I.

"Do you think her like me?"

"I wish to Heaven she were!" I exclaimed fervently. "I shouldn't be swirling round in a sort of maelstrom."

She looked steadily at me—I like her downrightness.

"Do you mind telling me what you mean?"

"I am in love with the personality of one woman and the face of another. And I never shall fall out of love with the face."

"And the personality?"

"God knows," I groaned.

"I never conceived it possible for any man to fall in love with a face so hopelessly unattractive," she said with a smile.

"It is beautiful," I cried.

She looked at me queerly for a few seconds, during which I had the sensation of something odd, uncanny having happened. I was fascinated. I found myself saying: "What did you mean by the 'sweet irresponsibility of man'?"

She put out her hand abruptly and said good-bye. I watched her disappear swiftly round a near corner, and

I went, my head buzzing with her, back to my hotel. In the evening I dined with Dr. Deane. I had no opportunity of seeing Valerie alone. In a whisper she begged forgiveness. I relented. Her beauty and charm would have mollified a cross rhinoceros. The love in her splendid eyes would have warmed a snow image. The pressure of her hand at parting brought back the old Valerie, and I knew I loved her desperately. But inwardly I groaned, because she had not the face of my dreams. I hated her beauty. As soon as the front door closed behind me, my head began to buzz again with the other Valerie.

I lay awake all night. The two Valeries wove themselves inextricably together in my hopes and longings. I worshipped a composite chimera. When the grey dawn stole through my bedroom window, the chimera vanished, but a grey dubiety dawned upon my soul. Day invested it with a ghastly light. I rose a shivering wreck and fled from Grandchester by the first train.

I have not been back to Grandchester. I am in Vienna, whither I returned as fast as the Orient Express could carry me. I go to bed praying that night will dispel my doubt. I wake every morning to my adamantine indecision. That I am consuming away with love for one of the two Valeries is the only certain fact in my uncertain existence. But which of the Valeries it is I cannot for the life of me decide.

If any woman (it is beyond the wit of man) could solve my problem and save me from a hopeless and lifelong celibacy she would earn my undying gratitude.

THREE men who had gained great fame and honour throughout the world met unexpectedly in front of the bookstall at Paddington Station. Like most of the great ones of the earth they were personally acquainted, and they exchanged surprised greetings.

Sir Angus McCurdie, the eminent physicist, scowled at the two others beneath his heavy black eyebrows.

" I'm going to a God-forsaken place in Cornwall called Trehenna," said he.

" That's odd ; so am I," croaked Professor Biggleswade. He was a little, untidy man with round spectacles, a fringe of greyish beard and a weak, rasping voice, and he knew more of Assyriology than any man, living or dead. A flippant pupil once remarked that the Professor's face was furnished with a Babylonic cuneiform in lieu of features.

" People called Deverill, at Foullis Castle ? " asked Sir Angus.

" Yes," replied Professor Biggleswade.

" How curious !   I am going to the Deverills, too," said the third man.

This man was the Right Honourable Viscount Doyne, the renowned Empire Builder and Administrator, around whose solitary and remote life popular imagination had woven many legends. He looked at the world through tired grey eyes, and the heavy, drooping, blonde moustache seemed tired too, and had dragged down the tired face into deep furrows. He was smoking a long black cigar.

"I suppose we may as well travel down together," said Sir Angus, not very cordially.

Lord Doyne said courteously : "I have a reserved carriage. The railway company is always good enough to place one at my disposal. It would give me great pleasure if you would share it."

The invitation was accepted, and the three men crossed the busy, crowded platform to take their seats in the great express train. A porter, laden with an incredible load of paraphernalia, trying to make his way through the press, happened to jostle Sir Angus McCurdie. He rubbed his shoulder fretfully.

"Why the whole land should be turned into a bear garden on account of this exploded superstition of Christmas is one of the anomalies of modern civilization. Look at this insensate welter of fools travelling in wild herds to disgusting places merely because it's Christmas ! "

"You seem to be travelling yourself, McCurdie," said Lord Doyne.

"Yes—and why the devil I'm doing it, I've not the faintest notion," replied Sir Angus.

"It's going to be a beast of a journey," he remarked some moments later, as the train carried them slowly out of the station. "The whole country is under snow —and as far as I can understand we have to change twice and wind up with a twenty-mile motor drive.

He was an iron-faced, beetle-browed, stern man, and this morning he did not seem to be in the best of tempers. Finding his companions inclined to be sympathetic, he continued his lamentation.

"And merely because it's Christmas I've had to

shut up my laboratory and give my young fools a holiday—just when I was in the midst of a most important series of experiments."

Professor Biggleswade, who had heard vaguely of and rather looked down upon such new-fangled toys as radium and thorium and helium and argon—for the latest astonishing developments in the theory of radio-activity had brought Sir Angus McCurdie his world-wide fame—said somewhat ironically :

" If the experiments were so important, why didn't you lock yourself up with your test-tubes and electric batteries and finish them alone ? "

" Man! " said McCurdie, bending across the carriage, and speaking with a curious intensity of voice, " d'ye know I'd give a hundred pounds to be able to answer that question ? "

" What do you mean ? " asked the Professor, startled.

" I should like to know why I'm sitting in this damned train and going to visit a couple of addle-headed society people whom I'm scarcely acquainted with, when I might be at home in my own good company furthering the progress of science."

" I myself," said the Professor, " am not acquainted with them at all."

It was Sir Angus McCurdie's turn to look surprised.

" Then why are you spending Christmas with them ? "

" I reviewed a ridiculous blank-verse tragedy written by Deverill on the Death of Sennacherib. Historically it was puerile. I said so in no measured terms. He wrote a letter claiming to be a poet and not an archæ-ologist. I replied that the day had passed when poets could with impunity commit the abominable crime of distorting history. He retorted with some futile argument, and we went on exchanging letters, until his invitation and my acceptance concluded the correspondence."

McCurdie, still bending his black brows on him, asked him why he had not declined. The Professor screwed up his face till it looked more like a cuneiform than ever. He, too, found the question difficult to answer, but he showed a bold front.

"I felt it my duty," said he, "to teach that preposterous ignoramus something worth knowing about Sennacherib. Besides, I am a bachelor and would sooner spend Christmas, as to whose irritating and meaningless annoyance I cordially agree with you, among strangers than among my married sisters' numerous and nerve-racking families."

Sir Angus McCurdie, the hard, metallic apostle of radio-activity, glanced for a moment out of the window at the grey, frost-bitten fields. Then he said :

"I'm a widower. My wife died many years ago and, thank God, we had no children. I generally spend Christmas alone."

He looked out of the window again. Professor Biggleswade suddenly remembered the popular story of the great scientist's antecedents, and reflected that as McCurdie had once run, a barefoot urchin, through the Glasgow mud, he was likely to have little kith or kin. He himself envied McCurdie. He was always praying to be delivered from his sisters and nephews and nieces, whose embarrassing demands no calculated coldness could repress.

"Children are the root of all evil," said he. " Happy the man who has his quiver empty."

Sir Angus McCurdie did not reply at once ; when he spoke again it was with reference to their prospective host.

"I met Deverill," said he, "at the Royal Society's Soirée this year. One of my assistants was demonstrating a peculiar property of thorium and Deverill seemed interested. I asked him to come to my laboratory the next day, and found he didn't know a damned thing about anything. That's all the acquaintance I have with him."

Lord Doyne, the great administrator, who had been wearily turning over the pages of an illustrated weekly chiefly filled with flamboyant photographs of obscure actresses, took his gold glasses from his nose and the black cigar from his lips, and addressed his companions.

"I've been considerably interested in your conversation," said he, "and as you've been frank, I'll be frank too. I knew Mrs. Deverill's mother, Lady Carstairs, very well years ago, and of course Mrs. Deverill when she was a child. Deverill I came across once in Persia—he had been sent on a diplomatic mission to Teheran. As for our being invited on such slight acquaintance, little Mrs. Deverill has the reputation of being the only really successful celebrity hunter in England. She inherited the faculty from her mother, who entertained the whole world. We're sure to find archbishops, and eminent actors, and illustrious divorcées asked to meet us. That's one thing. But why I, who loathe country-house parties and children and Christmas as much as Biggleswade, am going down there to-day, I can no more explain than you can. It's a devilish odd coincidence."

The three men looked at one another. Suddenly

McCurdie shivered and drew his fur coat around him.

"I'll thank you," said he, "to shut that window."

"It is shut," said Doyne.

"It's just uncanny," said McCurdie, looking from one to the other.

"What?" asked Doyne.

"Nothing, if you didn't feel it."

"There did seem to be a sudden draught," said Professor Biggleswade. "But as both window and door are shut, it could only be imaginary."

"It wasn't imaginary," muttered McCurdie.

Then he laughed harshly. "My father and mother came from Cromarty," he said with apparent irrelevance.

"That's the Highlands," said the Professor.

"Ay," said McCurdie.

Lord Doyne said nothing, but tugged at his moustache and looked out of the window as the frozen meadows and bits of river and willows raced past. A dead silence fell on them. McCurdie broke it with another laugh and took a whisky-flask from his handbag.

"Have a nip?"

"Thanks, no," said the Professor. "I have to keep to a strict dietary, and I only drink hot milk and water—and of that sparingly. I have some in a thermos bottle."

Lord Doyne also declining the whisky, McCurdie swallowed a dram and declared himself to be better. The Professor took from his bag a foreign review in which a German sciolist had dared to question his interpretation of a Hittite inscription. Over the man's ineptitude he fell asleep and snored loudly.

To escape from his immediate neighbourhood Mc-

Curdie went to the other end of the seat and faced
Lord Doyne, who had resumed his gold glasses and his
listless contemplation of obscure actresses.   McCurdie
lit a pipe, Doyne another black cigar.   The train
thundered on.

Presently they all lunched together in the restaurant
car.   The windows steamed, but here and there
through a wiped patch of pane a white world was revealed.   The snow was falling.   As they passed through
Westbury, McCurdie looked mechanically for the
famous white horse carved into the chalk of the down ;
but it was not visible beneath the thick covering of
snow.

"It'll be just like this all the way to Gehenna—
Trehenna, I mean," said McCurdie.

Doyne nodded.   He had done his life's work amid
all extreme fiercenesses of heat and cold, in burning
droughts, in simooms and in icy wildernesses, and a
ray or two more of the pale sun or a flake or two more
of the gentle snow of England mattered to him but
little.   But Biggleswade rubbed the pane with his
table-napkin and gazed apprehensively at the prospect.

"If only this wretched train would stop," said he,
"I would go back again."

And he thought how comfortable it would be to
sneak home again to his books and thus elude not
only the Deverills, but the Christmas jollities of his
sisters' families, who would think him miles away.
But the train was timed not to stop till Plymouth,
two hundred and thirty-five miles from London, and
thither was he being relentlessly carried.   Then he
quarrelled with his food, which brought a certain
consolation.

The train did stop, however, before Plymouth—indeed, before Exeter. An accident on the line had dislocated the traffic. The express was held up for an hour, and when it was permitted to proceed, instead of thundering on, it went cautiously, subject to continual stoppings. It arrived at Plymouth two hours late. The travellers learned that they had missed the connection on which they had counted and that they could not reach Trehenna till nearly ten o'clock. After weary waiting at Plymouth they took their seats in the little, cold local train that was to carry them another stage on their journey. Hot-water cans put in at Plymouth mitigated to some extent the iciness of the compartment. But that only lasted a comparatively short time, for soon they were set down at a desolate, shelterless wayside junction, dumped in the midst of a hilly snow-covered waste, where they went through another weary wait for another dismal local train that was to carry them to Trehenna. And in this train there were no hot-water cans, so that the compartment was as cold as death. McCurdie fretted and shook his fist in the direction of Trehenna.

"And when we get there we have still a twenty miles' motor drive to Foullis Castle. It's a fool name and we're fools to be going there."

"I shall die of bronchitis," wailed Professor Biggleswade.

"A man dies when it is appointed for him to die," said Lord Doyne, in his tired way; and he went on smoking long back cigars.

"It's not the dying that worries me," said McCurdie. "That's a mere mechanical process which every organic being from a king to a cauliflower has to pass . through. It's the being forced against my will and my reason to come on this accursed journey, which something tells me will become more and more accursed as we go on, that is driving me to distraction."

"What will be, will be," said Doyne.

"I can't see where the comfort of that reflection comes in," said Biggleswade.

"And yet you've travelled in the East," said Doyne. "I suppose you know the Valley of the Tigris as well as any man living."

"Yes," said the Professor. "I can say I dug my way from Tekrit to Bagdad and left not a stone unexamined."

"Perhaps, after all," Doyne remarked, "that's not quite the way to know the East."

"I never wanted to know the modern East," returned the Professor. "What is there in it of interest compared with the mighty civilizations that have gone before?"

McCurdie took a pull from his flask.

"I'm glad I thought of having a refill at Plymouth," said he.

At last, after many stops at little lonely stations, they arrived at Trehenna. The guard opened the door and they stepped out on to the snow-covered platform. An oil-lamp hung from the tiny pent-house roof that, structurally, was Trehenna Station. They looked around at the silent gloom of white undulating moorland, and it seemed a place where no man lived and only ghosts could have a bleak and unsheltered being. A porter came up and helped the guard with the luggage. Then they realized that the station was built on a small embankment, for, looking over the railing, they saw below the two great lamps of a motorcar. A fur-clad chauffeur met them at the bottom of

the stairs. He clapped his hands together and informed them cheerily that he had been waiting for
four hours. It was the bitterest winter in these parts
within the memory of man, said he, and he himself
had not seen snow there for five years. Then he
settled the three travellers in the great roomy touring-
car covered with a Cape-cart hood, wrapped them up in
many rugs and started.

After a few moments, the huddling together of their
bodies—for, the Professor being a spare man, there
was room for them all on the back seat—the pile of
rugs, the serviceable and all but air-tight hood, induced
a pleasant warmth and a pleasant drowsiness. Where
they were being driven they knew not. The perfectly
upholstered seat eased their limbs, the easy swinging
motion of the car soothed their spirits. They felt
that already they had reached the luxuriously appointed
home which, after all, they knew awaited them. Mc-
Curdie no longer railed, Professor Biggleswade forgot
the dangers of bronchitis, and Lord Doyne twisted
the stump of a black cigar between his lips without
any desire to relight it. A tiny electric lamp inside
the hood made the darkness of the world to right
and left and in front of the talc windows still darker.
McCurdie and Biggleswade fell into a doze. Lord
Doyne chewed the end of his cigar. The car sped on
through an unseen wilderness.

Suddenly there was a horrid jolt and a lurch and a
leap and a rebound, and then the car stood still, quivering like a ship that has been struck by a heavy sea. The
three men were pitched and tossed and thrown sprawling over one another on to the bottom of the car.
Biggleswade screamed. McCurdie cursed. Doyne
scrambled from the confusion of rugs and limbs and,

132

tearing open the side of the Cape-cart hood, jumped out. The chauffeur had also just leaped from his seat. It was pitch dark save for the great shaft of light down the snowy road cast by the head-lamps. The snow had ceased falling.

"What's gone wrong?"

"It sounds like the axle," said the chauffeur ruefully.

He unshipped a lamp and examined the car, which had wedged itself against a great drift of snow on the off side. Meanwhile McCurdie and Biggleswade had alighted.

"Yes, it's the axle," said the chauffeur.

"Then we're done," remarked Doyne.

"I'm afraid so, my lord."

"What's the matter? Can't we get on?" asked Biggleswade in his querulous voice.

McCurdie laughed. "How can we get on with a broken axle? The thing's as useless as a man with a broken back. Gad, I was right. I said it was going to be an infernal journey."

The little Professor wrung his hands. "But what's to be done?" he cried.

"Tramp it," said Lord Doyne, lighting a fresh cigar.

"It's ten miles," said the chauffeur.

"It would be the death of me," the Professor wailed.

"I utterly refuse to walk ten miles through a Polar waste with a gouty foot," McCurdie declared wrathfully.

The chauffeur offered a solution of the difficulty. He would set out alone for Foullis Castle—five miles farther on was an inn where he could obtain a horse and trap—and would return for the three gentlemen with another car. In the meanwhile they could take shelter in a little house which they had just passed, some half-mile up the road. This was agreed to. The chauffeur went on cheerily enough with a lamp, and the three travellers with another lamp started off in the opposite direction. As far as they could see they were in a long, desolate valley, a sort of No Man's Land, deathly silent. The eastern sky had cleared somewhat, and they faced a loose rack through which one pale star was dimly visible.

"I'm a man of science," said McCurdie as they trudged through the snow, "and I dismiss the supernatural as contrary to reason; but I have Highland blood in my veins that plays me exasperating tricks. My reason tells me that this place is only a commonplace moor, yet it seems like a Valley of Bones haunted by malignant spirits who have lured us here to our destruction. There's something guiding us now. It's just uncanny."

"Why on earth did we ever come?" croaked Biggleswade.

Lord Doyne answered: "The Koran says, 'Nothing can befall us but what God hath destined for us.' So why worry?"

"Because I'm not a Mohammedan," retorted Biggleswade.

"You might be worse," said Doyne.

Presently the dim outline of the little house grew perceptible. A faint light shone from the window. It stood unfenced by any kind of hedge or railing a few feet away from the road in a little hollow beneath some rising ground. As far as they could discern in the darkness when they drew near, the house was a mean, dilapidated hovel. A guttering candle stood on the inner sill of the small window and afforded a vague view into a mean interior. Doyne help up the lamp

so that its rays fell full on the door. As he did so, an
exclamation broke from his lips and he hurried forward, followed by the others. A man's body lay
huddled together on the snow by the threshold. He
was dressed like a peasant, in old corduroy trousers
and rough coat, and a handkerchief was knotted round
his neck. In his hand he grasped the neck of a broken
bottle. Doyne set the lamp on the ground and the
three bent down together over the man. Close by the
neck lay the rest of the broken bottle, whose contents
had evidently run out into the snow.

" Drunk ? " asked Biggleswade.

Doyne felt the man and laid his hand on his heart.

" No," said he, " dead."

McCurdie leaped to his full height. " I told you
the place was uncanny ! " he cried. " It's fey." Then
he hammered wildly at the door.

There was no response. He hammered again till
it rattled. This time a faint prolonged sound like the
wailing of a sea-creature was heard from within the
house. McCurdie turned round, his teeth chattering.

" Did ye hear that, Doyne ? "

" Perhaps it's a dog," said the Professor.

Lord Doyne, the man of action, pushed them aside
and tried the door-handle. It yielded, the door stood
open, and the gust of cold wind entering the house
extinguished the candle within. They entered and
found themselves in a miserable stone-paved kitchen,
furnished with poverty-stricken meagreness—a wooden
chair or two, a dirty table, some broken crockery, old
cooking utensils, a fly-blown missionary society almanac,
and a fireless grate. Doyne set the lamp on the table.

" We must bring him in," said he.

They returned to the threshold, and as they were

bending over to grip the dead man the same sound filled the air, but this time louder, more intense, a cry of great agony. The sweat dripped from McCurdie's forehead. They lifted the dead man and brought him into the room, and after laying him on a dirty strip of carpet they did their best to straighten the stiff limbs. Biggleswade put on the table a bundle which he had picked up outside. It contained some poor provisions —a loaf, a piece of fat bacon, and a paper of tea. As far as they could guess (and, as they learned later, they guessed rightly), the man was the master of the house, who, coming home blind drunk from some distant inn, had fallen at his own threshold and got frozen to death. As they could not unclasp his fingers from the broken bottle-necks they had to let him clutch it as a dead warrior clutches the hilt of his broken sword.

Then suddenly the whole place was rent with another and yet another long, soul-piercing moan of anguish.

"There's a second room," said Doyne, pointing to a door. "The sound comes from there."

He opened the door, peeped in, and then, returning for the lamp, disappeared, leaving McCurdie and Biggleswade in the pitch darkness, with the dead man on the floor.

"For Heaven's sake, give me a drop of whisky," said the Professor, "or I shall faint."

Presently the door opened and Lord Doyne appeared in the shaft of light. He beckoned to his companions.

"It is a woman in childbirth," he said in his even, tired voice. "We must aid her. She appears un-conscious. Does either of you know anything about such things?"

They shook their heads, and the three looked at each other in dismay. Masters of knowledge that had won them world-fame and honour, they stood helpless, abashed before this, the commonest phenomenon of nature.

"My wife had no child," said McCurdie.

"I've avoided women all my life," said Biggleswade.

"And I've been too busy to think of them. God forgive me," said Doyne.

The history of the next two hours was one that none of the three men ever cared to touch upon. They did things blindly, instinctively, as men do when they come face to face with the elemental. A fire was made, they knew not how, water drawn they knew not whence, and a kettle boiled. Doyne, accustomed to command, directed. The others obeyed. At his suggestion they hastened to the wreck of the car and came staggering back beneath rugs and travelling bags which could supply clean linen and needful things, for amid the poverty of the house they could find nothing fit for human touch or use. Early they saw that the woman's strength was failing, and that she could not live. And there, in that nameless hovel, with death on the hearthstone and death and life hovering over the pitiful bed, the three great men went through the pain and the horror and squalor of birth, and they knew that they had never yet stood before so great a mystery.

With the first wail of the newly born infant a last convulsive shudder passed through the frame of the unconscious mother. Then three or four short gasps for breath, and the spirit passed away. She was dead. Professor Biggleswade threw a corner of the sheet over her face, for he could not bear to see it.

They washed and dried the child as any crone of a midwife would have done, and dipped a small sponge

137

which had always remained unused in a cut-glass
bottle in Doyne's dressing-bag in the hot milk and
water of Biggleswade's thermos bottle and put it to
his lips ; and then they wrapped him up warm in some
of their own woollen undergarments, and took him
into the kitchen and placed him on a bed made of
their fur coats in front of the fire. As the last piece
of fuel was exhausted they took one of the wooden
chairs and broke it up and cast it into the blaze. And
then they raised the dead man from the strip of carpet
and carried him into the bedroom and laid him reverently by side of his dead wife, after which they left
the dead in the darkness and returned to the living. And
the three grave men stood over the wisp of flesh that
had been born a male into the world. Then, their task
being accomplished, reaction came, and even Doyne,
who had seen death in many lands, turned faint. But
the others, losing control of their nerves, shook like
men stricken with palsy.

Suddenly McCurdie cried in a high-pitched voice.
" My God ! Don't you feel it ? " and clutched Doyne
by the arm. An expression of terror appeared on his
iron features. " There ! It's here with us."

Little Professor Biggleswade sat on a corner of the
table and wiped his forehead.

" I heard it. I felt it. It was like the beating of
wings."

" It's the fourth time," said McCurdie. " The
first time was just before I accepted the Deverills' invitation. The second in the railway carriage this afternoon. The third on the way here. This is the fourth."

Biggleswade plucked nervously at the fringe of
whisker under his jaws and said faintly, " It's the
fourth time up to now. I thought it was fancy."

"I have felt it too," said Doyne. "It is the Angel of Death." And he pointed to the room where the dead man and woman lay.

"For God's sake let us get away from this," cried Biggleswade.

"And leave the child to die, like the others?" said Doyne.

"We must see it through," said McCurdie.

A silence fell upon them as they sat round in the blaze with the new-born babe wrapped in its odd swaddling clothes asleep on the pile of fur coats, and it lasted until Sir Angus McCurdie looked at his watch.

"Good Lord," said he, "it's twelve o'clock."

"Christmas morning," said Biggleswade.

"A strange Christmas," mused Doyne.

McCurdie put up his hand. "There it is again! The beating of wings." And they listened like men spellbound. McCurdie kept his hand uplifted, and gazed over their heads at the wall, and his gaze was that of a man in a trance, and he spoke :

"Unto us a child is born, unto us a son is given——"

Doyne sprang from his chair, which fell behind him with a crash.

"Man—what the devil are you saying?"

Then McCurdie rose and met Biggleswade's eyes staring at him through the great round spectacles, and Biggleswade turned and met the eyes of Doyne. A pulsation like the beating of wings stirred the air.

The three wise men shivered with a queer exaltation. Something strange, mystical, dynamic had happened. It was as if scales had fallen from their eyes and they saw with a new vision. They stood together humbly, divested of all their greatness, touching one another in the instinctive fashion of children, as if seeking mutual protection, and they looked, with one accord, irresist-ibly compelled, at the child.

At last McCurdie unbent his black brows and said hoarsely :

"It was not the Angel of Death, Doyne, but another Messenger that drew us here."

The tiredness seemed to pass away from the great administrator's face, and he nodded his head with the calm of a man who has come to the quiet heart of a perplexing mystery.

"It's true," he murmured. "Unto us a child is born, unto us a son is given. Unto the three of us."

Biggleswade took off his great round spectacles and wiped them.

"Gaspar, Melchior, Balthazar. But where are the gold, frankincense and myrrh ? "

"In our hearts, man," said McCurdie.

The babe cried and stretched its tiny limbs.

Instinctively they all knelt down together to, dis-cover, if possible, and administer ignorantly to its wants. The scene had the appearance of an adoration.

Then these three wise, lonely, childless men who, in furtherance of their own greatness, had cut them-selves adrift from the sweet and simple things of life and from the kindly ways of their brethren, and had grown old in unhappy and profitless wisdom, knew that an inscrutable Providence had led them, as it had led three Wise Men of old, on a Christmas morning long ago, to a nativity which should give them a new wisdom, a new link with humanity, a new spiritual outlook, a new hope.

And, when their watch was ended, they wrapped up the babe with precious care, and carried him with them, an inalienable joy and possession, into the great world.

140

THAT there was once a real Prince Rabomirski is beyond question. That he was Ottilie's father may be taken for granted. But that the Princess Rabomirski had a right to bear the title many folks were scandalously prepared to deny. It is true that when the news of the Prince's death reached Monte Carlo, the Princess, who was there at the time, showed various persons on whose indiscretion she could rely a holograph letter of condolence from the Tsar, and later unfolded to the amiable muddle-headed the intricacies of a lawsuit which she was instituting for the recovery of the estates in Poland ; but her detractors roundly declared the holograph letter to be a forgery and the lawsuit a fiction of her crafty brain. Princess, however, she continued to style herself in Cosmopolis, and Princess she was styled by all and sundry. And little Ottilie Rabomirski was called the Princess Ottilie.

Among the people who joined heart and soul with the detractors was young Vince Somerset. If there was one person whom he despised and hated more than Count Bernheim (of the Unholy Lombardic Empire) it was the Princess Rabomirski. In his eyes she was everything that a princess, a lady, a woman, and a mother should not be. She dressed ten years younger than was seemly, she spoke English like a barmaid and French like a cocotte, she gambled her way through Europe from year's end to year's end, and after neglecting Ottilie for twenty years, she was about to marry her to Bernheim. The last was the unforgivable offence.

The young man walked up and down the Casino Terrace of Illerville-sur-Mer, and poured into a friend's ear his flaming indignation. He was nine-and-twenty, and though he pursued the unpoetical avocation of sub-editing the foreign telegrams on a London daily news-paper, retained some of the vehemence of under-graduate days when he had chosen the career (now abandoned) of poet, artist, dramatist, and irrecon-cilable politician.

"Look at them !" he cried, indicating a couple seated at a distant table beneath the awning of the café. "Did you ever see anything so horrible in your life ? The maiden and the Minotaur. When I heard of the engagement to-day I wouldn't believe it until she herself told me. She doesn't know the man's abomination. He's a by-word of reproach through Europe. His name stinks like his infernal body. The live air reeks with the scent he pours upon himself. There can be no turpitude under the sun in which the wretch doesn't wallow. Do you know that he killed his first wife ? Oh, I don't mean that he cut her throat. That's far too primitive for such a com-plex hound. There are other ways of murdering a woman, my dear Ross. You kick her body and break her heart and defile her soul. That's what he did. And he has done it to other women."

"But, my dear man," remarked Ross, elderly and cynical, "he is colossally rich."

"Rich ! Do you know where he made his money ? In the cesspool of European finance. He's a Jew by race, a German by parentage, an Italian by upbringing and a Greek by profession. He has bucket-shops and low-down money-lenders' cribs and rotten companies all over the Continent. Do you remember Sequasto and Co. ? That was Bernheim. England's too hot to hold him. Look at him now he has taken off his hat. Do you know why he wears his greasy hair plastered over half his damned forehead ? It's to hide the mark of the Beast. He's Antichrist ! He's no more a Count than I am. And when I think of that Jezebel from the Mile End Road putting Ottilie into his arms, it makes me see red. By heavens, it's touch and go that I don't slay the pair of them."

"Very likely they're not as bad as they're painted," said his friend.

"She couldn't be," Somerset retorted grimly.

Ross laughed, looked at his watch, and announced that it was time for *apéritifs*. The young man assented moodily, and they crossed the Terrace to the café tables beneath the awning. It was the dying afternoon of a sultry August day, and most of Illerville had deserted tennis courts, *tir aux pigeons* and other distractions to listen lazily to the band in the Casino shade. The place was crowded ; not a table vacant. When the waiter at last brought one from the interior of the café, he dumped it down beside the table occupied by the unspeakable Bernheim and the little Princess Ottilie. Somerset raised his hat as he took his seat. Bernheim responded with elaborate politeness, and Princess Ottilie greeted him with a faint smile. The engaged pair spoke very little to each other. Bernheim lounged back in his chair smoking a cigar and looked out to sea with a bored expression. When the girl made a casual remark he nodded rudely without turning his head. Somerset felt an irresistible desire to kick him. His external appearance was of the type that irritated the young Englishman. He was too handsome in a hard, swaggering black-musta-chioed way; he exaggerated to offence the English style of easy dress; he wore a too devil-may-care Panama, a too obtrusive coloured shirt and club tie; he wore no waistcoat, and the hem of his new flannel trousers, turned up six inches, disclosed a stretch of tan-coloured silk socks clocked with gold matching elegant tan shoes. He went about with a broken-spirited poodle. He was inordinately scented. Somerset glowered at him, and let his drink remain untasted.

Presently Bernheim summoned the waiter, paid him for the tea the girl had been drinking and pushed back his chair.

"This hole is getting on my nerves," he said in French to his companion. "I am going into the *cercle* to play écarté. Will you go to your mother whom I see over there, or will you stay here?"

"I'll stay here," said the little Princess Ottilie.

Bernheim nodded and swaggered off. Somerset bent forward.

"I must see you alone to-night—quite alone. I must have you all to myself. How can you manage it?"

Ottilie looked at him anxiously. She was fair and innocent, of a prettiness more English than foreign, and the scare in her blue eyes made them all the more appealing to the young man.

"What is the good? You can't help me. Don't you see that it is all arranged?"

"I'll undertake to disarrange it at a moment's notice," said Somerset.

"Hush !" she whispered, glancing round ; "somebody will hear. Everything is gossiped about in this place."

"Well, will you meet me ?" the young man persisted.

"If I can," she sighed. "If they are both playing baccarat I may slip out for a little."

"As at spa."

She smiled and a slight flush came into her cheek.

"Yes, as at Spa. Wait for me on the *plage* at the bottom of the Casino steps. Now I must go to my mother. She would not like to see me talking to you."

"The Princess hates me like poison. Do you know why ?"

"No, and you are not going to tell me," she said demurely. "*Au revoir.*"

When she had passed out of earshot, Ross touched the young man's arm.

"I'm afraid, my dear Somerset, you are playing a particularly silly fool's game."

"Have you never played it ?"

"Heaven forbid !"

"It would be a precious sight better for you if you had," growled Somerset.

"I'll take another quinquina," said Ross.

"Did you see the way in which the brute treated her ?" Somerset exclaimed angrily. "If it's like that before marriage, what will it be after ?"

"Plenty of money, separate establishments, perfect independence and happiness for each."

Somerset rose from the table.

"There are times, my good Ross," said he, "when I absolutely hate you."

Somerset had first met the Princess Rabomirski and

145

her daughter three years before, at Spa. They were staying at the same hotel, a very modest one which, to Somerset's mind, ill-accorded with the Princess's pretensions. Bernheim was also in attendance, but he disposed his valet, his motor-car, and himself in the luxurious Hôtel d'Orange, as befitted a man of his quality ; also he was in attendance not on Ottilie, but on the Princess, who at that time was three years younger and a trifle less painted. Now, at Illerville-sur-Mer the trio were stopping at the Hôtel Splendide, a sumptuous hostelry where season prices were far above Somerset's moderate means. He contented himself with the little hotel next door, and hated the Hôtel Splendide and all that it contained, save Ottilie, with all his heart. But at Spa, the Princess was evidently in low water from which she did not seem to be rescued by her varying luck at the tables. Ottilie was then a child of seventeen, and Somerset was less attracted by her delicate beauty than by her extraordinary loneliness. Day after day, night after night he would come upon her sitting solitary on one of the settees in the gaming-rooms, like a forgotten fan or flower, or wandering wistfully from table to table, idly watching the revolving wheels. Sometimes she would pause behind her mother's or Bernheim's chair to watch their game ; but the Princess called her a little *porte-malheur* and would drive her away. In the mornings, or on other rare occasions, when the elder inseparables were not playing roulette, Ottilie hovered round them at a distance, as disregarded as a shadow that followed them in space of less dimensions, as it were, wherever they went. In the Casino rooms, if men spoke to her, she replied in shy monosyllables and shrank away. Somerset, who had made regular acquaintance with the Princess at the hotel and taken a chivalrous pity on the girl's loneliness, she admitted first to a timid friendship, and then to a childlike intimacy. Her face would brighten and her heart beat a little faster when she saw his young, well-knit figure appear in the distance ; for she knew he would come straight to her and take her from the hot rooms, heavy with perfumes and tobacco, on to the cool balcony, and talk of all manner of pleasant things. And Somerset found in this neglected, little sham Princess what his youth was pleased to designate a flower-like soul. Those were idyllic hours. The Princess, glad to get the embarrassing child out of the way, took no notice of the intimacy. Somerset fell in love.

It lasted out a three-years' separation, during which he did not hear from her. He had written to several addresses, but a cold Post Office returned his letters undelivered, and his only consolation was to piece together from various sources the unedifying histories of the Princess Rabomirski and Count Bernheim of the Bloodsuckers' Empire. He came to Illerville-sur-Mer for an August holiday. The first thing he did when shown into his hotel bedroom was to gaze out of window at the beach and the sea. The first person his eyes rested upon was the little Princess Ottilie issuing, alone as usual, from the doors of the next hotel.

He had been at Illerville a fortnight—a fortnight of painful joy. Things had changed. Their interviews had been mostly stolen, for the Princess Rabomirski had rudely declined to renew the acquaintance and had forbidden Ottilie to speak to him. The girl, though apparently as much neglected as ever, was guarded against him with peculiar ingenuity. Somerset, aware that Ottilie, now grown from a child into an exquisitely beautiful and marriageable young woman, was destined by a hardened sinner like the Princess for a wealthier husband than a poor newspaper man with no particular prospects, could not, however, quite understand the reasons for the virulent hatred of which he was the object. He overheard the Princess one day cursing her daughter in execrable German for having acknowledged his bow a short time before. Their only undisturbed time together was in the sea during the bathing hour. The Princess, hating the pebbly beach which cut to pieces her high-heeled shoes, never watched the bathers ; and Bernheim, who did not bathe (Somerset, prejudiced, declared that he did not even wash), remained in his bedroom till the hour of *déjeuner*. Ottilie, attended only by her maid, came down to the water's edge, threw off her *peignoir*, and plunging into the water, found Somerset waiting.

Now Somerset was a strong swimmer. Moderately proficient at all games as a boy and an undergraduate, he had found that swimming was the only sport in which he excelled, and he had cultivated and maintained the art. Oddly enough, the little Princess Ottilie, in spite of her apparent fragility, was also an excellent and fearless swimmer. She had another queer delight for a creature so daintily feminine, the *salle d'armes*, so that the muscles of her young limbs were firm and well ordered. But the sea was her passion. If an additional bond between Somerset and herself were needed, it would have been this. Yet, though it is a pleasant thing to swim far away into the loneliness of the sea with the object of one's affections, the conditions do not encourage sustained conversation on subjects of vital interest. On the day when Somerset learned that his little princess was engaged to Bernheim, he burned to tell her more than could be spluttered out in ten fathoms of water. So he urged her to an assignation.

At half-past ten she joined him at the bottom of the Casino steps. The shingly beach was deserted, but on the terrace above the throng was great, owing to the breathless heat of the night.

"Thank Heaven you have come," said he. "Do you know how I have longed for you?"

She glanced up wistfully into his face. In her simple cream dress and burnt straw hat adorned with white roses round the brim, she looked very fair and childlike.

"You mustn't say such things," she whispered. "They are wrong now. I am engaged to be married."

"I won't hear of it," said Somerset. "It is a horrible nightmare—your engagement. Don't you know that I love you? I loved you the first minute I set my eyes on you at Spa."

Princess Ottilie sighed, and they walked along the boards behind the bathing-machines, and down the rattling beach to the shelter of a fishing-boat, where they sat down, screened from the world with the murmuring sea in front of them. Somerset talked of his love and the hatefulness of Bernheim. The little Princess sighed again.

"I have worse news still," she said. "It will pain you. We are going to Paris to-morrow, and then on to Aix-les-Bains. They have just decided. They say the baccarat here is silly, and they might as well play for bon-bons. So we must say good-bye to-night— and it will be good-bye for always."

"I will come to Aix-les-Bains," said Somerset.

"No—no," she answered quickly. "It would only

bring trouble on me and do no good. We must part
to-night. Don't you think it hurts me ? "

" But you must love me," said Somerset.

" I do," she said simply, "and that is why it hurts.
Now I must be going back."

" Ottilie," said Somerset, grasping her hands.
" Need you ever go back ? "

" What do you mean ? " she asked.

" Come away from this hateful place with me—now,
this minute. You need never see Bernheim again as
long as you live. Listen. My friend Ross has a
motor-car. I can manage it—so there will be only us
two. Run into your hotel for a thick cloak, and meet
me as quickly as you can behind the tennis-courts. If
we go full speed we'll catch the night-boat at Dieppe.
It will be a wild race for our life happiness. Come."

In his excitement he rose and pulled her to her feet.
They faced each other for a few glorious moments,
panting for breath, and then Princess Ottilie broke
down and cried bitterly.

" I can't, dear, I can't. I must marry Bernheim.
It is to save my mother from something dreadful. I
don't know what it is—but she went on her knees to
me, and I promised."

" If there's a woman in Europe capable of getting
out of her difficulties unaided it is the Princess Rabomirski," said Somerset. " I am not going to let you
be sold. You are mine, Ottilie, and by Heaven, I'm
going to have you. Come."

He urged, he pleaded, he put his strong arms around
her as if he would carry her away bodily. He did
everything that a frantic young man could do. But
the more the little Princess wept, the more inflexible
she became. Somerset had not realized before this

steel in her nature. Raging and vehemently urging, he accompanied her back to the Casino steps.

"Would you like to say good-bye to me to-morrow morning, instead of to-night?" she asked, holding out her hand.

"I am never going to say good-bye," cried Somerset.

"I shall slip out to-morrow morning for a last swim —at six o'clock," she said, unheeding his exclamation. "Our train goes at ten." Then she came very close to him.

"Vince dear, if you love me, don't make me more unhappy than I am."

It was an appeal to his chivalry. He kissed her hand, and said :

"At six o'clock."

But Somerset had no intention of bidding her a final farewell in the morning. If he followed her the world over he would snatch her out of the arms of the accursed Bernheim and marry her by main force. As for the foreign telegrams of the *Daily Post*, he cared not how they would be sub-edited. He went to bed with lofty disregard of Fleet Street and bread and butter. As for the shame from which Ottilie's marriage would save her sainted mother, he did not believe a word of it. She was selling Ottilie to Bernheim for cash down. He stayed awake most of the night plotting schemes for the rescue of his Princess. It would be an excellent plan to insult Bernheim and slay him outright in a duel. Its disadvantages lay in his own imperfections as a duellist, and for the first time he cursed the benign laws of his country. At length he fell asleep ; woke up to find it daylight, and leaped to his feet in a horrible scare. But a sight of his watch reassured him. It was only five o'clock. At half-past he put on a set of

bathing things and sat down by the window to watch
the hall door of the Hôtel Splendide. At six, out came
the familiar figure of the little Princess, draped in her
white *peignoir*. She glanced up at Somerset's window.
He waved his hand, and in a minute or two they were
standing side by side at the water's edge. It was far
away from the regular bathing-place marked by the
bathing cabins, and farther still from the fishing end
of the beach where alone at that early hour were signs
of life visible. The town behind them slept in warmth
and light. The sea stretched out blue before them un-
rippled in the still air. A little bank of purple cloud
on the horizon presaged a burning day.

The little Princess dropped her *peignoir* and kicked
off her straw-soled shoes, and gave her hand to her
companion. He glanced at the little white feet which
he was tempted to fall down and kiss, and then at the
wistful face below the blue-silk foulard knotted in
front over the bathing-cap. His heart leaped at her
bewildering sweetness. She was the morning incar-
nate.

She read his eyes and flushed pink.

" Let us go in," she said.

They waded in together, hand-in-hand, until they
were waist-deep. Then they struck out, making for
the open sea. The sting of the night had already passed
from the water. To their young blood it felt warm.
They swam near together. Ottilie using a steady
breast stroke and Somerset a side stroke, so that he
could look at her flushed and glistening face. The
blue of the sea and the blue of the sky and the blue
of the silk foulard made the blue of her eyes magically deep.

" There seems to be nothing but you and I in God's

universe, Ottilie," said he. She smiled at him. He drew quite close to her.

"If we could only go on straight until we found an enchanted island which we could have as our kingdom."

"The sea must be our kingdom," said Ottilie.

"Or its depths. Shall we dive down and look for the 'ceiling of amber, the pavement of pearl' and the 'red gold throne in the heart of the sea' for the two of us?"

"We should be happier than in the world," replied the little Princess.

They swam on slowly, dreamily, in silence. The mild waves lapped against their ears and their mouths. The morning sun lay at their backs, and its radiance fell athwart the bay. Through the stillness came the faint echo of a fisherman on the far beach hammering at his boat. Beyond that and the gentle swirl of the water there was no sound. After a while they altered their course so as to reach a small boat that lay at anchor for the convenience of the stronger swimmers. They clambered up and sat on the gunwale, their feet dangling in the sea.

"Is my princess tired?" he asked.

She laughed in merry scorn.

"Tired? Why, I could swim twenty times as far. Do you think I have no muscle? Feel. Don't you know I fence all the winter?"

She braced her bare arm. He felt the muscle; then, relaxing it, by drawing down her wrist, he kissed it very gently.

"Soft and strong—like yourself," said he. Ottilie said nothing, but looked at her white feet through the transparent water. She thought that in letting him

153

kiss her arm and feeling as though he had kissed right
through to her heart, she was exhibiting a pitiful
lack of strength. Somerset looked at her askance,
uncertain. For nothing in the world would he have
offended.

" Did you mind ? " he whispered.

She shook her head and continued to look at her
feet. Somerset felt a great happiness pulse through
him.

" If I gave you up," said he, " I should be the poorest
spirited dog that ever whined."

" Hush ! " she said, putting her hand in his. " Let
us think only of the present happiness."

They sat silent for a moment, contemplating the
little red-roofed town of Illerville-sur-Mer, which
nestled in greenery beyond the white sweep of the
beach, and the rococo hotels and the casino, whose
cupolas flashed gaudily in the morning sun. From the
north-eastern end of the bay stretched a long line of
sheer white cliff as far as the eye could reach. Towards
the west it was bounded by a narrow headland running
far out to sea.

" It looks like a frivolous little Garden of Eden,"
said Somerset, " but I wish we could never set foot
in it again."

" Let us dive in and forget it," said Ottilie.

She slipped into the water. Somerset stood on the
gunwale and dived. When he came up and had shaken
the salt water from his nostrils, he joined her in two
or three strokes.

" Let us go round the point to the little beach the
other side."

She hesitated. It would take a long time to swim
there, rest, and swim back. Her absence might be

noticed. But she felt reckless. Let her drink this hour of happiness to the full. What mattered anything that could follow ? She smiled assent, and they struck out steadily for the point. It was good to have the salt smell and the taste of the brine and the pleasant smart of the eyes and to feel their mastery of the sea. As they threw out their flashing white arms and topped each tiny wave they smiled in exultation. To them it seemed impossible that anyone could drown. For the buoyant hour they were creatures of the element. Now and then a gull circled before them, looked at them unconcerned, as if they were in some way his kindred, and swept off into the distance. A tired white butterfly settled for a moment on Ottilie's head ; then light-heartedly fluttered away seawards to its doom. They swam on and on, and they neared the point. They slackened for a moment, and he brought his face close to hers.

" If I said ' Let us swim on for ever and ever,' would you do it ? "

" Yes," she said, looking deep into his eyes.

After a while they floated restfully. The last question and answer seemed to have brought them a great peace. They were conscious of little save the mystery of the cloudless ether above their faces and the infinite sea that murmured in their ears strange harmonies of Love and Death—harmonies woven from the human yearnings of every shore and the hushed secrets of eternal time. So close were they bodily together that now and then hand touched hand and limb brushed limb. A happy stillness of the soul spread its wings over them and they felt it to be a consecration of their love. Presently his arm sought her, encircled her, brought her head on his shoulder.

"Rest a little," he whispered.

She closed her eyes, surrendered her innocent self to the flooding rapture of the moment. The horrors that awaited her passed from her brain. He had come to the lonely child like a god out of heaven. He had come to the frightened girl like a new terror. He was by her side now, the man whom of all men God had made to accomplish her womanhood and to take all of soul and body, sense and brain that she had to give. Their salt lips met in a first kiss. Words would have broken the spell of the enchantment cast over them by the infinite spaces of sea and sky. They drifted on and on, the subtle, subconscious movement of foot and hand keeping them afloat. The little Princess moved closer to him so as to feel more secure around her the circling pressure of his arm. He laughed a man's short, exultant laugh, and gripped her more tightly. Never had he felt his strength more sure. His right arm and his legs beat rhythmically and he felt the pulsation of the measured strokes of his companion's feet and the water swirled past his head, so that he knew they were making way most swiftly Of exertion there was no sense whatever. He met her eyes fixed through half-shut lids upon his face. Her soft young body melted into his. He lost count of time and space. Now and then a little wave broke over their faces, and they laughed and cleared the brine from their mouths and drew more close together.

"If it wasn't for that," she whispered once, "I could go to sleep."

Soon they felt the gentle rocking of the sea increase and waves broke more often over them. Somerset was the first to note the change. Loosening his hold of Ottilie, he trod water and looked around. To his amazement they were still abreast of the point, but far out to sea. He gazed at it uncomprehendingly for an instant, and then a sudden recollection smote him like a message of death. They had caught the edge of the current against which swimmers were warned, and the current held them in its grip and was sweeping them on while they floated foolishly. A swift glance at Ottilie showed him that she too realized the peril. With the outgoing tide it was almost impossible to reach the shore.

" Are you afraid ? " he asked.

She shook her head. " Not with you."

He scanned the land and the sea. On the arc of their horizon lay the black hull of a tramp steamer going eastwards. Far away to the west was a speck of white and against the pale sky a film of smoke. Landwards beyond the shimmering water stretched the sunny bay of the casino. Its gilt cupolas shot tiny flames. The green-topped point, its hither side deep in shadow, reached out helplessly for them. Somerset and Ottilie still paused, doing nothing more than keeping themselves afloat, and they felt the current drifting them ever seawards.

" It looks like death," he said gravely. " Are you afraid to die ? "

Again Ottilie said, " Not with you."

He looked at the land, and he looked at the white speck and the puff of smoke. Then suddenly his heart leaped with the thrilling inspiration of a wild impossibility.

" Let us leave Illerville and France behind us. Death is as certain either way."

The little Princess looked at him wonderingly.

" Where are we going ? "

"To England."

"Anywhere but Illerville," she said.

He struck out seawards, she followed. Each saw the other's face white and set. They had current and tide with them, they swam steadily, undistressed. After a silence she called to him.

"Vince, if we go to our kingdom under the sea, you will take me down in your arms?"

"In a last kiss," he said.

He had heard (as who has not) of Love being stronger than Death. Now he knew its truth. But he swore to himself a great oath that they should not die.

"I shall take my princess to a better kingdom," he said later.

Presently he heard her breathing painfully. She could not hold out much longer.

"I will carry you," he said.

An expert swimmer, she knew the way to hold his shoulders and leave his arms unimpeded. The contact of her light young form against his body thrilled him and redoubled his strength. He held his head for a second high out of the water and turned half round.

"Do you think I am going to let you die—now?"

The white speck had grown into a white hull, and Somerset was making across its track. To do so he must deflect slightly from the line of the current. His great battle began.

He swam doggedly, steadily, husbanding his strength. If the vessel justified his first flash of inspiration, and if he could reach her, he knew how he should act. As best he could, for it was no time for speech, he told Ottilie his hopes. He felt the spray from her lips upon his cheek, as she said :

" It seems sinful to wish for greater happiness than this."

After that there was utter silence between them. At first he thought exultingly of Bernheim and the Princess Rabomirski, and the rage of their wicked hearts ; of the future glorified by his little Princess of the unconquerable soul : of the present's mystic consummation of their marriage. But gradually mental concepts lost sharpness of definition. Sensation began to merge itself into a half-consciousness of stroke on stroke through the illimitable waste. Despite the laughing morning sunshine, the sky became dark and lowering. The weight on his neck grew heavier. At first Ottilie had only rested her arms. Now her feet were as lead and sank behind him ; her clasp tightened about his shoulders. He struggled on through a welter of sea and mist. Strange sounds sang in his ears, as if over them had been clamped great sea-shells. At each short breath his throat gulped down bitter water. A horrible pain crept across his chest. His limbs seemed paralysed and yet he remained above the surface. The benumbed brain wondered at the miracle. . . .

The universe broke upon his vision as a blurred mass of green and white. He recognized it vaguely as his kingdom beneath the sea, and as in a dream he remembered his promise. He slipped round. His lips met Ottilie's. His arms wound round about her, and he sank, holding her tightly clasped.

Strange things happened. He was pulled hither and thither by sea monsters welcoming him to his kingdom. In a confused way he wondered that he could breathe so freely in the depths of the ocean. Unutterable happiness stole upon him. The Kingdom

159

was *real*. His sham Princess would be queen in very truth. But where was she?

He opened his eyes and found himself lying on the deck of a ship. A couple of men were doing funny things to his arms. A rosy-faced man in white ducks and a yachting cap stood over him with a glass of brandy. When he had drunk the spirit, the rosy man laughed.

"That was a narrow shave. We got you just in time. We were nearly right on you. The young woman is doing well. My wife is looking after her."

As soon as he could collect his faculties, Somerset asked:

"Are you the *Mavis*?"

"Yes."

"I felt sure of it. Are you Sir Henry Ransome?"

"That's my name."

"I heard you were expected at Illerville to-day," said Somerset. "That is why I made for you."

The two men who had been doing queer things with his arms wrapped him in a blanket and propped him up against the deck cabin.

"But what on earth were you two young people doing in the middle of the English Channel?" asked the owner of the *Mavis*.

"We were eloping," said Somerset.

The other looked at him for a bewildered moment and burst into a roar of laughter. He turned to the cabin door and disappeared, to emerge a moment afterwards followed by a lady in a morning wrapper.

"What do you think, Marian? It's an elopement."

Somerset smiled at them.

" Have you ever heard of the Princess Rabomirski ?
You have ?   Well, this is her daughter.   Perhaps you
know of the Count Bernheim who is always about
with the Princess ? "

" I trod on him last winter at Monte Carlo," said Sir
Henry Ransome.

" He survives," said Somerset, " and has bought the
Princess Ottilie from her mother.   He's not going to
get her.   She belongs to me.   My name is Somerset,
and I am foreign sub-editor of the *Daily Post*."

" I am very pleased to make your acquaintance,
Mr. Somerset," said Sir Henry with a smile.   " And
now what can I do for you ? "

" If you can lend us some clothes and take us to
any part on earth save Illerville-sur-Mer, you will
earn our eternal gratitude."

Sir Henry looked doubtful.   " We have made our
arrangements for Illerville," said he.

His wife broke in.

" If you don't take these romantic beings straight
to Southampton, I'll never set my foot upon this
yacht again."

" It was you, my dear, who were crazy to come to
Illerville."

" Don't you think," said Lady Ransome, " you
might provide Mr. Somerset with some dry
things ? "

Four hours afterwards Somerset sat on deck by
the side of Ottilie, who, warmly wrapped, lay on a long
chair.   He pointed to the far-away coastline of the
Isle of Wight.

" Behold our kingdom ! " said he.

The little Princess laughed.

161

"That is not our kingdom."

"Well, what is?"

"Just the little bit of space that contains both you and me," she said.

THE girl stood at the end of the little stone jetty, her hair and the ends of her cheap fur boa and her skirts all fluttering behind her in the stiff northeast gale. Why anyone should choose to stand on a jetty on a raw December afternoon with the wind in one's teeth was a difficult problem for a comfort-loving, elderly man like myself, and I pondered over it as I descended the slope leading from the village to the sea. It was nothing, thought I, but youth's animal delight in physical things. A few steps, however, brought me in view of her face in half-profile, and I saw that she did not notice wind or spray, but was staring out to sea with an intolerable wistfulness. A quick turn in the path made me lose the profile. I crossed the road that ran along the shore and walked rapidly along the jetty. Arriving within hailing distance, I called her.

" Pauline."

She pivoted round like a weather-cock in a gust and with a sharp cry leaped forward to meet me. Her face was aflame with great hope and joy. I have seen to my gladness that expression once before worn by a woman. But as soon as this one recognized me, the joy vanished, killed outright.

" Oh, it's you," she said, with a quivering lip.

" I am sorry, my dear," said I, taking her hand. " I can't help it. I wish from my heart I were somebody else."

She burst into tears. I put my arm around her and
drew her to me, and patted her and said "There,
there!" in the blundering masculine way. Having
helped to bring her into the world twenty years before,
I could claim fatherly privileges.

"Oh, Doctor," she sobbed, dabbing her pretty
young eyes with a handkerchief. "Do forgive me.
Of course I am glad to see you. It was the shock.
I thought you were a ghost. No one ever comes to
Ravetot."

"Never?" I asked mildly.

The tears flowed afresh. I leaned against the parapet of the jetty for comfort's sake, and looked around
me. Ravetot-sur-Mer was not the place to attract
visitors in December. A shingle beach with a few
fishing-boats hauled out of reach of the surf; a miniature casino, like an impudently large summer-house,
shuttered-up, weather-beaten and desolate; a weather-
beaten, desolate, and shuttered-up Hôtel de l'Univers,
and a perky deserted villa or two on the embankment;
a cliff behind them, topped by a little grey church;
the road that led up the gorge losing itself in the turn
—and that was all that was visible of Ravetot-sur-
Mer. A projecting cliff bounded the bay at each side,
and in front seethed the grey, angry Channel. It was
an Aceldama of a spot in winter; and only a matter
of peculiar urgency had brought me thither. Pauline
and her decrepit rascal of a father were tied to Ravetot
by sheer poverty. He owned a pretty villa half a mile
inland, and the rent he obtained for it during the summer enabled them to live in some miraculous way the
rest of the year. They, the Curé and the fisher-folk,
were the sole winter inhabitants of the place. The
nearest doctor lived at Merville, twenty kilometres

164

away, and there was not even an educated farmer in the neighbourhood. Yet I could not help thinking that my little friend's last remark was somewhat disingenuous.

"Are you quite sure, my dear," I said, "that no one ever comes to Ravetot?"

"Has father told you?" she asked tonelessly.

"No. I guessed it. I have extraordinary powers of divination. And the Somebody has been making my little girl miserable."

"He has broken my heart," said Pauline.

I pulled the collar of my fur-lined coat above my ears which the north-east wind was biting. Being elderly and heart-whole, I am sensitive to cold. I proposed that we should walk up and down the jetty while she told me her toubles, and I hooked her arm in mine.

"Who was he?" I asked. "And what was he doing here?"

"Oh, Doctor, what does it matter?" she answered tearfully. "I never want to see him again."

"Don't fib," said I. "If the confounded blackguard were here now——"

"But he isn't a blackguard!" she flashed. "If he were I shouldn't be so miserable. I should forget him. He is good and kind, and noble, and everything that is right. I couldn't have expected him to act otherwise—it was awful, horrible—and when you called me by name I thought it was he——"

"And the contradictious feminine did very much want to see him?" said I.

"I suppose so," she confessed.

I looked down at her pretty face and saw that it was wan and pinched.

"You have been eating little and sleeping less. For how long?" I demanded sternly.

"For a week," she said pitifully.

"We must change all that. This abominable hole is a kind of cold storage for depression."

She drew my arm tighter. She had always been an affectionate little girl, and now she seemed to crave human sympathy and companionship.

"I don't mind it now. It doesn't in the least matter where I am. Before he came I used to hate Ravetot, and long for the gaiety and brightness of the great world. I used to stand here for hours and just long and long for something to happen to take us away; and it seemed no good. Here I was for the rest of time —with nothing to do day after day but housework and sewing and reading, while father sat by the fire, with his little roulette machine and Monte Carlo averages and paper and pencil, working out the wonderful system that is going to make our fortune. We'll never have enough money to go to Monte Carlo for him to try it, so that is some comfort. One would have thought he had had enough of gambling."

She made the allusion, very simply, to me—an old friend. Her father had gambled away a fortune, and in desperation had forged another man's name on the back of a bill for which he had suffered a term of imprisonment. His relatives had cast him out. That was why he lived in poverty-stricken seclusion at Ravetot-sur-Mer. He was not an estimable old man, and I had always pitied Pauline for being so parented. Her mother had died years ago. I thought I would avoid the painful topic.

"And so," said I, after we had gone the length of the jetty in silence and had turned again, "one day when the lonely little princess was staring out to sea and longing for she knew not what, the young prince out of the fairy-tale came riding up behind her—and stayed just long enough to make her lose her heart—and then rode off again."

"Something like it—only worse," she murmured. And then, with a sudden break in her voice, " I will tell you all about it. I shall go mad if I don't. I haven't a soul in the world to speak to. Yes. He came. He found me standing at the end of the jetty. He asked his way, in French, to the cemetery, and I recognized from his accent that he was English like myself. I asked him why he wanted to go to the cemetery. He said that it was to see his wife's grave. The only Englishwoman buried here was a Mrs. Everest, who was drowned last summer. This was the husband. He explained that he was in the Indian Civil Service, was now on leave. Being in Paris he thought he would like to come to Ravetot, where he could have quiet, in order to write a book."

"I understood it was to see his wife's grave," I remarked.

" He wanted to do that as well. You see, they had been separated for some years—judicially separated. She was not a nice woman. He didn't tell me so ; he was too chivalrous a gentleman. But I had learned about her from the gossip of the place. I walked with him to the cemetery. I know a well-brought-up girl wouldn't have gone off like that with a stranger."

" My dear," said I, "in Ravetot-sur-Mer she would have gone off with a hippogriffin."

She pressed my arm. " How understanding you are, Doctor dear."

" I have an inkling of the laws that govern humanity," I replied. "Well, and after the pleasant trip to the cemetery?"

"He asked me whether the café at the top of the hill was really the only place to stay at in Ravetot. It's dreadful, you know—no one goes there but fishermen and farm labourers—and it *is* the only place. The hotel is shut up out of the season. I said that Ravetot didn't encourage visitors during the winter. He looked disappointed, and said that he would have to find quiet somewhere else. Then he asked whether there wasn't any house that would take him in as a boarder?"

She paused.

"Well?" I inquired.

"Oh, Doctor, he seemed so strong and kind, and his eyes were so frank. I knew he was everything that a man ought to be. We were friends at once, and I hated the thought of losing him. It is not gay at Ravetot with only Jeanne to talk to from week's end to week's end. And then we are so poor—and you know we do take in paying guests when we can get them."

"I understand perfectly," said I.

She nodded. That was how it happened. Would a nice girl have done such a thing? I replied that if she knew so much of the ways of nice girls as I did, she would be astounded. She smiled wanly and went on with her artless story. Of course Mr. Everest jumped at the suggestion. It is not given to every young and unlamenting widower to be housed beneath the same roof as so delicious a young woman as Pauline. He brought his luggage and took possession of the best spare room in the Villa, while Pauline and old, slatternly Jeanne, the *bonne à tout faire*, went about with agitated

168

minds and busy hands attending to his comfort. Old Widdrington, however, in his morose chimney-corner, did not welcome the visitor. He growled and grumbled and rated his daughter for not having doubled the terms. Didn't she know they wanted every penny they could get ? Something was wrong with his roulette machine which ought to be sent to Paris for repairs. Where was the money to come from ? Pauline's father is the most unscrupulous, selfish old curmudgeon of my acquaintance !

Then, according to my young lady's incoherent and parenthetic narrative, followed idyllic days. Pauline chattered to Mr. Everest in the morning, walked with him in the afternoon, pretended to play the piano to him in the evening, and in between times sat with him at meals. The inevitable happened. She had met no one like him before—he represented the strength and the music of the great world. He flashed upon her as the realization of the vague visions that had floated before her eyes when she stared seawards in the driving wind. That the man was a bit in love with her seems certain. I think that one day, when a wayside shed was sheltering them from the rain, he must have kissed her. A young girl's confidences are full of details ; but the important ones are generally left out. They can be divined, however, by the old and experienced. At any rate, Pauline was radiantly happy, and Everest appeared contented to stay indefinitely at Ravetot and watch her happiness.

Thus far the story was ordinary enough. Given the circumstances it would have been extraordinary if my poor little Pauline had not fallen in love with the man and if the man's heart had not been touched. If he had found the girl's feelings too deep for his response and had precipitately bolted from a confused sense of acting honourably towards her, the story would also have been commonplace. The cause of his sudden riding away was peculiarly painful. Somehow I cannot blame him ; and yet I am vain enough to imagine that I should have acted otherwise.

One morning Everest asked her if Jeanne might search his bedroom for a twenty-franc piece which he must have dropped on the floor. In the afternoon her father gave her twenty francs to get a postal order ; he was sending to Paris for some fresh mechanism for his precious roulette-wheel. Everest accompanied her to the little post office. They walked arm in arm through the village like an affianced couple, and I fancy he must have said tenderer things than usual on the way, for at this stage of the story she wept. When she laid the louis on the slab below the *guichet*, she noticed that it was a new Spanish coin. Spanish gold is rare. She showed it to Everest, and meeting his eyes read in them a curious questioning. The money order obtained, they continued their walk happily, and Pauline forgot the incident. Some days passed. Everest grew troubled and preoccupied. One livelong day he avoided her society altogether. She lived through it in a distressed wonder, and cried herself to sleep that night. How had she offended ? The next morning he gravely announced his departure. Urgent affairs summoned him to Paris. In dazed misery she accepted the payment of his account and wrote him a receipt. His face was set like a mask, and he looked at her out of cold, stern eyes which frightened her. In a timid way she asked him if he were going without one kind word.

"There are times, Miss Widdrington," said he, "when no word at all is the kindest."

"But what have I done?" she cried.

"Nothing at all but what is good and right. You may think whatever you like of me. Good-bye!"

He grasped his Gladstone bag, and through the window she saw him give it to the fisher-lad who was to carry it three miles to the nearest wayside station. He disappeared through the gate, and so out of her life. Fat, slatternly Jeanne came upon her a few moments later moaning her heart out, and administered comfort. It was very hard for Mademoiselle—but what could Mademoiselle expect? Monsieur Everest could not stay any longer in the house. Naturally. Of course, Monsieur was a little touched in the brain, with his eternal calculations—he was not responsible for his actions. Still, Monsieur Everest did not like Monsieur to take money out of his room. But, Great God of Pity! did not Mademoiselle know that was the reason of Monsieur Everest going away?

"It was father who had stolen the Spanish louis," cried Pauline in a passion of tears, as we leaned once more against the parapet of the jetty. "He also stole a fifty-franc note. Then he was caught red-handed by Mr. Everest rifling his despatch-box. Jeanne overheard them talking. It is horrible, horrible! How he must despise me! I feel wrapped in flames when I think of it—and I love him so—and I haven't slept for a week—and my heart is broken."

I could do little to soothe this paroxysm, save let it spend itself against my great-coat, while I again put my arm around her. The grey tide was leaping in and the fine spray dashed in my face. The early twilight began to settle over Ravetot, which appeared more desolate than ever."

"Never mind, my dear," said I, "you are young, and as your soul is sweet and clean, you will get over this."

"Never," she moaned.

"You will leave Ravetot-sur-Mer and all its associations, and the brightness of life will drive all the shadows away."

"No. It is impossible. My heart is broken and I only want to stay here at the end of the jetty until I die."

"I shall die, anyhow," I remarked with a shiver, "if I stay here much longer, and I don't want to. Let us go home."

She assented. We walked away from the sea and struck the gloomy inland road. Then I said, somewhat meaningly :

"Haven't you the curiosity to inquire why I left my comfortable house in London to come to this God-forsaken hole ? "

"Why did you, Doctor dear ? " she asked listlessly.

"To inform you that your cross old aunt Caroline is dead, that she has left you three thousand pounds a year under my trusteeship till you are five-and-twenty, and that I am going to carry off the rich and beautiful Miss Pauline Widdrington to England to-morrow."

She stood stock-still, looking at me open-mouthed.

"Is it true ? " she gasped.

"Of course," said I.

Her face was transfigured with a sudden radiance. Amazement, rapture, youth——the pulsating wonder of her twenty years danced in her eyes. In her excitement she pulled me by the lapels of my coat——

"*Doctor!* Doctor! Three thousand pounds a year! England! London! Men and women! Everything I've longed for! All the glad and beautiful things of life!"

"Yes, my dear."

She took my hands and swung them backwards and forwards.

"It's Heaven! Delicious Heaven!" she cried.

"But what about the broken heart?" I said maliciously.

She dropped my hands, sighed, and her face suddenly assumed an expression of portentous misery.

"I was forgetting. What does anything matter now? I shall never get over it. My heart *is* broken."

"Devil a bit, my dear," said I.

THE SCOURGE

I

UP to the death of his wife, that is to say for fifty-six years, Sir Hildebrand Oates held himself to be a very important and upright man, whose life not only was unassailable by slander, but even through the divine ordering of his being exempt from criticism. To the world and to himself he represented the incarnation of British impeccability, faultless from the little pink crown of his head to the tips of his toes correctly pedicured and unstained by purples of retributive gout. Except in church, where a conventional humility of attitude is imposed, his mind was blandly *conscia recti*. No ghost of sins committed disturbed his slumbers. He had committed no sin. He could tick off the Ten Commandments one by one with a serene conscience. He objected to profane swearing ; he was a strict sabbatarian ; he had honoured his father and his mother and had erected a monument over their grave which added another fear of death to the beholder ; he neither thieved nor murdered, nor followed in the footsteps of Don Juan, nor in those of his own infamous namesake ; and being blessed in the world's goods, coveted nothing possessed by his neighbour—not even his wife, for his neighbours' wives could not compare in wifely meekness with his own. In thought, too, he had not sinned. Never, so far as he remembered, had he spoken a

ribald word, never, indeed, had he laughed at an un-
savoury jest. It may be questioned whether he had
laughed at any kind of joke whatsoever.

Sir Hildebrand stood for many things : for Public
Morality ; his name appeared on the committees of all
the societies for the suppression of all the vices : for
sound Liberalism and Incorruptible Government ; he
had poured much of his fortune into the party coffers
and, to his astonishment, a gracious (and minister-har-
assed) Sovereign had conveyed recognition of his virtues
in the form of a knighthood. For the sacred rights of
the people ; as Justice of the Peace he sentenced
vagrants who slept in other people's barns to the
severest penalties. For Principle in private life ; in
spite of the rending of his own heart and the agonized
tears of his wife, he had cast off his undutiful children,
a son and a daughter who had been guilty of the sin of
disobedience and had run away taking their creaking
destinies in their own hands. For the Sanctity of
Home Life ; night and morning he read prayers
before the assembled household and dismissed any
maidservant who committed the impropriety of con-
versing with a villager of the opposite sex. From
youth up, his demeanour had been studiously grave
and punctiliously courteous. A man of birth and
breeding, he made it his ambition to be what he, with
narrow definition, termed "a gentleman of the old
school"; but being of Whig lineage, he had sat in
Parliament as an hereditary Liberal and believed in
Progressive Institutions.

It is difficult to give a flashlight picture of a human
being at once so simple and so complex. An ardent
Pharisee may serve as an epigrammatic characteriza-
tion. Hypocrite he was not. No miserable sinner

more convinced of his rectitude, more devoid of pretence, ever walked the earth. Though his narrowness of view earned him but little love from his fellow-humans, his singleness of purpose, aided by an ample fortune, gained a measure of their respect. He lived irreproachably up to his standards. In an age of general scepticism he had unshakable faith. He believed intensely in himself. Now this passionate certitude of infallibility found, as far as his life's drama is concerned, its supreme expression in his relation to his wife, his children, and his money.

He married young. His wife brought him a fortune for which he was sole trustee, a couple of children, and a submissive obedience unparalleled in the most correct of Moslem households. Eresby Manor, where they had lived for thirty years, was her own individual property, and she drew for pocket-money some five hundred pounds a year. A timid, weak, sentimental soul, she was daunted from the first few frosty days of honeymoon by the inflexible personality of her husband. For thirty years she passed in the world's eye for little else than his shadow.

" My dear, you must allow me to judge in such matters," he would say in reply to mild remonstrance. And she deferred invariably to his judgment. When his son Godfrey and his daughter Sybil went their respective unfilial ways, it was enough for him to remark with cold eyes and slight, expressive gesture :

" My dear, distressing as I know it is to you, their conduct has broken my heart and I forbid the mention of their names in this house."

And the years passed and the perfect wife, though, in secret, she may have mourned like Rachel for her children, obeyed the very letter of her husband's law.

There remains the third vital point, to which I must refer, if I am to make comprehensible the strange story of Sir Hildebrand Oates. It was money—or, more explicitly, the diabolical caprice of finance—that first shook Sir Hildebrand's faith, not, perhaps, in his own infallibility, but in the harmonious co-operation of Divine Providence and himself. For the four or five years preceding his wife's death his unerring instinct in financial affairs failed him. Speculations that promised indubitably the golden fruit of the Hesperides produced nothing but Dead Sea apples. He lost enormous sums of money. Irritability constricted both his brow and the old debonair " s " at the end of his signature. And when the County Guarantee Investment Society of which he was one of the original founders and directors called up unpaid balance on shares, and even then hovered on the verge of scandalous liquidation, Sir Hildebrand found himself racked with indignant anxiety.

He was sitting at a paper-strewn table in his library, a decorous library, a gentleman's library, lined from floor to ceiling with bookcases filled with books that no gentleman's library should be without, and trying to solve the eternal problem why two and two should not make forty, when the butler entered announcing the doctor.

"Ah, Thompson, glad to see you. What is it? Have you looked at Lady Oates? Been a bit queer for some days. These east winds. I hold them responsible for half the sickness of the county."

He threw up an accusing hand. If the east wind had been a human vagabond brought before Sir Hildebrand Oates, Justice of the Peace, it would have whined itself into a Zephyr. Sir Hildebrand's eyes

looked blue and cold at offenders. From a stature of
medium height he managed to extract the dignity of
six-foot-two. Beneath a very long and very straight
nose a grizzling moustache, dependent on the muscles
of the thin lips as to whether it should go up or down,
symbolized, as it were, the scales of justice. Sketches
of accurately trimmed grey whiskers also indicated
the exact balance of his mind. But to show that he
was human and not impassionately divine, his thin
hair once black, now greenish, was parted low down
on the left side and brought straight over, leaving the
little pink crown to which I have before alluded. His
complexion was florid, disavowing atrabiliar prejudice.
He had the long blunted chin of those secure of their
destiny. He was extraordinarily clean.

The doctor said abruptly : " It's nothing to do with
east winds. It's internal complications. I have to
tell you she's very seriously ill."

A shadow of impatience passed over Sir Hildebrand's
brow.

" Just like my wife," said he, " to fall ill when I'm
already half off my head with worry."

" The County Guarantee——? "

Sir Hildebrand nodded. The misfortunes of the
Society were public property, and public too, within
the fairly wide area of his acquaintance, was the knowledge of the fact that Sir Hildebrand was heavily in-
volved therein. Too often had he vaunted the bene-
ficent prosperity of the concern to which he had given
his august support. At his own dinner-table men had
dreaded the half-hour after the departure of the ladies,
and at his club men had fled from him as they flee from
the Baconian mythologist.

" It is a worry," the doctor admitted. " But

financial preoccupations must give way "—he looked
Sir Hildebrand clear in the eyes—"must give way
before elementary questions of life and death."

"Death ?" Sir Hildebrand regarded him blankly.
How dare Death intrude in so unmannerly a fashion
across his threshold ?

"I should have been called in weeks ago," said the
doctor. "All I can suggest now is that you should get
Sir Almeric Home down from London. I'll telephone
at once, with your authority. An operation may
save her."

"By all means. But tell me—I had no idea—I
wanted to send for you last week, but she's so obstinate
—said it was mere indigestion."

"You should have sent for me all the same."

"Anyhow," said Sir Hildebrand, "tell me the
worst."

The doctor told him and departed. Sir Hildebrand
walked up and down his library, a man undeservedly
stricken. The butler entered. Pringle, the chauffeur, desired audience.

Admitted, the man plunged into woeful apology.
He had been trying the Mercédès on its return from
an overhaul, and as he turned the corner by Rush-
worth Farm a motor lorry had run into him and
smashed his head-lamps.

"I told you when I engaged you," said Sir Hildebrand, "that I allowed no accidents."

"It's only the lamps. I was driving most careful.
The driver of the lorry owns himself in the wrong,"
pleaded the chauffeur.

"The merits or demerits of the case," replied Sir
Hildebrand, "do not interest me. It's an accident.
I don't allow accidents. You take a month's notice."

"Very well, Sir Hildebrand, but I do think it——"

"Enough," said Sir Hildebrand, dismissing him. "I have nothing more to hear from you or to say to you."

Then, when he was alone again, Sir Hildebrand reflected that noble resignation under misfortune was the part of a Christian gentleman, and in chastened mood went upstairs to see his wife. And in the days that followed, when Sir Almeric Home, summoned too late, had performed the useless wonders of his magical craft and had gone, Sir Hildebrand, most impeccable of husbands, visited the sick-room twice a day, making the most correct inquiries, beseeching her to name desires capable of fulfilment, and urbanely prophesying speedy return to health. At the end of the second visit he bent down and kissed her on the forehead. The ukase went forth to the servants' hall that no one should speak above a whisper, for fear of disturbing her ladyship, and the gardeners had orders to supply the sick-room with a daily profusion of flowers. Mortal gentleman could show no greater solicitude for a sick wife—save perhaps bring her a bunch of violets in his own hand. But with an automatic supply of orchids, why should he think of so trumpery an offering?

Lady Oates died. Sir Hildebrand accepted the stroke with Christian resignation. The Lord giveth and the Lord taketh away. Yet his house was desolate. He appreciated her virtues, which were many. He went categorically through her attributes : A faithful wife, a worthy mother of unworthy children, a capable manager, a submissive helpmate, a country gentle-woman of the old school who provided supremely for her husband's material comforts and never trespassed into the sphere of his intellectual and other masculine activities. His grief at the loss of his Eliza was sincere. The impending crash of the County Guarantee Investment Society ceased to trouble him. His own fortune had practically gone. Let it go. His dead wife's remained—sufficient to maintain his position in the county. As Dr. Thompson had rightly said, the vulgarities of finance must give way to the eternal sublimities of death. His wife, with whom he had lived for thirty years in a conjugal felicity unclouded save by the unforgivable sins of his children now exiled through their own wilfulness to remote parts of the Empire, was dead. The stupendous fact eclipsed all other facts in a fact-riveted universe. Lady Oates, who, after the way of women of limited outlook, had always taken a great interest in funerals, had the funeral of her life. The Bishop of the Diocese conducted the funeral service. The County, headed by the old Duke of Dunster, his neighbour, followed her to the grave.

II

"She was a good Christian woman, Haversham," said Sir Hildebrand later in the day. "I did not deserve her. But I think I may feel that I did my best all my life to ensure her happiness."

"No doubt, of course," replied Haversham, the county lawyer. "Er—don't you think we might get this formal business over? I've brought Lady Oates's will in my pocket."

He drew out a sealed envelope. Sir Hildebrand held out his hand. The lawyer shook his head. "I'm executor—it's written on the outside—I must open it."

"You executor? That's rather strange," said Sir Hildebrand.

Haversham opened the envelope, adjusted his glasses, and glanced through the document. Then he took off his glasses and, his brows wrinkled, and a queer look, half scared, half malicious, in his eyes, gazed at Sir Hildebrand.

"I must tell you, my dear Oates," said he, after a moment or so, "that I had nothing to do with the making of this. Nothing whatsoever. Lady Oates called at my office about two years ago and placed the sealed envelope in my charge. I had no idea of the contents till this minute."

"Let me see," said Sir Hildebrand; and again he stretched out his hand.

Haversham, holding the paper, hesitated for a few seconds. "I'm afraid I must read it to you, there being no third party present."

"Third party? What do you mean?"

"A witness. A formal precaution." The lawyer again put on his glasses. "The introductory matter is the ordinary phraseology of the printed form one buys at stationers' shops—naming me executor." Then he read aloud :

"I will and bequeath to my husband, Sir Hildebrand Oates, Knight, the sum of fifteen shillings to buy himself a scourge to do penance for the arrogance, uncharitableness and cruelty with which he has treated myself and my beloved children for the last thirty years. I bequeath to my son Godfrey the house and estate of Eresby Manor and all the furniture, plate, jewels, livestock and everything of mine comprised therein. The residue of my possessions I bequeath to my son Godfrey and my daughter Sybil, in equal shares. I leave it to my children to act generously by my old servants, and my horses and dogs."

Sir Hildebrand's florid face grew purple. He looked fishy-eyed and open-mouthed at the lawyer, and gurgled horribly in his throat. Haversham hastily rang a bell. The butler appeared. Between them they carried Sir Hildebrand up to bed and sent for the doctor.

III

When Sir Hildebrand recovered, which he did quickly, he went about like a man in a daze, stupefied by his wife's hideous accusation and monstrous ingratitude. It was inconceivable that the submissive angel with whom he had lived and the secret writer of those appalling words should be one and the same person. Surely, insanity. That invalidated the will. But Haversham pointed out that insanity would have to be proved, which was impossible. The will contained no legal flaw. Lady Oates's dispositions would have to be carried out.

" It leaves me practically a pauper," said Sir Hildebrand, whereat the other, imperceptibly, shrugged his shoulders.

He realized, in cold terror, that the house wherein he dwelt was his no longer. Even the chairs and tables belonged to his son, Godfrey. His own personal belongings could be carried away in a couple of hand-carts. Instead of thousands his income had suddenly dwindled to a salvage of a few hundreds a year. From his position in the county he had tumbled with the suddenness and irreparability of Humpty-Dumpty ! All the vanities of his life sprang on him and choked him. He was a person of no importance whatever. He gasped. Had mere outside misfortune beset him, he doubtless would have faced his downfall with the

184

courage of a gentleman of the old school. His soul
would have been untouched. But now it was stabbed,
and with an envenomed blade. His wife had brought
him to bitter shame. . . . " Arrogance, uncharitableness, cruelty." The denunciation rang in his head day
and night. He arrogant, uncharitable, cruel ? The
charge staggered reason. His indignant glance sweeping backwards through the years could see nothing in
his life but continuous humility, charity, and kindness.
He had not deviated a hair's-breadth from irreproachable standards of conduct. Arrogant ? When Sybil,
engaged in consequence of his tender sagacity to a
neighbouring magnate, a widowed ironmaster, eloped,
at dead of night on her wedding eve, with a penniless
subaltern in the Indian Army, he suffered humiliation
before the countryside with manly dignity. No less
humiliating had been his position and no less resigned
his attitude when Godfrey, declining to obey the
teetotal, non-smoking, early-to-bed, early-to-break-
fast rules of the house, declining also to be ordained
and take up the living of Thereon in the gift of the
Lady of the Manor of Eresby, went off, in undutiful
passion, to Canada to pursue some godless and precarious career. Uncharitableness ? Cruelty ? His
children had defied him, and with callous barbarity
had cut all filial ties. And his wife ? She had lived
in cotton-wool all her days. It was she who had been
cruel—inconceivably malignant.

IV

Sir Hildebrand, after giving Haversham, the lawyer,
an account of his stewardship—in his wild invest-
ments he had not imperilled a penny of his wife's
money—resigned his county appointments, chair-

manships and presidentships and memberships of committees, went to London and took a room at his club. Rumour of his fallen fortunes spread quickly. He found himself neither shunned nor snubbed, but not welcomed in the inner smoke-room coterie before which, as a wealthy and important county gentleman, he had been wont to lay down the law. No longer was he Sir Oracle. Sensitive to the subtle changes, he attributed them to the rank snobbery of his fellow-members. No doubt he was right. The delicate point of snobbery that he did not realize was the difference between the degrees of sufferance accorded to the rich bore and the poor bore. In the eyes of the club, Sir Hildebrand Oates was the poor bore. He became freezingly aware of a devastating loneliness. In the meanwhile his children had written the correctest of letters. Deep grief for mother's death was the keynote of each. With regard to wordly matters, Sybil confessed that the legacy made a revolution in her plans for her children's future, but would not affect her present movements, as she could not allow her husband to abandon a career which promised to be brilliant. She would be home in a couple of years. The son, Godfrey, welcomed the unexpected fortune. The small business he had got together just needed this capital to expand into gigantic proportions. It would be two or three years before he could leave it. In the meantime, he hoped his father would not dream of leaving Eresby Manor. Neither son nor daughter seemed to be aware of Sir Hildebrand's impoverishment. Also, neither of them expressed sympathy for, or even alluded to, the grief that he himself must be suffering. The omission puzzled him ; for he had the lawyer's assurance that they should remain ignorant, as far as lay in his power, of the dreadful text of the will.   Did the omission arise from doubt in their minds as to his love for their mother and the genuineness of his sorrow at her death ?   To solve the riddle, Sir Hildebrand began to think as he had never thought before.

V

Arrogance, uncharitableness, and cruelty.   To wife and children.   For thirty years.   Fifteen shillings to buy a scourge wherewith to do penance.   He could think of nothing else by day or night.   The earth beneath his feet which he had deemed so solid became a quagmire, so that he knew not where to step.   And the serene air darkened.   The roots of his being suffered cataclysm.   Either his wife had been some mad monster in human form, or her terrible indictment had some basis of truth.   The man's soul writhed in the flame of the blazing words.   A scourge for penance. Fifteen shillings to buy it with.   In due course he received the ghastly cheque from Haversham.   His first impulse was to tear it to pieces ; his second, to fold it up and put it in his letter-case,   At the end of a business meeting with Haversham a day or two later, he asked him point-blank :

"Why did you insult me by sending me the cheque for fifteen shillings ? "

"It was a legal formality with which I was bound to comply."

"*De minimis non curat lex,*" said Sir Hildebrand. "No one pays barley-corn rent or farthing damages or the shilling consideration in a contract.   Your action implies malicious agreement with Lady Oates's opinion of me."

187

He bent his head forward and looked at Haversham with feverish intensity. Haversham had old scores to settle. The importance, omniscience, perfection, and condescending urbanity of Sir Hildebrand had rasped his nerves for a quarter of a century. If there was one living man whom he hated whole-heartedly, and over whose humiliation he rejoiced, it was Sir Hildebrand Oates. He yielded to the swift temptation. He rose hastily and gathered up his papers.

"If you can find me a human creature in this universe who doesn't share Lady Oates's opinion, I will give him every penny I am worth."

He went out, and then overcome with remorse for having kicked a fallen man, felt inclined to hang himself. But he knew that he had spoken truly. Meanwhile Sir Hildebrand walked up and down the little visitors' room at the club, where the interview had taken place, passing his hand over his indeterminate moustache and long blunt chin. He felt neither anger nor indignation—but rather the dazed dismay of a prisoner to whom the judge deals a severer sentence than he expected. After a while he sat at a small table and prepared to write a letter connected with the business matters he had just discussed with Haversham. But the words would not come, his brain was fogged; he went off into a reverie, and awoke to find himself scribbling in arabesque, "Fifteen shillings to buy a scourge."

After a solitary dinner at the club that evening he discovered in a remote corner of the smoking-room, a life-long acquaintance, an old schoolfellow, one Colonel Bagot, reading a newspaper. He approached.

"Good evening, Bagot."

Colonel Bagot raised his eyes from the paper, nodded,

188

and resumed his reading. Sir Hildebrand deliberately
wheeled a chair to his side and sat down.

"Can I have a word or two with you?"

"Certainly, my dear fellow," Bagot replied, putting
down his paper.

"What kind of a boy was I at school?"

"What kind of a . . . what the deuce do you
mean?" asked the astonished Colonel.

"I want you to tell me what kind of a boy I was,"
said Sir Hildebrand gravely.

"Just an ordinary chap."

"Would you have called me modest, generous, and
kind?"

"What in God's name are you driving at?" asked
the Colonel, twisting himself round on his chair.

"At your opinion of me. Was I modest, generous,
and kind? It's a vital question."

"It's a damned embarrassing one to put to a man
during the process of digestion. Well, you know,
Oates, you always were a queer beggar. If I had had
the summing up of you I should have said: 'Free
from vice.'"

"Negative."

"Well, yes—in a way—but——"

"You've answered me. Now another. Do you
think I treated my children badly?"

"Really, Oates—oh, confound it!" Angrily he
dusted himself free from the long ash that had fallen
from his cigar. "I don't see why I should be asked
such a question."

"I do. You've known me all your life. I want you
to answer it frankly."

Colonel Bagot was stout, red, and choleric. Sir
Hildebrand irritated him. If he was looking for trouble,

189

he should have it. " I think you treated them abomin-ably—there ! " said he.

" Thank you," said Sir Hildebrand.

" What ? " gasped Bagot.

" I said 'thank you.' And lastly—you have had many opportunities of judging—do you think I did all in my power to make my wife happy ? "

At first Bagot made a gesture of impatience. His position was both grotesque and intolerable. Was Oates going mad ? Answering the surmise, Sir Hilde-brand said :

" I'm aware my question is extraordinary, perhaps outrageous ; but I am quite sane. Did she look crushed, down-trodden, as though she were not allowed to have a will of her own ? "

It was impossible not to see that the man was in a dry agony of earnestness. Irritation and annoyance fell like garments from Bagot's shoulders.

" You really want to get at the exact truth, as far as I can give it you ? "

" From the depth of my soul," said Sir Hildebrand.

" Then," answered Bagot, quite simply, " I'm sorry to say unpleasant things. But I think Lady Oates led a dog's life—and so does everybody."

" That's just what I wanted to be sure of," said Sir Hildebrand, rising. He bent his head courteously. " Good night, Bagot," and he went away with dreary dignity.

VI

A cloud settled on Sir Hildebrand's mind through which he saw immediate things murkily. He passed days of unaccustomed loneliness and inaction. He walked the familiar streets of London like one in a dream. One afternoon he found himself gazing with unspeculative eye into the window of a small Roman Catholic Repository where crucifixes and statues of the Virgin and Child and rosaries and religious books and pictures were exposed for sale. Until realization of the objects at which he had been staring dawned upon his mind, he had not been aware of the nature of the shop. The shadow of a smile passed over his face. He entered. An old man with a long white beard was behind the counter.

"Do you keep scourges?" asked Sir Hildebrand.

"No, sir," replied the old man, somewhat astonished.

"That's unfortunate—very unfortunate," said Sir Hildebrand, regarding him dully. "I'm in need of one."

"Even among certain of the religious orders the Discipline is forbidden nowadays," replied the old man.

"Among certain others it is practised?"

"I believe so."

"Then scourges are procurable. I will ask you to get one—or have one made according to religious pattern. I will pay fifteen shillings for it."

"It could not possibly cost that—a mere matter of wood and string."

"I will pay neither more nor less," said Sir Hildebrand, laying on the counter the cheque which he had endorsed and his card. "I—I have made a vow. It's a matter of conscience. Kindly send it to the club address."

He walked out of the shop somewhat lighter of heart, his instinct for the scrupulous satisfied. The abominable cheque no longer burned through letter-case and raiment and body and corroded his soul. He had devoted the money to the purpose for which it was ear-marked. The precisian was soothed. In puzzling darkness he had also taken an enormous psychological stride.

The familiar club became unbearable, his fellow-members abhorrent. Friends and acquaintances outside—and they were legion—who, taking pity on his loneliness, sought him out and invited him to their houses, he shunned in a curious terror. He was for ever meeting them in the streets. Behind their masks of sympathy he read his wife's deadly accusation and its confirmation which he had received from Haversham and Bagot. When the scourge arrived—a business-like instrument in a cardboard box—he sat for a long time in his club bedroom drawing the knotted cords between his fingers, lost in retrospective thought. . . . And suddenly a scene flashed across his mind. Venice. The first days of their honeymoon. The sun-baked Renaissance façade of a church in a *campo* bounded by a canal where their gondola lay waiting. A tattered, one-legged, becrutched beggar holding out his hat by the church door. . . . He, Hildebrand, stalked majestically past, his wife following. Near the *fondamenta* he turned and discovered her in the act of tendering from her purse a two-lire piece to the beggar who had hobbled expectant in her wake. Hildebrand interposed a hand ; the shock accidentally jerked the coin from hers. It rolled. The one-legged beggar threw himself prone, in order to seize it. But it rolled into the canal. An agony of despair and supplication mounted from the tatterdemalion's eyes.

"Oh, Hildebrand, give him another."

"Certainly not," he replied. "It's immoral to encourage mendicity."

She wept in the gondola. He thought her silly, and

192

told her so. They landed at the Molo and he took her
to drink chocolate at Florian's on the Piazza. She
bent her meek head over the cup and the tears fell
into it. A well-dressed Venetian couple who sat at
the next table stared at her, passed remarks, and giggled
outright with the ordinary and exquisite Italian
politeness.

"My dear Eliza," said Hildebrand, "if you can't
help being a victim to sickly sentimentality, at least, as
my wife, you must learn to control yourself in public."

And meekly she controlled herself and drank her
salted chocolate. In compliance with a timidly expressed desire, and in order to show his forgiveness,
he escorted her into the open square, and like any
vulgar Cook's tourist bought her a paper cornet of
dried peas, wherewith, to his self-conscious martyrdom,
she fed the pigeons. Seeing an old man some way off
do the same, she scattered a few grains along the curled-
up brim of her Leghornh at; and presently, so still
she was and gracious, an iridescent swarm enveloped
her, eating from both hands outstretched and en-
circling her head like a halo. For the moment she was
the embodiment of innocent happiness. But Hildebrand thought her notoriously absurd, and when he
saw Lord and Lady Benham approaching them from
the Piazzetta, he stepped forward and with an abrupt
gesture sent the pigeons scurrying away. And she
looked for the vanished birds with much the same
scared piteousness as the one-legged beggar had looked
for the lost two-lire piece.

After thirty years the memory of that afternoon
flamed vivid, as he drew the strings of the idle scourge
between his fingers. And then the puzzling darkness
overspread his mind.

After a while he replaced the scourge in the cardboard box and summoned the club valet.

"Pack up all my things," said he. "I am going abroad to-morrow by the eleven o'clock train from Victoria."

VII

Few English-speaking and, stranger still, few German-speaking guests stay at the Albergo Tonelli in Venice. For one thing, it has not many rooms ; for another, it is far from the Grand Canal ; and for yet another, the fat proprietor Ettore Tonelli and his fatter wife are too sluggish of body and brain to worry about *forestieri* who have to be communicated with in outlandish tongues, and, for their supposed comfort, demand all sorts of exotic foolishness such as baths, punctuality, and information as to the whereabouts of fusty old pictures and the exact tariff of gondolas. The house was filled from year's end to year's end with Italian commercial travellers ; and Ettore's ways and their ways corresponded to a nicety. The Albergo Tonelli was a little red-brick fifteenth-century palazzo, its Lombardic crocketed windows gaily picked out in white, and it dominated the *campiello* wherein it was situated. In the centre of the tiny square was a marble well-head richly carved, and by its side a pump from which the inhabitants of the vague tumble-down circumambient dwellings drew the water to wash the underlinen which hung to dry from the windows. A great segment of the corner diagonally opposite the Albergo was occupied by the bare and rudely swelling brick apse of a seventeenth-century church. Two inconsiderable thoroughfares, *calle* five foot wide, lead from the *campiello* to the wide world of Venice.

It was hither that Sir Hildebrand Oates, after a week of nerve-shattering tumult at one of the great Grand Canal hotels, and after horrified examination of the question of balance of expenditure over income, found his way through the kind offices of a gondolier to whom he had promised twenty francs if he could conduct him to the forgotten church, the memorable scene of the adventure of the beggar and the two-franc piece. With unerring instinct the gondolier had rowed him to Santa Maria Formosa, the very spot. Sir Hildebrand troubled himself neither with the church nor the heart-easing wonder of Palma Vecchio's Santa Barbara within, but, with bent brow, traced the course of the lame beggar from the step to the *fondamenta*, and the course of the rolling coin from his Eliza's hand into the canal. Then he paused for a few moments deep in thought, and finally drew a two-lire piece from his pocket, and, recrossing the Campo, handed it gravely to a beggar-woman, the successor of the lame man, who sat sunning herself on the spacious marble seat by the side of the great door. When he returned to the hotel he gave the gondolier his colossal reward and made a friend for life. Giuseppe, delighted at finding an English gentleman who could converse readily in Italian—for Sir Hildebrand, a man of considerable culture, possessed a working knowledge of three or four European languages—expressed his gratitude on subsequent excursions, by overflowing with picturesque anecdote, both historical and personal. A pathetic craving for intercourse with his kind and the solace of obtaining it from one remote from his social environment drew Sir Hildebrand into queer sympathy with a genuine human being. Giuseppe treated him with a respectful familiarity which he had never before encountered in a member of the lower classes. One afternoon, on the silent *lagune* side of the Giudecca, turning round on his cushions, he confided to the lean, bronzed, rhythmically working figure standing behind him, something of the puzzledom of his soul. Giuseppe, in the practical Italian way, interpreted the confidences as a desire to escape from the tourist-agitated and fantastically expensive quarters of the city into some unruffled haven. That evening he interviewed the second cousin of his wife, the Signora Tonelli of the Albergo of that name, and the next day Sir Hildebrand took possession of the front room overlooking the *campiello*, on the *piano nobile* or second floor of the hotel.

And here Sir Hildebrand Oates, Knight, once Member of Parliament, Lord of the Manor, Chairman of Quarter Sessions, Director of great companies, orchid rival of His Grace the Duke of Dunster, important and impeccable personage, the exact temperature of whose bath water had been to a trembling household a matter of as much vital concern as the salvation of their own souls—entered upon a life of queer discomfort, privation and humility. For the first time in his life he experienced the hugger-mugger makeshift of the bed-sitting-room—a chamber, too, cold and comfortless, with one scraggy rug by the bedside to mitigate the rigour of an inlaid floor looking like a galantine of veal, once the pride of the palazzo, and meagrely furnished with the barest objects of necessity, and these of monstrous and incongruous ugliness ; and he learned in the redolent restaurant downstairs the way to eat spaghetti like a contented beast and the relish of sour wine and the overrated importance of the cleanliness of cutlery. In his dignified acceptance of surroundings

that to him were squalid, he manifested his essential
breeding. The correct courtesy of his demeanour
gained for the *illustrissimo signore inglese* the whole-
hearted respect of the Signore and Signora Tonelli.
And the famous scourge nailed (symbolically) over his
hard little bed procured him a terrible reputation for
piety in the *parrocchia*. After a while, indeed, as soon
as he had settled to his new mode of living, the inveter-
ate habit of punctilio caused him, almost unconsciously,
to fix by the clock his day's routine. Called at eight
o'clock, a kind of eight conjectured by the good-
humoured, tousled sloven of a chambermaid, he
dressed with scrupulous care. At nine he descended
for his morning coffee to the chill deserted restaurant—
for all the revolution in his existence he could not
commit the immorality of breakfasting in his bedroom. At half-past he regained his room, where, till
eleven, he wrote by the window overlooking the urchin-
resonant *campiello*. Then with gloves and cane, to
outward appearance the immaculate, the impeccable
Sir Hildebrand Oates of Eresby Manor, he walked
through the narrow, twisting streets and over bridges
and across *campi* and *campiello* to the Piazza San
Marco. As soon as he neared the east-end of the great
square, a seller of corn and peas approached him,
handed him a paper cornet, from which Sir Hildebrand,
with awful gravity, fed the pigeons. And the pigeons
looked for him, too ; and they perched on his arms
and his shoulders and even on the crown of his Hom-
burg hat, the brim of which he had, by way of solemn
rite, filled with grain, until the gaunt, grey, unsmiling
man was hidden in fluttering iridescence. And tourists
and idlers used to come every day and look at him, as
at one of the sights of Venice. The supply finished,

Sir Hildebrand went to the Café Florian on the south of the Piazza and ordering a *sirop* which he seldom drank, read the *Corriere de la Sera*, until the midday gun sent the pigeons whirring to their favourite cornices. Then Sir Hildebrand retraced his steps to the Albergo Tonelli, lunched, read till three, wrote till five, and again went out to take the air. Dinner, half an hour's courtly gossip in the cramped and smelly apology for a lounge, with landlord or a commercial traveller disinclined for theatre or music-hall, or the absorbing amusement of Venice, walking in the Piazza or along the Riva Schiavoni, and then to read or write till bedtime.

No Englishman of any social position can stand daily in the Piazza San Marco without now and then coming across acquaintances, least of all a man of such importance in his day as Sir Hildebrand Oates. He accepted the greetings of chance-met friends with courteous resignation.

"We're at the Hôtel de l'Europe. Where are you staying, Sir Hildebrand?"

"I live in Venice, I have made it my home. You see the birds accept me as one of themselves."

"You'll come and dine with us, won't you?"

"I should love to," Sir Hildebrand would reply; "but for the next month or so I am overwhelmed with work. I'm so sorry. If you have any time to spare, and would like to get off the beaten track, let me recommend you to wander through the Giudecca on foot. I hope Lady Elizabeth is well. I'm so glad. Will you give her my kindest regards? Good-bye." And Sir Hildebrand would make his irreproachable bow and take his leave. No one learned where he had made his home in Venice. In fact, no one but Messrs.

Thomas Cook and Son knew his address. He banked with them and they forwarded his letters to the Albergo Tonelli.

It has been said that Sir Hildebrand occupied much of his time in writing, and he himself declared that he was overwhelmed with work. He was indeed engaged in an absorbing task of literary composition, and his reference library consisted in thirty or forty leather-covered volumes each fitted with a clasp and lock, of which the key hung at the end of his watch-chain; and every page of every volume was filled with his own small, precise handwriting. He made slow progress, for the work demanded concentrated thought and close reasoning. The rumour of his occupation having spread through the *parrocchia*, he acquired, in addition to that of a pietist, the reputation of an *erudito*. He became the pride of the *campiello*. When he crossed the little square, the inhabitants pointed him out to less fortunate out-dwellers. There was the great English noble who had made vows of poverty, and gave himself the Discipline and wrote wonderful works of Theology. And men touched their hats and women saluted shyly, and Sir Hildebrand punctiliously, and with a queer pathetic gratitude, responded. Even the children gave him a " Buon giorno, Signore," and smiled up into his face, unconscious of the pious scholar he was supposed to be, and of the almighty potentate that he had been. Once, yielding to an obscure though powerful instinct, he purchased in the Merceria a packet of chocolates, and on entering his *campiello* presented them, with stupendous gravity concealing extreme embarrassment, to a little gang of urchins. Encouraged by a dazzling success, he made it a rule to distribute sweetmeats every Saturday morning to

the children of the *campiello*. After a while he learned
their names and idiosyncrasies, and held solemn though
kindly speech with them, manifesting an interest in
their games and questioning them sympathetically as
to their scholastic attainments. Sometimes gathering
from their talk a notion of the desperate poverty of
parents, he put a lire or two into grubby little fists,
in spite of a lifelong conviction of the immorality of
indiscriminate almsgiving ; and dark, haggard mothers
blessed him, and stood in his way to catch his smile.
All of which was pleasant, though exceedingly puzzling
to Sir Hildebrand Oates.

VIII

Between two and three years after their mother's
death, Sir Hildebrand's son and daughter, who bore
each other a devoted affection and carried on a con-
stant correspondence, arranged to meet in England,
Godfrey travelling from Canada, Sybil, with her children, from India. The first thing they learned (from
Haversham, the lawyer) was the extent of their father's
financial ruin. They knew—many kind friends had
told them—that he had had losses and had retired
from public life ; but, living out of the world, and
accepting their childhood's tradition of his incalcul-
able wealth, they had taken it for granted that he continued to lead a life of elegant luxury. When Haversham, one of the few people who really knew, informed
them (with a revengeful smile) that their father could
not possibly have more than a hundred or two a
year, they were shocked to the depths of their clean,
matter-of-fact English souls. The Great Panjan-
drum, arbiter of destinies, had been brought low, was
living in obscurity in Italy. The pity of it ! As they

interchanged glances the same thought leaped into the eyes of each.

"We must look him up and see what can be done," said Godfrey.

"Of course, dear," said Sybil.

"I offered him the use of Eresby, but he was too proud to take it."

"And I never offered him anything at all," said Sybil.

"I should advise you," said Haversham, "to leave Sir Hildebrand alone."

Godfrey, a high-mettled young man and one who was accustomed to arrive at his own decisions, and moreover did not like Haversham, gripped his sister by the arm.

"Whatever advice you give me, Mr. Haversham, I will take just when I think it necessary."

"That is the attitude of most of my clients," replied Haversham dryly, "whether it is a sound attitude or not——" He waved an expressive hand.

"We'll go and hunt him up, anyway," said Godfrey. "If he's impossible, we can come back. If he isn't—so much the better. What do you say, Sybil?"

Sybil said what he knew she would say.

"Sir Hildebrand's address is vague," remarked Haversham. "Cook's, Venice."

"What more, in Hades, do we want?" cried the young man.

So, after Sybil had made arrangements for the safe keeping of her offspring, and Godfrey and herself had written to announce their coming, the pair set out for Venice.

"We are very sorry, but we are unable to give you

Sir Hildebrand Oates's address," said Messrs. Thomas Cook and Son.

Godfrey protested. "We are his son and daughter," he said, in effect. "We have reason to believe our father is living in poverty. We have written and he has not replied. We must find him."

Identity established, Messrs. Thomas Cook and Son disclosed the whereabouts of their customer. A gondola took brother and sister to the *campo* facing the west front of the church behind which lay the *campiello* where the hotel was situated. Their hearts sank low as they beheld the mildewed decay of the Albergo Tonelli, lower as they entered the cool, canal-smelling *trattoria*—or restaurant, the main entrance to the Albergo. Signore Tonelli in shirt-sleeves greeted them. What was their pleasure?

"Sir Hildebrand Oates?"

At first from his rapid and incomprehensible Italian they could gather little else than the fact of their father's absence from home. After a while the reiteration of the words *ospedale inglese* made an impression on their minds.

"*Malade?*" asked Sybil, trying the only foreign language with which she had a slight acquaintance.

"*Si, si!*" cried Tonelli, delighted at eventual understanding.

And then a Providence-sent bagman who spoke a little English came out and interpreted.

The *illustrissimo signore* was ill. A pneumonia. He had stood to feed the pigeons in the rain, in the north-east wind, and had contracted a chill. When they thought he was dying, they sent for the English doctor who had attended him before for trifling ailments, and unconscious he had been transported to the

English hospital in the Giudecca. And there he was
now. A thousand pities he should die. The dearest
and most revered man. The whole neighbourhood
who loved him was stricken with grief.. They prayed
for him in the church, the signore and signora could see
it there, and vows of candles had been made to the Virgin, the Blessed Mother, for he too loved all children.
Signore Tonelli, joined by this time by his wife,
exaggerated perhaps in the imaginative Italian way..
But every tone and gesture sprang from deep sincerity..
Brother and sister looked at each other in dumb wonder..

"*Ecco, Elizabetta!*" Tonelli, commanding the doorway of the restaurant, summoned an elderly woman
from the pump by the well-head and discoursed volubly..
She approached the young English couple and also
volubly discoursed. The interpreter interpreted.
They gained confirmation of the amazing fact that
in this squalid, stone-flagged, rickety little square, Sir
Hildebrand had managed to make himself beloved.
Childhood's memories rose within them, half-caught,
but haunting sayings of servants and villagers which
had impressed upon their minds the detestation in
which he was held in their Somersetshire home.

Godfrey turned to his sister. "Well, I'm damned,"
said he.

"I should like to see his rooms," said Sybil.

The interpreter again interpreted. The Tonellis
threw out their arms. Of course they could visit the
apartment of the *illustrissimo signore*. They were led
upstairs and ushered into the chill, dark bed-sitting-
room, as ascetic as a monk's cell, and both gasped
when they beheld the flagellum hanging from its nail
over the bed. They requested privacy. The Tonellis
and the bagman-interpreter retired.

" What the devil's the meaning of it ? " said Godfrey.

Sybil, kind-hearted, began to cry. Something
strange and piteous, something elusive had happened.
The awful, poverty-stricken room chilled her blood,
and the sight of the venomous scourge froze it. She
caught and held Godfrey's hand. Had their father
gone over to Rome and turned ascetic ? They looked
bewildered around the room. But no other sign,
crucifix, rosary, sacred picture, betokened the pious
convert. They scanned the rough deal bookshelf. A
few dull volumes of English classics, a few works on
sociology in French and Italian, a flagrantly staring
red *Burke's Landed Gentry*, and that was practically
all the library. Not one book of devotion was visible,
save the Bible, the Book of Common Prayer, and a
little vellum-covered Elzevir edition of Saint Augustine's *Flammulæ Amoris*, which Godfrey remembered
from childhood on account of its quaint wood-cuts.
They could see nothing indicative of religious life but
the flagellum over the bed—and that seemed curiously
new and unused. Again they looked around the bare,
characterless room, characteristic only of its occupant
by its scrupulous tidiness ; yet one object at last
attracted their attention. On a deal writing-table by
the window lay a thick pile of manuscript. Godfrey
turned the brown paper covering. Standing together, brother and sister read the astounding title-
page :

" An inquiry into my wife's justification for the
following terms of her will :

" ' I will and bequeath to my husband, Sir Hildebrand Oates, Knight, the sum of fifteen shillings to
buy himself a scourge to do penance for the arrogance,

uncharitableness and cruelty with which he has treated myself and my beloved children for the last thirty years.'

"This dispassionate inquiry I dedicate to my son Godfrey and my daughter Sybil."

Brother and sister regarded each other with drawn faces and mutually questioning eyes.

"We can't leave this lying about," said Godfrey. And he tucked the manuscript under his arm.

The gondola took them through the narrow waterways to the Grand Canal of the Giudecca, where, on the Zattere side, all the wave-worn merchant shipping of Venice and Trieste and Fiume and Genoa finds momentary rest, and across to the low bridge-archway of the canal cutting through the island, on the side of which is Lady Layard's modest English hospital. Yes, said the matron, Sir Hildebrand was there. Pneumonia. Getting on as well as could be expected ; but impossible to see him. She would telephone to their hotel in the morning.

That night, until dawn, Godfrey read the manuscript, a document of soul-gripping interest. It was neither an *apologia pro vita sua*, nor a breast-beating *peccavi* cry of confession ; but a minute analysis of every remembered incident in the relations between his family and himself from the first pragmatical days of his wedding journey. And judicially he delivered judgments in the terse, lucid French form. "Whereas I, etc., etc. . . ." and "whereas my wife, etc., etc. . . ."—setting forth and balancing the facts— "it is my opinion that I acted arrogantly," or "uncharitably," or "cruelly." Now and again, though rarely, the judgments went in his favour. But invariably the words were added : "I am willing, however, in this case, to submit to the decision of any arbitrator or court of appeal my children may think it worth while to appoint."

The last words, scrawled shakily in pencil, were:

"I have not, to my great regret, been able to bring this record up to date; but as I am very ill and, at my age, may not recover, I feel it my duty to say that, as far as my two years' painful examination into my past life warrants my judgment, I am of the opinion that my wife had ample justification for the terms she employed regarding me in her will. Furthermore, if, as is probable, I should die of my illness, I should like my children to know that long ere this I have deeply desired in my loneliness to stretch out my arms to them in affection and beg their forgiveness, but that I have been prevented from so doing by the appalling fear that, I being now very poor and they being very rich, my overtures, considering the lack of affection I have exhibited to them in the past, might be misinterpreted. The British Consul here, who has kindly consented to be my executor, will . . ."

And then strength had evidently failed him and he could write no more.

The next morning Godfrey related to his sister what he had read and gave her the manuscript to read at her convenience; and together they went to the hospital and obtained from the doctor his somewhat pessimistic report; and then again they visited the Albergo Tonelli and learned more of the strange, stiff and benevolent life of Sir Hildebrand Oates. Once more they mounted to the cold cheerless room where their father had spent the past two years. Godfrey unhooked the scourge from the nail.

"What are you going to do?" Sybil asked, her eyes full of tears.

"I'm going to burn the damned thing. Whether he lives or dies, the poor old chap's penance is at an end. By God! he has done enough." He turned upon her swiftly. "You don't feel any resentment against him now, do you?"

"Resentment?" Her voice broke on the word and she cast herself on the hard little bed and sobbed.

IX

And so it came to pass that a new Sir Hildebrand Oates, with a humble and a contrite heart, which we are told the Lord doth not despise, came into residence once more at Eresby Manor, agent for his son and guardian of his daughter's children. Godfrey transferred his legal business from Haversham to a younger practitioner in the neighbourhood to whom Sir Hildebrand showed a stately deference. And every day, being a man of habit—instinctive habit which no revolution of the soul can alter—he visited his wife's grave in the little churchyard, a stone's-throw from the manor-house, and in his fancy a cloud of pigeons came iridescent, darkening the air. . . .

The county called, but he held himself aloof. He was no longer the all-important unassailable man. He had come through many fires to a wisdom undreamed of by the county. Human love had touched him with its simple angel wing—the love of son and daughter, the love of the rude souls in the squalid Venetian *campiello*; and the patter of children's feet, the soft and trusting touch of children's hands, the glad welcome of children's voices, had brought him back to the elemental wells of happiness.

One afternoon, the butler, entering the dining-room with the announcement "His Grace, the Duke of——" gasped, unable to finish the title. For there was Sir Hildebrand Oates—younger at fifty-nine than he was at thirty—lying prone on the hearthrug, with a pair of flushed infants astride on the softer portions of his back, using the once almighty man as a being of little account. Sir Hildebrand turned his long chin and long nose up towards his visitor, and there was a new smile in his eyes.

"Sorry, Duke," said he, "but you see, I can't get up."

I

"DICK," said Viviette, "ought to go about in skins like a primitive man."

Katherine Holroyd looked up from her needlework. She was a gentle, fair-haired woman of thirty, with demure blue eyes which regarded the girl with a mingling of pity, protection, and amusement.

"My dear," she said, "whenever I see a pretty girl fooling about with a primitive man I always think of a sweet little monkey I once knew, who used to have great sport with a lyddite shell. Her master kept it on his table as a paper-weight, and no one knew it was loaded. One day she hit the shell in the wrong place— and they're still looking for the monkey. Don't think Dick is the empty shell."

Whereupon she resumed her work, and for a few moments the click of thimble and needle alone broke the summer stillness. Viviette lay idly on a long garden chair admiring the fit of a pair of dainty tan shoes, which she twiddled with graceful twists of the ankles some five feet from her nose. At Mrs. Holroyd's remark she laughed after the manner of one quite contented with herself—a low, musical laugh, in harmony with the blue June sky and the flowering chestnuts and the song of the thrushes.

"My intentions with regard to Dick are strictly honourable," she remarked. "We've been engaged for the last eleven years, and I still have his engagement ring. It cost three-and-sixpence."

"I only want to warn you, dear," said Mrs. Holroyd. "Anyone can see that Dick is in love with you, and if you don't take care you'll have Austin falling in love with you too."

Viviette laughed again. "But he has already fallen! I don't think he knows it yet ; but he has. It's great fun being a woman, isn't it, dear ? "

"I don't know that I've ever found it so," Katherine replied with a sigh. She was a widow, and had loved her husband, and her sky was still tinged with grey.

Viviette, quick to catch the sadness in the voice, made no reply, but renewed the contemplation of her shoe-tips.

"I'm afraid you're an arrant little coquette," said Katherine indulgently.

"Lord Banstead says I'm a little devil," she laughed.

If she was in some measure a coquette she may be forgiven. What woman can have suddenly revealed to her the thrilling sense of her sex's mastery over men without snatching now and then the fearful joy of using her power ? She was one-and-twenty, her heart still unawakened, and she had returned to her childhood's home to find men who had danced her on their knees bending low before her, and proclaiming themselves her humble vassals. It was intoxicating. She had always looked up to Austin with awe, as one too remote and holy for girlish irreverence. And now ! No wonder her sex laughed within her.

Until she had gone abroad to finish her education, she had lived in the old, grey manor-house that dreamed in the sunshine of the terrace below which she was sitting, ever since they had brought her thither, an orphaned child of three. Mrs. Ware, her guardian,

was her adopted mother ; the sons, Dick and Austin
Ware, her brothers—the engagement, when she was
ten and Dick one-and-twenty, had hardly fluttered the
fraternal relationship. She had left them a merry,
kittenish child. She had returned a woman, slender,
full-bosomed, graceful, alluring, with a maturity of
fascination beyond her years. Enemies said she had
gipsy blood in her veins. If so, the infusion must have
taken place long, long ago, for her folks were as proud
of their name as the Wares of Ware House. But, for
all that, there was a suggestion of the exotic in the
olive and cream complexion, and the oval face pointing
at the dimpled chin ; something of the woodland in
her lithe figure and free gestures ; from her swimming,
dark eyes one could imagine something fierce and
untamable lying beneath her laughing idleness. Katherine Holroyd called her a coquette, Austin whatever
the whim of a cultured fancy suggested, and Lord Banstead a little devil. As for Dick, he called her nothing.
His love was too great ; his vocabulary too small.

Lord Banstead was a neighbour who, in the course
of three months, had proposed several times to Viviette.

" I'm not very much to look at," he remarked on
the first of these occasions—he was a weedy, pallid
youth of six-and-twenty—"and the title's not very
old, I must admit. Governor only a scientific Johnnie, Margetson, the celebrated chemist, you know, who
discovered some beastly gas or other and got made a
peer—but I can sit with the other old rotters in the
House of Lords, you know, if I want. And I've got
enough to run the show, if you'll keep me from chuck-
ing it away as I'm doing. It'd be a godsend if you'd
marry me, I give you my word."

" Before I have anything to do with you," replied

Viviette, who had heard Dick express his opinion of Lord Banstead in forcible terms, "you'll have to forswear sack, and—and a very big AND———"

Lord Banstead, not being learned in literary allusions, looked bewildered. Viviette laughed.

"I'll translate if you like. You'll have to give up unlimited champagne and whisky and lead an ostensibly respectable life."

Whereupon Lord Banstead called her a little devil and went off in dudgeon to London and took fluffy-haired little ladies out to supper. When he returned to the country he again offered her his title, and being rejected a second time, again called her a little devil, and went back to the fashionable supper-room. A third and a fourth time he executed this complicated manœuvre ; and now news had reached Viviette that he was in residence at Farfield, where he was boring himself exceedingly in his father's scientific library.

"I suppose he'll be coming over to-day," said Viviette.

"Why do you encourage him ?" asked Katherine.

"I don't," Viviette retorted. "I snub him unmercifully. If I am a coquette it's with real men, not with the by-product of a chemical experiment."

Katherine dropped her work and her underlip, and turned reproachful blue eyes on the girl.

"Viviette !"

"Oh, she's shocked ! Saint Nitouche is shocked !" Then, with a change of manner, she rose and, bending over Katherine's chair, kissed her. "I'm sorry, dear," she said, in pretty penitence. "I know it was an abominable and unladylike thing to say, but my tongue sometimes runs away with my thoughts. Forgive me."

At that moment a man dressed in rough tweeds and

leggings, who had emerged from the stable side of the manor-house, crossed the terrace, and, descending the steps, walked over the lawn towards the two ladies. He had massive shoulders and a thick, strong neck, coarse reddish hair, and a moustache of a lighter shade. Blue eyes looked with a curious childish pathos out of a face tanned by sun and weather. He slouched slightly in his gait, like the heavy man accustomed to the saddle. This was Dick Ware, the elder of the brothers and heir to fallen fortunes, mortgaged house and lands, and he gave the impression of failure, of a man who, in spite of thews and sinews, had been unable to grapple with circumstance.

Viviette left Katherine to her needlework, and advanced to meet him. At her spontaneous act of welcome a light came into his eyes. He removed from his lips the short corn-cob pipe he was smoking.

" I've just been looking at the new mare. She's a beauty. I know I oughtn't to have got her, but she was going dirt-cheap—and what can a man do when he's offered a horse at a quarter its value ? "

" Nothing, my dear Dick, save pay four times as much as he can afford."

" But we had to get a new beast," he argued seriously. " We can't go about the country in a donkey-cart. If I hadn't bought one, Austin would, for the sake of the family dignity—and I do like to feel independent of Austin now and then."

" I wish you were entirely independent of Austin," said Viviette, walking with him up the lawn.

" I can't, so long as I stay here doing nothing. But if I went out to Canada or New Zealand, as I want to do, who would look after my mother ? I'm tied by the leg."

"I'd look after mother," said Viviette. "And you'd write me nice long letters, saying how you were getting on, and I would send you nice little bulletins, and we should all be very happy."

"Do you want to get rid of me, Viviette?"

"I want you to have your heart's desire."

"You know what my heart's desire is," he said unsteadily.

"Why, to raise sheep or drive cattle, or chop down trees in the backwoods," she replied, lifting demure eyebrows. "Oh, Dick, don't be foolish. See— there's mother just come out."

With a light laugh she escaped and ran up the steps to meet an old lady, rather infirm, who, with the aid of a stick, was beginning to take her morning walk up and down the terrace. Dick followed her moodily.

"Good morning, mother," said he, bending down to kiss her.

Mrs. Ware put up her cheek, and received the salute with no great show of pleasure.

"Oh, how you smell of tobacco smoke, Dick. Where's Austin? Please go and find him. I want to hear what he has to say about the stables."

"What can he say, mother?"

"He can advise us and help us to put the muddle right," said Mrs. Ware.

These stables had been a subject of controversy for some time. The old ones having fallen into disgraceful disrepair, Dick had turned architect and erected new ones himself. As shelters for beasts, they were comparatively sound; as appanages to an Elizabethan manor-house, they were open to adverse criticism. Austin, who had come down from London a day or two before to spend his Whitsuntide holiday at home,

had promised his mother to make inspection and
report.

"But what does Austin know about stables?"
Viviette asked, as soon as Dick had slouched away in
search of his brother.

"Austin knows about everything, my dear," replied
the old lady decisively. "Not only is Austin a bril-
liantly clever man, but he's a successful barrister, and
a barrister's business is to know all about everything.
Give me your arm, dear, and let us walk up and down
a little till they come."

Presently Dick returned with Austin, whom he had
found smoking a cigar in a very meditative manner
in front of the stables. Dick's face was gloomy, but
Austin's was bright, as he came briskly up and, cigar
in hand, stooped to his mother. She put her arms
round his neck, kissed him affectionately, and inquired
after his sleep and his comfort and the quality of his
breakfast.

"Doesn't Austin smell of tobacco smoke, mother?"
asked Dick.

"Austin," replied Mrs. Ware, "has a way of smoking and not smelling of it."

Austin laughed gaily. "I believe if I fell into a
pond you'd say I had a way of coming up dry."

Dick turned to Viviette, and muttered with some
bitterness : "And if I fell into a dry ditch she'd say I
came up slimy."

Viviette, touched by pity, raised a bewitching face.
"Dry or slimy, you would be just the same dear old
Dick," she whispered.

"And what about the stables?" asked Mrs. Ware.

"Oh, they're not bad. They're rather creditable ;
but," Austin added, turning with a laugh to his brother,

"the mother will fidget, you know, and the somewhat —let us say rococo style of architecture has got on her nerves. I think the whole thing had better come down, don't you?"

"If you like," said Dick gruffly. He had given way to Austin all his life. What was the use of opposing him now?

"Good. I'll send young Rapson, the architect, along to make a design. Don't you worry, old chap, I'll see it through."

Young, brisk, debonair, flushed with success and the sense of the mastery of life, he did not notice the lowering of Dick's brows, which deepened into almost a scowl when he turned frankly admiring eyes on Viviette, and drew her into gay, laughing talk, nor did he catch the hopelessness in the drag of Dick's feet as he went off to gaze sorrowfully at the fallen pride of his heart, the condemned stables.

But Viviette, who knew, as Austin did not, of Dick's disappointment, soon broke away and joined him in front of the amorphous shed of timber. She took him by the arm.

"Come for a stroll in the orchard."

He suffered himself to be led through the stable-yard gate. She talked to him of apple blossoms. He listened for some time in silence. Then he broke out.

"It's an infernal shame," said he.

"It is," said Viviette. "But you needn't put on such a glum face when I'm here especially to comfort you. If you're not glad to see me I'll go back to Austin. He's much more amusing than you."

"I suppose he is. Yes, go back to him. I'm a fool. I'm nobody. No, don't, Viviette; forgive me," he cried, catching her as she turned away somewhat haughtily. " I didn't mean it, but things are getting beyond my endurance."

Viviette seated herself on a bench beneath the apple blossoms.

" What things ? "

" Everything. My position. Austin's airy ways."

" But that's what makes him so charming."

" Yes, confound him. My ways are about as airy as a hippopotamus's. Look here, Viviette. I'm fond of Austin, God knows—but all my life he has been put in front of me. He has had all the chances ; I've had none. With my father when he was alive, with my mother, it has always been Austin this and Austin that. He was the head of the school when I, the elder, was a lout in the lower fourth. He had a brilliant University career and went into the world and is making a fortune. I'm only able to ride and shoot and do country things. I've stuck here with only this mortgaged house belonging to me and the hundred or so a year I get out of the tenants. I'm not even executor under my father's will. It's Austin. Austin pays mother the money under her marriage settlement. If things go wrong Austin is sent for to put them right. It never seems to occur to him that it's my house. Oh of course I know he pays the interest on the mortgage and makes my mother an allowance—that's the humiliation of it."

He sat with his elbows on his knees and his head in his hands, staring at the grass.

" But surely you could find some work to do, Dick ? "

He shrugged his great shoulders. " They stuck me once in an office in London. I suffocated and added up things wrong and told the wrong lies to the wrong people, and ended up by breaking the junior partner's head !"

"You had some satisfaction out of it, at any rate," laughed Viviette.

A faint reminiscent smile crossed his face. "I suppose I had. But it didn't qualify me for a successful business career. No. I might do something in a new country. I must get away from this. I can't stand it. But yet— as I've told you all along, I'm tied—hand and foot."

"And so you're very miserable, Dick."

"How can I help it ?"

Viviette edged a little away from him, and said, rather resentfully :

"I don't call that polite, seeing that I have come back to live with you."

He turned on her with some fierceness. "Don't you see that your being here makes my life all the more impossible ? How can I be with you day after day without wanting you ? I've never given a thought to another woman in my life. I want to hold you so tight in my arms that not the ghost of another man can ever come between us. You know it."

Viviette shredded an apple blossom that had fallen into her lap. The fingers that held the petal tingled, and a flush rose in her cheek.

"I do know it," she said in a low voice. "You're always telling me. But, Dick "—she flashed a mischievous glance at him—" while you're holding me— although it would be very nice—we should starve."

"Then let us starve," he cried vehemently.

"Oh, no. Oh, most decidedly no. Starvation would be so unbecoming. I should get to be a fright —a bundle of bones and a rundle of skin—and you'd be horrified—I couldn't bear it."

" If you would only say you cared a scrap for me it would be easier," he pleaded.

" I should have thought it would be harder."

" Anyhow, say it—say it this once—just this once."

She bent her head to hide a smile, and said in a voice adorably soft :

" Dick, shut your eyes."

" Viviette ! " he cried, with sudden hope.

" No. Shut your eyes. Turn round. Now tell me," she continued, when he had turned obediently, "just what I've got on. No ! "—she held him by the shoulders,—" you're not to move."

Now, she was wearing a white blouse and a blue skirt and tan shoes, and a yellow rose was pinned at her bosom.

" What dress am I wearing ? "

" A light-coloured thing," said Dick.

" And what's it trimmed with ? "

" Lace," said the unfortunate man. Lace, indeed !

" And what coloured boots ? "

" Black," said Dick, at a venture.

" And what flower ? "

" I don't know—a pink rose, I think."

She started up. " Look," she cried gaily. " Oh, Dick ! I'll never marry you till you have the common decency to look at me—never ! never ! never ! I dressed myself this beautiful morning just to please you. Oh, Dick ! Dick, you've lost such a chance."

She stood with her hands behind her back regarding him mockingly, as Eve in the first orchard must have regarded Adam when he was more dull and masculine than usual—when, for instance, she had attired herself in hibiscus flowers which he took for the humdrum, everyday fig-leaves.

"I'm a born duffer," said Dick pathetically. "But your face is all that I see when I look at you."

"That's very pretty," she retorted. "But you ought to see more. Now let us talk sense. Mind, if I sit on that bench again you're to talk sense."

Dick sighed. "Very well," said he.

That was the history of all his love-making. She drew him on to passionate utterance, and then, with a twist of her wit and a twirl of her skirts, she eluded him. When she had thus put herself out of his reach, he felt ashamed. What right had he, dull, useless, lumbering, squiredomless squire, to ask a woman like Viviette to marry him? How could he support a wife? As it was, he lived a pensioner on Austin's bounty. Could he ask Austin to feed his wife and family as well? This thought, which always came to him as soon as his passion was checked, filled him with deep humiliation. Viviette had reason on her side when she said, "Let us talk sense."

He glowered at his fate, and tugged his tawny moustache for some time in silence. Then Viviette began to talk to him prettily of things that made up his country interests, his dogs, the garden, the personalities of the country-side. Soon she had him laughing, which pleased and flattered her, as it proved her power over the primitive man. Indeed, at such moments, she felt very tenderly towards him, and would have liked to pat his cheeks and crown him with flowers, thus manifesting her favour by dainty caresses. But she refrained, knowing that primitive men are too dense to interpret such demonstrations rightly, and limited herself to less compromising words.

"I am going to tell you a secret," he said at last, in

a shamefaced way. " You mustn't laugh at me—
promise me you won't."

" I promise," said Viviette solemnly.

" I am thinking of going in for local politics—Rural
District Council, you know."

Viviette nodded her head approvingly. " A village
Hampden—in Tory clothing ? "

" They're running things on party lines down here.
The influence of Westhampton is Radical, and fills the
Council with a lot of outsiders. So they've got together
a Conservative Committee, and are going to run a good
strong man for a vacancy. I've given them to understand that I'll be a candidate if they'll have me. I'd
like to be one. It's a rubbishy thing, dear, but somehow it would give me a little interest in life."

" I don't think it a rubbishy thing at all," said
Viviette. " A country gentleman ought to have a
hand in rural administration. I do hope you'll get in.
When will you know that the committee have selected
you ? "

" There's a meeting this evening. I ought to know
to-night or to-morrow morning."

" Are you very keen on it ? "

" Very," said Dick. And he added proudly, " It
was my own idea."

" But you're not as keen on that as on going abroad ? "

" Ah, that ! " said Dick. " That, bar one, is the
dearest wish of my heart. And who knows ? it might
enable me to carry out the other."

The sound of a gong within the house floated through
the still June air. Viviette rose.

" I must tidy myself for lunch."

They walked to the house together. On parting
she put out both her hands.

"Do be reasonable, Dick, and don't look for slights in what you call Austin's airy ways. He is awfully fond of you, and would not hurt you for the world."

At the luncheon table, however, Austin did hurt him, in utter unconsciousness, by his gay command of the situation, his eager talk with Viviette of things Dick did not understand, places he had not visited, books he had never read, pictures he had never seen. It was heartache rather than envy. He did not grudge Austin his scholarship and brilliance. But his soul sank at the sight of Austin and Viviette moving as familiars in a joyous world as remote from him as Neptune. Mrs. Ware kept Katherine Holroyd engaged in mild talk of cooks and curates, while the other two maintained their baffling conversation, half banter, half serious, on a bewildering number of topics, and poor Dick remained as dumb as the fish and cutlets he was eating. He sat at the head of the table, Mrs. Ware at the foot. On his right hand sat Katherine Holroyd, on his left Viviette, and between her and his mother was Austin. With Viviette talking to Austin and Mrs. Ware to Katherine, he felt lonely and disregarded in a kind of polar waste of snowy tablecloth. Once Katherine, escaping from Mrs. Ware's platitudinous ripple, took pity on him, and asked him when he was going to redeem his promise and show her his collection of armour and weapons. Dick brightened. This was the only keen interest he had in life outside things of earth and air and stream. He had inherited a good family collection, and had added to it occasionally, as far as his slender means allowed. He had read deeply, and understood his subject.

"Whenever you like, Katherine," he said.

"This afternoon?"

" I'm afraid they want polishing up and arranging. I've got some new things which I've not placed. I've rather neglected them lately. Let us say to-morrow afternoon. Then they'll all be spick and span for you."

Katherine assented. " I've been down here so often and never seen them," she said. " It seems odd, considering the years we've known each other."

" I only took it up after father's death," said Dick. " And since then, you know, you haven't been here so very often."

" It was only the last time that I discovered you took an interest in the collection. You hid your light under a bushel. Then I went to London and heard that you were a great authority on the subject."

Dick's tanned face reddened with pleasure.

" I do know something about it. You see, guns and swords and pistols are in my line. I'm good at killing things. I ought to have been a soldier, only I couldn't pass examinations, so I sort of interest myself in the old weapons and do my killing in imagination."

" You give a regular lecture, don't you ? "

" Well, you know," said Dick modestly, " a lot of them are historical. There's a mace used by a bishop, an ancestor of ours. He couldn't wield a sword in battle, so he cottoned on to that, and in order to salve his conscience before using it he would cry out ' Gare ! gare ! '—and they say that's what our name comes from—see ? ' Ware—Ware.' He was the founder of our family—though, of course, he oughtn't to have been. And then we have the duelling pistols my great-grandfather shot Lord Estcourt with. They're beautiful things—in the case just as he left it after the duel, with powder, balls, and caps, all complete. It's a romantic story——"

"My dear Dick," interposed Mrs. Ware, with fragile, uplifted hand, "please don't offend us with these horrible family scandals. Katherine dear, are you going to the vicar's garden-party this afternoon? If you are, will you take a message to Mrs. Cook?"

So Katherine being monopolized, Dick was silenced, and as Austin and Viviette were talking in a lively but unintelligible way about a thing, or a play, or a horse called Nietzsche, he relapsed into the heavy, full-blooded man's animal enjoyment of his food and th e sensitive's consciousness of heartache.

When the ladies had left the table and the coffee had been brought in, and the men's cigars were lit, Austin said:

"What a magnificently beautiful creature she has grown into."

"Whom do you mean?" asked Dick.

"Why, Viviette, of course. She's the most fascinating thing I've come across for years."

"Do you think so?" said Dick shortly.

"Don't you?"

Dick shrugged his shoulders. Austin laughed.

"What a stolid old beggar you are. To you, she's just the same little girl that used to run about here in short frocks. If she were a horse you'd have a catalogue yards long of her points."

"But as she's a lady," said Dick, tugging his moustache, "I don't care to catalogue them."

Austin laughed again. "Fairly scored!" He raised his cup to his lips, took a sip, and set it down again.

"Why on earth," said he with some petulance, "can't mother give us decent coffee?"

II

Dick went heavy-hearted to bed that night, pronouncing himself to be the most miserable of God's creatures, and calling on Providence to remove him speedily from an unsympathetic world. He had said good night to the ladies at eleven o'clock when the three went upstairs to bed, and had forthwith gone to spend the rest of the evening in the friendly solitude of his armoury. Emerging thence an hour later into the hall, he had come upon a picturesque, but heart-rending, spectacle. There, on the third step of the grand staircase, stood Viviette, holding in one hand a candle, and extending the other to Austin, who, with sleek head bent, was pressing it to his lips. In the candle-light her hair threw disconcerting shadows over her elfin face, and her great eyes seemed to glow with an intensity that poor Dick had never seen in them before. As soon as he had appeared she had broken into her low laugh, drawn away her hand from Austin, and, descending the steps, extended it in much the same regal manner to Dick.

"Good night again, Dick," she said sweetly. "Austin and I have been having a little talk."

But he had disregarded the hand, and, with a gruff "Good night," had returned to his armoury, slamming the door behind him. There he had nourished his wrath on more whisky and soda than was good for him, and crawled upstairs in the small hours to miserable sleeplessness.

This was the beginning of Dick's undoing, the gods (abetted by Viviette) employing their customary procedure of first driving him mad. But Viviette was not

225

altogether a guilty abettor. Indeed, all day long, she had entertained high notions of acting fairy godmother, and helping Dick along the road to fortune and content. He himself, she learned, had taken no steps to free himself from his present mode of life. He had not even confided in Austin. Viviette ran over the list of her influential friends. There was Lady Winsmere, a dowager countess of seventy, surrounded by notabilities, at whose house she stayed now and then in London. On the last occasion an Agent-General for one of the great Colonies had sat next her at dinner. Then there was her friend Mrs. Penderby, whose husband gathered enormous wealth in some mysterious way in Mark Lane. Why should she not go up to London and open a campaign on Dick's behalf, secure him an appointment, and come back flourishing it before his dazzled and delighted eyes? The prospect was enchanting. The fairy godmother romance of it fascinated her girlish mind. But first she must clear the ground at home. There must be no opposition from Austin. He must be her ally.

When a woman get an idea like this into her head she must execute it, as the Americans say, right now. A man waits, counts up all the barriers, and speculates on the strength and courage of the lions in the path— but a woman goes straight forward, and does not worry about the lions till they bite her. Viviette resolved to speak to Austin at once ; but, owing to a succession of the little ironies of circumstance, she found no opportunity of doing so all the afternoon or evening. It was only when, standing at the top of the stairs, she had seen Dick go off to the armoury, and Austin return to the drawing-room——for the men had bidden the ladies good night in the hall—that she saw her chance. She went downstairs and opened the drawing-room door.

"I don't want to go to bed after all. Do you think you can do with me a little longer?"

"A great deal longer," he said, drawing a chair for her, and arranging the shade of a lamp so that the light should not shine full in her eyes. "I was just thinking how dull the room looked without you—as if all the flowers had suddenly been taken away."

"I suppose I am decorative," she said blandly.

"You're bewitching. What instinct made you choose that shade of pale green for your frock? If I had seen it in the pattern I should have said it was impossible for your colouring. But now it seems to be the only perfect thing you could wear."

She laughed her little laugh of pleasure, and thanked him prettily for the compliment. They bandied gay words for a while.

"Oh, I'm so glad you have come down—even for this short visit," said Viviette, at last. "I was pining for talk, for wit, for a breath of the great world beyond these sleepy meadows. You bring all that with you."

Austin leaned forward. "How do you know I'm not bringing even more?"

The girl's eyes drooped before his gaze. Then she fluttered a glance at him in which there was a gleam of mockery.

"You bring the most valuable gift of all—appreciation of my frocks. I love people to notice them. Now Dick is frock-blind. Why is that?"

"He's a dear old duffer," said Austin.

"I don't think he's happy," said Viviette, who, in her feminine way, had worked round to the subject of the interview.

"He did seem rather cut up about the stables," Austin admitted. "But the things are an eyesore, and mother was worrying herself to death about them."

"It isn't only the stables," said Viviette. "Dick is altogether discontented."

Austin looked at her in amazement. "Discontented?"

"He wants something to do."

"Nonsense," he laughed, with the air of a man certain of his facts. "He's as happy as a king here. He shoots and hunts—looks after the place—runs the garden and potters about in his armoury—in fact, does just what he likes all day long. He goes to bed without a care sharing his pillow, and, when he wakes up, gets into comfortable country clothes instead of a tight-fitting suit of responsibilities. For a man of his tastes he leads an ideal existence."

He threw away the end of the cigarette he was smoking, as though to say that the argument was finished. But Viviette regarded him with a smile—the smile of woman's superior wisdom. How astonishingly little he knew of Dick!

"Do you really think there is one contented being on earth?" she asked. "Even I know better than that."

Austin maintained that Dick ought to be contented.

"Dependent for practically all he has on you?"

"I've never let him feel it," he said quickly.

"He does, though. He wants to get away—to earn his own living—make a way for himself."

"That's the first I've heard of it," said Austin, genuinely surprised. "I really thought he was perfectly contented here. Of course, now and then he's grumpy—but he always has had fits of grumpiness. What kind of work does he want?"

"Something to do with sheep or cattle—in Arizona or New Zealand—the place doesn't matter—any open-air life."

Austin lit another cigarette and walked about the room. He was a man of well-regulated habits, and did not like being taken unawares. Dick ought to have told him. Then there was their mother. Who would look after her? Dick was a dispensation of Providence.

"Perhaps I might be a deputy dispensation, mightn't I?" said Viviette. "I don't think mother is so desperately attached to Dick as all that. It could be arranged somehow or other. And Dick is growing more and more wretched about it every day. Every day he pours out his woes to me till I can almost howl with misery."

"What do you want me to do?"

"Not to stand in his way if he gets a chance of going abroad."

"Of course I won't," cried Austin eagerly. "It never entered my head that he wanted to go away. I would do anything in the world for his happiness, poor old chap. I love Dick very deeply. In spite of his huge bulk and rough ways there's something of the woman in him that makes one love him."

They catalogued Dick's virtues, and then Viviette unfolded her scheme. One or other of the powerful personages whom, in her young confidence, she proposed to attack, would surely know of some opening abroad.

"Even humble I sometimes hear of things," said Austin. "Only a day or two ago old Lord Overton asked me if I knew of a man who could manage a timber forest he's got in Vancouver——"

Viviette jumped up and clapped her hands.

"Why that's the very thing for Dick!" she cried exultingly.

"God bless my soul!" said Austin. "So it is. I never thought of it."

"If you get it for him I'll thank you in the sweetest way possible." She glanced at him swiftly, under her eyelids. "I promise you I will."

"Then I'll certainly get it," replied Austin.

Austin then went into details. Lord Overton wanted a man of education—a gentleman—one who could ride and shoot and make others work. He would have to superintend the planting and the cutting and the transportation of timber, and act as agent for the various farms Lord Overton possessed in the wide district. The salary would be £700 a year. The late superintendent had suddenly died, and Lord Overton wanted a man to go out at once and fill his place. If only he had thought of Dick!

"But you're thinking of him now. It can't be too late—men with such qualifications aren't picked up at every street corner."

"That's quite true," said Austin. "And as for my recommendation," he added in his confident way, "Lord Overton and I are on such terms that he would not hesitate to give the appointment to a brother of mine. I'll write at once."

"And we'll say nothing to Dick until we've got it all in black and white."

"Not a word," said he.

Then they burst out laughing like happy conspirators, and enjoyed beforehand the success of their plot.

"The old place will be very strange without him," said Austin.

A shadow passed over Viviette's bright face. The manor-house would indeed be very lonely. Her occupation as Dick's liege lady, confidante, and tormentor would be gone. Parting from him would be a wrench. There would be a dreadful scene at the last moment, in which he would want to hold her right in his arms and make her promise to join him in Vancouver. She shivered a little; then tossed her head as if to throw off the disturbing thoughts.

" Don't let us look at the dismal side of things. It's selfish. All we want is Dick's happiness." She glanced at the clock and started up. " It's midnight. If Katherine knew I was here she would lecture me."

" It's nothing very dreadful," he laughed. " Nor is Katherine's lecture."

" I call her Saint Nitouche—but she's a great dear, isn't she ? Good night."

He accompanied her to the foot of the stairs and lit her candle. On the third stair she paused.

" Remember—in all this it's I who am the fairy godmother."

" And I," said Austin, " am nothing but the fairy godmother's humble and devoted factotum." He took the hand which she extended and, bending over it, kissed it gallantly.

Then by unhappy chance out came Dick from the armoury, and beheld the spectacle which robbed him of his peace of mind.

The next morning, when Dick came down gloomily to breakfast, she was very gentle with him, and administered tactfully to his wants. She insisted on going to the sideboard and carving his cold ham, of which he ate prodigious quantities after a hot first course, and when she put the plate before him laid a caressing touch on his shoulder. She neglected Austin in a barefaced manner, and drew Dick into reluctant and then animated talk on his prize roses and a setter pup just recovering from distemper. After the meal she went with him round the garden, inspected both roses and puppy, and manifested great interest in a trellis he was constructing for the accommodation later in the summer of some climbing cucumbers, at present only visible as modest leaves in flower-pots. Neither made any reference to the little scene of the night before. Morning had brought to Dick the conviction that in refusing her hand and slamming the door he had behaved in an unpardonably bearish manner; and he could not apologize for his behaviour unless he confessed his jealousy of Austin, which, in all probability, would have subjected him to the mockery of Viviette—a thing which, above all others, he dreaded, and against which he knew himself to be defenceless. Viviette, too, found silence golden. She knew perfectly well why Dick had slammed the door. An explanation would have been absurd. It would have interfered with her relations with Austin, which were beginning to be exciting. But she loved Dick in her heart for being a bear, and evinced both her compunction and her appreciation in peculiar graciousness.

"You've never asked me to try the new mare," she said. "I don't think it a bit kind of you."

"Would you care to?" he asked eagerly.

"Of course I should. I love to see you with horses. You and the trap and the horse seem to be as much one mechanism as a motor-car."

"I can make a horse do what I want," he said, delighted at the compliment. "We'll take the dog-cart. When will you come? This morning?"

232

"Yes—let us say eleven. It will be lovely."

"I'll have it round at eleven o'clock. You'll see. She's a flyer."

"So am I," she said with a laugh, and pointed to the front gate, which a garden lad had just run to open to admit a young man on horseback.

"Oh, lord! it's Banstead," said Dick with a groan.

"Au revoir—eleven o'clock," said Viviette, and she fled.

Lord Banstead dismounted, gave his horse to the lad, and came up to Dick. He was an unhealthy, dissipated-looking young man, with lustreless eyes, a characterless chin, and an underfed moustache. He wore a light blue hunting stock, fastened by a ruby fox in full gallop, and a round felt hat with a very narrow flat brim, beneath which protruded strands of Andrew Ague-cheek hair.

"Hallo, Banstead," said Dick, not very cordially.

"Hallo," said the other, halting before the rose-bed, where Dick was tying up some blooms with bast. He watched him for a moment or two. Conversation was not spontaneous.

"Where's Viviette?" he asked eventually.

"Who?" growled Dick.

"Rot. What's the good of frills? Miss Hastings."

"Busy. She'll be busy all the morning."

"I rather wanted to see her."

"I don't think you will. You might ring at the front door and send in your card."

"I might," said Banstead, lighting a cigar. He had tried this method of seeing Viviette before, but without success. There was another pause. Dick snipped off an end of bast.

"You're up very early," said he.

233

"Went to bed so bally sober I couldn't sleep," replied the misguided youth. "Not a soul in the house, I give you my word. So bored last night I took a gun and tried to shoot cats. Shot a damn cock pheasant by mistake, and had to bury the thing in my own covers. If I'm left to myself to-night I'll get drunk and go out shooting tenants. Come over and dine."

"Can't," said Dick.

"Do. I'll open a bottle of the governor's old port. Then we can play billiards, or piquet, or cat's-cradle, or any rotten thing you like."

Dick excused himself curtly. Austin had come down for Whitsuntide, and a lady was staying in the house. Lord Banstead pushed his hat to the back of his head.

"Then what the devil am I to do in this hole of a place?"

"Don't know," said Dick.

"You fellows in the country are so unfriendly. In town I never need dine alone. Anyone's glad to see me. Feeding all by myself in that dining-room fairly gives me the pip."

"Then come and dine here," said Dick, unable to refuse a neighbour hospitality.

"Right," said Banstead. "That is really like the Samaritan Johnnie. I'll come with pleasure."

"Quarter to eight."

Banstead hesitated. "Couldn't you make it a quarter past?"

Dick stared. "Alter our dinner-hour? You've rather a nerve, haven't you, Banstead?"

"I wouldn't suggest it if we weren't pals," replied the other, grinning somewhat shamefacedly. "But the fact is I've got an appointment late this afternoon."

The fatuity of vicious and coroneted youth outstripped his discretion. "There's a devilish pretty girl, you know, at the Green Man at Little Barton ; I don't know whether I can get away in time."

Dick stuffed his bast in his pocket, and muttered things uncomplimentary to Banstead.

"Dinner's at a quarter to eight. You can take it or leave it," said he.

"I suppose I've jolly well got to take it," said Banstead, unruffled. "Anything's better than going through dinner from soup to dessert all alone under the fishy eye of that butling image of a Jenkins. He was thirty years in my governor's service, and doesn't understand my ways. I guess I'll have to chuck him."

A perspiring, straw-hatted postman lurched along the gravel drive with the morning's post. He touched his hat to Dick, delivered the manor-house packet into his hands, and departed.

"I'll sort these in the morning-room," said Dick, moving in the direction of the house, and Lord Banstead, hoping to see Viviette, followed at his heels. The control of the family post was one of the few privileges Dick retained as master of the house. His simple mind still regarded the receipt and despatch of letters as a solemn affair of life, and every morning he went through the process of distribution with ceremonial observance. In the morning-room they found Austin and Viviette, the former writing in a corner, the latter reading a novel by the French window that opened on to the terrace. Dick went up to a table, and began to sort the letters into various heaps. Austin greeted Lord Banstead none too warmly, and, with scarcely an apology, went back to his writing. He disapproved of Banstead, who was of a type particularly antagonistic to the young, clean and successful barrister. When Viviette had informed him of the youth's presence in the garden, he had exclaimed impatiently :

" It ought to be somebody's business to go round the world occasionally with a broom and sweep away spiders like that."

Viviette, mindful of the invective, received Lord Banstead with a smile of amusement. As she had two protectors against a fifth proposal of marriage, she stood her ground.

" I expected you to come over yesterday," she said.

" No, did you really ? " he exclaimed, a flush rising to his pale cheeks. " If I had thought that, I should have come."

" You've made up for it by arriving early to-day, at any rate," said Viviette.

" And I'm making up for it further by coming to dinner to-night. Dick asked me," he added, seeing the polite questioning in her eyes.

" That will be very nice," she said. " You can talk to mother. You see, Dick talks to Mrs. Holroyd, who is staying with us, Austin talks to me, so poor mother is left out in the cold. She'll enjoy a nice long talk with you."

When Banstead took the chorus out to supper he had the ready repartee of his kind. In such a case he would have told the lady not to pull his leg. But the delicate mockery in Viviette's face seemed to forbid the use of this figure of speech, and as his vocabulary did not readily allow him to formulate the idea in other terms he said nothing, but settled his stock and looked at her adoringly. At last he bent forward, after a glance at the protectors, and said in a low tone :

" Come out into the garden. I've something to say to you."

" Why not say it here ? " she replied in her ordinary voice.

Banstead bit his lip. He would have liked to call her a little devil. But he reflected that if he did she would be quite capable of repeating the phrase aloud, somewhat to the astonishment of Dick and Austin, who might ask for embarrassing explanations. Instead he bent still nearer, and whispered :

" I can only say it to you alone. I've been awake all night thinking of it—give you my word."

" Wait till to-morrow morning, and by then you may have slept upon it." she counselled.

" You'll drive me to drink ! " he murmured.

She rose with a laugh. " In that case I must go. I ought to be labelled ' dangerous.' Don't you think so, Dick ? Besides, I'm going for a drive, and must put on my things. These my letters ? Au revoir." And with a wave of her hand she left them.

Banstead lingered by the threshold and took up an illustrated paper. The maid, in response to Dick's summons, bore away the letters for the rest of the household. Austin and Dick concerned themselves with their correspondence, Dick's chiefly consisting of gardeners' catalogues.

For a while there was silence. It was broken by a loud laugh from Austin.

" Dick ! I say, Dick ! What do you think these village idiots have asked me to do ? To accept their nomination and stand as a Rural District Councillor ! Me ! "

Dick quickly crossed to the table where his brother was sitting.

"That's my letter, old chap. I must have put it in your heap by mistake. The invitation is meant for me."

"You?" laughed Austin. "Why, what do you want to fool about with village politics for? No. The letter is meant for me right enough."

"I can't understand it," said Dick.

Lord Banstead looked up from his paper.

"That the Rural District Council? I'm on the committee. Had a meeting yesterday. I'm chairman of the silly rotters."

"Then your silly rotter of an honorary secretary," cried Dick angrily, "has sent Austin the letter of invitation that was meant for me."

"Oh, no, he didn't," said Banstead. "It's all right. They chucked you, old son. Now I remember. I promised to explain."

"Dick turned aside. "Oh, you needn't explain," he said bitterly.

"But I must. They had their reasons, you know. They thought they'd rather have a brainy nobleman like your brother than a good old rotter like you. You're——"

"Oh, hold your tongue, Banstead," cried Austin, rising and putting his hand on Dick's shoulder. "Really, my dear old Dick, you're the right person to stand. They only thought a lawyer could help them—but I'm far too busy—of course, I decline. I'm deeply pained, Dick, at having hurt you. I'll write to the committee and point out how much fitter, as a country gentleman, you are for the duties than I am. They're bound to ask you."

Dick swung away passionately, his lips quivering with anger and mortification beneath his great moustache.

" Do you think I would accept ?   I'm damned if I
would.   Do you expect me to pick up everything
you've thrown in the mud and feel grateful ?   I'm
damned if I will ! "

He flung out of the room on to the terrace and strode
away in a rage.

"Seems to take it badly," remarked Banstead,
looking at his disappearing figure.   "I had better say
good-bye."

"Good-bye," said Austin.   And he added, as he
accompanied him with grim politeness to the front
gate, "If you exercise the same tact in the chair as
you've done here, your meetings must be a huge success."

He returned with a shrug of the shoulders to his
table in the morning-room.   He was deeply attached
to Dick, but a lifelong habit of regarding him as a
good-natured, stupid, and contented giant blinded him
to the storm that was beginning to rage in the other's
soul.   The occurrence was unfortunate.   It wounded
the poor old fellow's vanity.   Banstead's blatant folly
had been enough to set any man in a rage.   But, after
all, Dick was a common-sense creature, and, recognizing
that Austin was in no way to blame, he would soon
get over it.   Meanwhile, there was awaiting him the
joyful surprise of Vancouver, which would soon put
such petty mortifications out of his head.   Thus Austin
consoled himself, and settled down to the serious
matters of his correspondence.

Viviette, coming in later in hat and jacket, found
him busily writing.   He looked up at her admiringly
as she stood against the background of light framed
by the great French window.

"Am I presentable ? " she asked, with a smile,
interpreting his glance.

"Each modification of your dress makes you seem more bewitching than the last."

"I trimmed this hat myself," she said, coming into the room, and looking at herself in a Queen Anne mirror on the wall.

"That's why it's so becoming," said Austin.

She wheeled round on him with a laugh. "You really ought to say something cleverer than that!"

"How can I," he replied, "when you drive my wits away?"

"Poor me," she said. And then, suddenly, "Where's Dick?"

"What do you want Dick for?"

"He promised to take me for a drive." She consulted the watch on her wrist. "It's past eleven now."

"I'm afraid poor Dick is rather upset. He seems to have been counting on being nominated to stand for the Rural District Council, and the imbeciles invited me instead."

"Oh, how could they?" she cried, smitten with a great pity. "How could they be so stupid and cruel? I know all about it. He told me yesterday. He must be bitterly disappointed."

Austin did not tell her of Lord Banstead's tactful explanation of the committee's action. He was a fastidious man, and did not care to soil his mind with the memory of Banstead's existence. If he had described the scene, the young man's vulgarity, his own attempt at conciliation, and Dick's passionate outburst—the course of the drama that was shaping itself might have been altered. But the stars in their courses were fighting against Dick. Austin only said:

"If we get him this appointment, it will be ample compensation, anyhow."

"Please don't say 'if,'" exclaimed Viviette, "we must get it."

"Unless Lord Overton has already found a man, which is unlikely, owing to the general suspension of business at Whitsuntide, it's practically a certainty."

"When shall we know?"

"My letter's written and is waiting for the post. If he replies by return we shall hear the day after to-morrow."

"That is such a long time to wait. Do you know what to-morrow is?"

"Wednesday," said Austin.

"It's Dick's birthday." She clapped her hands at a happy inspiration, and hung on his arm. "Oh, Austin! If we could only give him the appointment as a birthday present!"

Her touch, her fresh charm, the eagerness in her eyes, roused him to unwonted enthusiasm. In his sane moments he did not care a fig for anybody's birthday. What man ever does? He proclaimed the splendour of her idea. But how was it to be realized?

"Send a long prepaid telegram to Lord Overton, of course," said Viviette triumphantly. (How unresourceful are men!) "Then we can get an answer to-day."

"You forget the nearest telegraph office is at Witherby, seven miles off."

"But Dick and I are going for a drive. I'll make him go to Witherby and I'll send the telegram. Write it."

She drew him in her caressing way to the table, seated him in the chair, and laid the block of telegram forms before him. He scribbled industriously, and when he had finished handed her the sheets.

"There!"

He fished in his pockets for money, but Viviette checked him. She was the fairy godmother in this fairy-tale, and fairy godmothers always held the purse. She glanced again at her watch. It was ten minutes past eleven.

"Perhaps he's waiting with the trap for me all the time. Au revoir."

"I'll see you off," said Austin.

They went together into the hall and opened the front door. The new mare and the dog-cart in charge of the stable-lad were there, but no Dick.

"Where's Mr. Ware?"

"Don't know, miss."

Then the Devil entered into Viviette. There is no other explanation. The Devil entered into her.

"We must get to Witherby and back before lunch. You drive me over instead of Dick."

They exchanged glances. Austin was young. He was in love with her. Dick had committed the unpardonable offence of being late. It would serve him right.

"I'll come," said he, disappearing in search of cap and gloves.

Viviette went into the hall and scribbled a note.

"Dear Dick,—You're late. Austin and I have the most important business to transact at Witherby, so he's driving me over. We're preparing a great surprise for you.—Viviette."

"Give this to Mr. Ware," she said to the stable-boy as she prepared to get into the dog-cart.

The boy touched his cap and ran to open the gate. Viviette light mounted by Austin's side. They had just turned into the road when Dick came racing

242

through the hall and saw them disappear. He walked up the drive, and met the boy coming down, who handed him the note, with some words, which he did not hear. He watched the boy out of sight. Then he tore the note unread into tiny fragments, stamped them furiously into the mould of the nearest bed, and, flying into his armoury, threw himself into a chair and cursed the day that ever Austin was born.

III

The drive was a memorable one for many reasons. First, the new mare flew along at an exhilarating trot, as if showing off her qualities to her new masters. Then the morning sunshine flooded the soft, undulating Warwickshire country, and slanted freshly through the bordering elms in sweet-scented lanes. Summer flaunted its irresponsible youth in the faces of matronly, red-brick manor-house, old grey church, and crumbling cottage, danced about among the crisp green leaves, kissed the wayside flowers, and tossing up human hearts in sheer gaiety, played the very deuce with them. The drive also had its altruistic side. They were on an errand of benevolence. Austin, his mind conscious of nothing but right, felt the unusual glow of unselfish devotion to another's interests. When he had awakened that morning he had had misgivings as to the advisability of sending Dick to another hemisphere. After all, Dick was exceedingly useful at Ware House, and saved him a great deal of trouble. An agent would have to be appointed to replace him, whose salary—not a very large one, in view of the duties to be performed, but still a salary—would have to be provided out of his, Austin's, pocket. Who, again, could undertake the permanent care of his mother ? Viviette would stay at home for some little time ; but she would be marrying one of these fine days—a day which Austin had reason for hoping would not be very remote. He would have to make Heaven knows what arrangements for Mrs. Ware and the general upkeep of the manor-house, while he was in London carrying on his profession. Decidedly, Dick had been a godsend, and his absence would be a calamity. In sending him out to Vancouver Austin had all the unalloyed, pure pleasure of self-sacrifice.

They talked of Dick and Dick's birthday and Dick's happiness most of the way to Witherby. The telegram despatched, prepaid with the porterage by Viviette, Austin felt that he had done his duty by his brother, and deserved some consideration on his own account. And here it was that the summer began its game with their hearts. On such sportive occasions it is not so much what is said that matters. A conversation that might be entirely conventional between comparative strangers in a fog may become the most romantic interchange of sentiment imaginable between intimates in the sunshine. There are tones, there are glances, there are half-veiled allusions, there are—in a dog-cart, especially when it jolts—thrilling contacts of arm and arm. There is man's undisguised tribute to beauty ; there is beauty's keen feminine appreciation of the tribute. There is a manner of saying "we" which counts for more than the casual conjunction of the personalities.

"This is our day, Viviette," said Austin. "I shall always remember it."

"So shall I. We must put a white mark against it in our diaries."

"With white ink ? "

"Of course. Black would never do, nor red, nor violet."

"But where shall we get it?"

"I'll make us some when I get home out of white cloud and lilies and sunshine and a bit of the blue sky."

Laughter fluttered through her veins. Yesterday she had teasingly boasted to Katherine that Austin was in love with her. Now she knew it. He proclaimed it in a thousand ways. A note of exultation in his laugh, like that in a blackbird's call, alone proclaimed it. Instinct told her of harmless words she might use which would bring the plain avowal. But the hour was too delicate. As yet nothing was demanded. All was given. Her woman's vanity blossomed deliciously in the atmosphere of a man's love. Her heart had not yet received the inevitable summons to respond. She left it, careless in the gay hands of summer.

When they drew up before the front door of Ware House he lifted her from the dog-cart and set her laughing on her feet.

"How strong you are," she cried.

"I'm not a giant, like Dick," said he, "but I'm strong enough to do what I like with a bit of a thing like you."

She entered the hall and glanced at him provokingly over her shoulder.

"Don't be too sure of that."

"Whatever I like," he repeated, striding towards her.

But Viviette laughed, and fled lightly up the stairs, and on the landing blew him an ironical kiss from her finger-tips.

When Viviette came down for lunch, she found Dick awaiting her in the hall. With a lowering face he watched her descend and, his hand on the newel, confronted her.

"Well?" said he indignantly.

"Well?" she said, cheerfully smiling.

"What have you got to say for yourself?"

"Lots of things. I had a lovely drive. I got through all my business, and I have a beautiful appetite. Also I don't like standing on a stair."

At her look he drew aside and let her pass into the hall.

"You promised to drive with me," he said, following her to a chair in which she sat. "Driving with me is no great catch, perhaps; but a promise is a promise."

"You were late," said Viviette.

"My mother kept me—some silly nonsense about vegetables. You must have known it was something I couldn't help."

"I really don't see why you're so angry, Dick," she said, lifting candid eyes. "I explained why we had gone in my note."

"I didn't read the note," said Dick wrathfully. "A thousand notes couldn't have explained it. I tore the note into little pieces."

Viviette rose. "If that's the way you treat me," she said, piqued, "I have nothing more to say to you."

"It's the way you're treating me," he cried, with a clumsy man's awkward attempt at gesture. "I know I'm not clever. I know I can't talk to you as sweetly as other people; but I'm not a dog, and I deserve some consideration. Perhaps, after all, I might have the brains to jest and toss about words and shoot off

246

epigrams. I'll try, if you like. Let us see. Here. A man who entrusts his heart to a woman has a jade for his banker. That's devilish smart, isn't it ? Now then—there must be some repartee to it. What is it ? "

Viviette looked at him proudly, and moving in the direction of the morning-room door, said with much dignity :

" That depends on the way in which the woman you are talking to has been brought up. My repartee is—good morning."

Dick, suddenly repentant, checked her.

" No, Viviette. Don't go. I'm a brute and a fool. I didn't mean it. Forgive me. I would rather go on the rack than hurt your little finger. But it maddens me—can't you believe it ? It maddens me to see Austin——"

She broke into a little laugh and smiled dazzlingly on him.

" I do believe you're jealous ! " she interrupted.

" Good heavens ! " he cried passionately. " Haven't I cause ? Austin has everything his heart can desire. He has always had it. I had nothing—nothing but one little girl I love. Austin, with all the world at his feet, comes down here, and what chance has a rough yokel like me against Austin ? My God ! It's the one ewe lamb."

He raised his clenched fists and brought them down against his sides and turned away. The allusion and a consciousness of Vancouver brought a smile into Viviette's eyes. She had a woman's sense of humour, which is not always urbane. When he turned to meet her she shook her head reprovingly.

" And David put Uriah into the forefront of the battle, and carried off poor little Bathsheba. No one

247

seemed to have concerned himself with what Bathsheba thought of it all. Don't you consider she ought
to have some choice in the matter—whether she should
follow the sprightly David or cling to the melancholy
Uriah ? "

"Oh, don't jest like that, Viviette," he cried. "It
hurts ! "

"I'm sorry, Dick," she said innocently. "But
really, Bathsheba has her feelings. What am I to
do ? "

"Choose, dear, between us. Choose now—in
Heaven's name, choose."

"But, Dick dear," said Viviette, all that was
wickedly feminine in her shouting her sex's triumph
song, "I want a longer time to choose between two
hats ! "

Dick stamped his foot. "Then Austin has been
robbing me ! I'm growing desperate, Viviette, tell me
now. Choose."

He seized her arms in his strong hands. She felt a
delicious little thrill of fear. But knowing her strength
she looked up at him with a childish expression and
said plaintively : "Oh, Dick, dear, I'm so hungry."

He released her arms. She rubbed them ruefully.
"I'm sure you've made horrid red rings. Fancy
choosing a hard, uncomfortable hat like that ! "

He was about to make some rejoinder when the
presence of Mrs. Ware and Katherine Holroyd at the
top of the stairs put an end to the encounter. The
victory, such as it was, remained with Viviette.

At lunch, Austin, his veins still tingling with the
summer, laughed and jested light-heartedly. What a
joy it was to get away from stuffy courts of justice into
the pure Warwickshire air ! What a joy to drink of

the wine of life ! What was that ? Only those that drank of the wine could tell.

"What about the poor devils that only get the dregs ? " muttered Dick.

Austin declared that the real wine had no dregs. He called his mother and Katherine Holroyd to witness. Mrs. Ware was not sure. Old port had to be very carefully decanted. Did he remember the fuss his dear father used to make about it ? She was very glad there was no more left—for Dick would be sure to drink it and it would go to his head.

"Or his toes ? " cried Viviette.

When Austin explained Viviette's meaning to his mother, who had not an allusive habit of mind, she acquiesced placidly. Port was not good for gouty people. Their poor father suffered severely. Austin listened to her reminiscences and turned the talk to the drive. It had been more like driving through Paradise with Pegasus harnessed to Venus's car than anything else. He must take his mother out and show her what a good judge of horseflesh was dear old Dick.

"As she's my mare, perhaps I might have the privilege," said Dick.

Austin cried out, in all good faith : " My dear old boy, is there anything especially mine or yours in this house ? "

Katherine, a keen observer, broke quickly into the talk.

" There's Dick's armoury. That's his own particular and private domain. You're going to explain it all to me this afternoon, aren't you ? You promised yesterday."

She drew Dick into talk away from the others. The lecture on the armoury was fixed for three o'clock, when she would be free from the duty from which, during her stay at the manor-house, she had relieved Viviette, of postprandial reading of the newspaper to Mrs. Ware. But her interest in his hobby for once failed to awaken his enthusiasm. The dull jealousy of Austin, against which his honest soul had struggled successfully all his life long, had passed beyond his control. These few days of Austin's Whitsun visit had changed his cosmic view. Petty rebuffs, such as the matters of the stables and the Rural District Council, which formerly he would have regarded in the twilight of his mind as part of the unchangeable order of things in which Austin was destined to shine resplendently and he to glimmer—Austin the arc-lamp and he the tallow-dip—became magnified into grievances and insults intolerable. Esau could not have raged more against Jacob, the supplanter, than did Dick, when Austin carried off Viviette from beneath his nose. Until this visit of Austin he had no idea that he would find a rival in his brother. The discovery was a shock, causing his world to reel and setting free all the pent-up jealousies and grievances of a lifetime. Everything he had given up to Austin, if not willingly, at least graciously, hiding beneath the rough, tanned hide of his homely face all pain, disappointment, and humiliation. But now Austin had come and swooped off with his one ewe lamb. Not that Viviette had encouraged him by more than the real but mocking affection with which she had treated her bear foster-brother ever since her elfin childhood. In a dim way he realized this, and absolved her from blame. Less dimly, also, he felt his mental and social inferiority, his lack of warrant in offering her marriage. But his great, rugged manhood wanted her, the woman, with an imperious, savage need which took all the training of civilization to repress. Viviette alone in her maidenly splendour, he could have fought it down. But the vision of another man entering, light-hearted and debonair, into those precincts maddened him, let loose primitive instincts of hatred and revenge, and robbed him of all interest in the toys with which men used to slay each other centuries ago.

Austin, being nearest the door, opened it for the ladies to pass out. Viviette, going out last, looked up at him with one of her witch's glances.

" Don't be very long," she said

Before Austin could resume his seat Dick leaped up.

" Austin, look here ; I've something to say to you."

" Well ? " said Austin.

Dick pulled out a cigar, bit the end off, and finding that he had ripped the outer skin, threw it angrily into the fireplace.

" My dear old boy," said Austin, " what in the name of all that's neurotic is the matter ? "

" I've something to say to you," Dick repeated. "Something that concerns myself, my life. I must throw myself on your generosity."

Austin, his head full of philanthropy, thrust his hands into his pockets and smiled indulgently on Dick.

" Don't, old chap, I know all about it. Viviette has told me everything."

Dick, his head full of passion, staggered in amazement.

" Viviette has told you ? "

" Of course ; why shouldn't she ? "

Dick groped his way to the door. It were better for both that he should not stay. Austin, left alone, laughed, not unkindly. Dear old Dick ! It was a shame to tease him—but what a different expression his honest face would wear to-morrow! When the maid brought in his coffee he sipped it with enjoyment, forgetful for once of its lack of excellence.

There was one person, however, in the house who saw things clearly ; and the more clearly she saw them the less did they seem satisfactorily ordered. This was Katherine Holroyd, a sympathetic observer and everybody's intimate. She had known the family since her childhood spent in a great neighbouring house which had now long since passed from her kin into alien hands. She had known Viviette when she first came, with her changeling face, a toddling child of three, to the manor-house. She had grown up with the brothers. Until her marriage the place had been her second home. Her married life, mostly spent abroad, had somewhat broken the intimacy. But her widowhood after the first few hopeless months had renewed it, although her visits were comparatively rare. On the other hand, her little daintily furnished London house in Victoria Square was always open to such of the family as happened to be in town. Now, as Austin was the most frequently in town, seeing that he lived there all the year round, with the exception of the long vacation and odd flying visits to War-wickshire, to Austin was her door most frequently open. A deep affection existed between them, deeper perhaps than either realized. To be purely brotherly in attitude towards a woman whom you are fond of and who is not your sister, and to be purely sisterly in your attitude towards a man whom you are fond of and who is not your brother, are ideals of spiritual emotion very difficult to attain in this respectably organized but sex-ridden world.

During the dark time of her early widowhood it was to Austin's delicate tact and loyalty that she owed her first weak grasp on life. It was he that had brought her to a sense of outer things, to a realization that in spite of her own grey sky there was still a glory on the earth. He was her trusted friend, ally, and adviser, who never failed her, and she contemplated him always with a heart full of somewhat exaggerated gratitude —which is as far on the road to love as it is given to many women to travel.

She had barely reached the top of the hall stairs, on her way to spend her reading hour with Mrs. Ware, when she saw Dick come out of the dining-room with convulsed and angry face, the veins standing out on his thick bull's neck. She felt frightened. Something foolish and desperate would happen before long. She resolved to give Austin a warning word. With an excuse to Mrs. Ware she went down again to the dining-room, and found Austin in the cosiest and sunniest frame of mind imaginable. Obviously there had been no serious quarrel between the brothers

"Can I have a few minutes with you, Austin?"

"A thousand," he said gaily. "What has gone wrong?"

"It is nothing to do with me," she said.

He looked amusedly into her eyes. "I know. It's about Viviette. Confess."

"Yes," she replied soberly, "it's about Viviette."

"You've seen it. I make no bones about it. You can believe the very worst. I have fallen utterly and hopelessly in love with her. I am at your mercy."

This beginning was not quite what Katherine had expected. He had taken matters out of her hands. She had not anticipated a downright confession. She felt conscious of a little dull and wholly reprehensible ache at her heart. She sighed.

"Aren't you pleased, Katherine?" he asked with a man's selfishness.

"I suppose I must be—for your sake. But I must also sigh a little. I knew you would be falling in love sooner or later—only I hoped it would be later. But *que veux-tu?* It is the doom of all such friendships."

"I don't see anything like a doom about it, my dear," said he. "The friendship will continue. Viviette loves you dearly."

She took up a peach from a dish to her hand, regarded it for a moment absent-mindedly, and delicately replaced it.

"Our friendship will continue, of course. But the particular essence of it, the little sentimentality of ownership, will be gone, won't it?"

Austin rose and bent over Katherine's chair in some concern. "You're not distressed, Katherine?"

"Oh, no. You have been such a kind, loyal friend to me during a very dark and lonely time—brought sunshine into my life when I needed it most—that I should be a wicked woman if I didn't rejoice at your happiness. And we have been nothing more than friends."

"Nothing more," said Austin.

She was smiling now, and he caught a gleam of mischief in her eyes.

"And yet there was an afternoon last winter——"

His face coloured. "Don't throw my wickedness in my face. I remember that afternoon. I came in fagged, with the prospect of dinner at the club and a dismal evening over a brief in front of me, and found you sitting before the fire, the picture of rest and comfortableness and companionship. I think it was the homely smell of hot buttered toast that did it. I nearly asked you to marry me."

"And I had been feeling particularly lonely," she laughed.

"Would you have accepted me?"

"Do you think that it is quite a fair question?"

"We have always been frank with one another since our childhood," said he.

She smiled. "Has Viviette accepted you?"

He broke away from her with a gay laugh, and lit a cigarette.

"Your feminine subtlety does you credit, Katherine."

"But has she?"

"Well, no—not exactly."

"Will she?"

He brought his hand down on the table. "By heavens, I'll make her! I've got most of the things I've wanted during my life, and it'll be odd if I don't get the thing I want more than all the rest put together. Now answer my question, my dear Katherine," he continued teasingly. "Would you have married me?"

The smile faded from Katherine's face. She could not parry the question as she had done before, and it probed depths. She said very seriously and sweetly:

"I should have done, Austin, as I always shall do, whatever you ask me to do. I'm glad you didn't ask me—very glad—for the love a woman gives a man died within me, you know."

He took her hand and kissed it.

"My dear," said he, "you are the truest friend that ever man had."

There was a short pause. Austin looked out of the

255

window and Katherine wiped away some moisture in her eyes. This scene of sentimentality was not at all what she had come for. Soon she rose with a determined air and joined Austin by the window.

"It was as a true friend that I wanted to speak to you to-day. To warn you."

"About what?"

"About Dick. Austin, he's madly in love with Viviette too."

Austin stared at her for a moment incredulously. "Dick in love—in love with Viviette?" Then he broke into a peal of laughter. "My dear Katherine! Why, it's absurd! It's preposterous! It's too funny."

"But seriously, Austin."

"But seriously," he said, with laughing eyes, "such an idea has never penetrated into old Dick's wooden skull. You dear women are always making up romance. He and Viviette are on the same old fairy and great brown bear terms that they have been ever since they first met. She makes him dance on his hind legs —he wants to hug her—she hits him over the nose— and he growls."

"I warn you," said Katherine. "Great brown bears in love are dangerous."

"But he isn't in love," he argued light-heartedly. "If he were he would want to stay with Viviette. But he's eating his heart out apparently, to leave us all and go and plough fields and herd cattle abroad. The life he lives here, my good mother's somewhat arbitrary ways, and one thing and another have at last got on his nerves. I wonder now how the dear old chap has stood it so long. That's what is wrong with him, not blighted affection."

"I can only tell you what I know," said Katherine.

"If you won't believe me, it's not my fault. Keep your eyes open and you will see."

"And you keep your eyes open to-morrow morning and *you* will see," he said, with his bright self-confidence.

So Katherine sighed at the obtuseness and inconvincibility of man and went to read the leader in the *Daily Telegraph* to Mrs. Ware. Austin, with a smile on his lips, wandered out into the sunshine in search of Viviette.

Before they parted, however, Katherine turned by the door.

"Are you coming to the armoury to hear Dick's lecture?"

"Of course," said Austin gaily. "The dear old chap loves an audience."

IV

Dick's great-grandfather (Wild Dick Ware, as he used to be called by the country-side), besides other enormities of indiscretion, committed an architectural crime. Having begun to form the collection of arms which was Dick's pride and hobby, he felt the need of a fencing gallery where they could be displayed to advantage. None of the rooms in the house were suitable. Building a new wing would cost too much. So, like a good old English gentleman, accustomed to get what he wanted, he ruthlessly cut off a slice of the nobly proportioned morning-room, containing a beautifully mullioned casement at the side, knocked a French window through one end, so that he could wander in and out from the terrace, knocked a door through the other so that it opened on a corner of the hall, forgot all about the fireplace, and left his descendants to make the best of things.

257

This long, narrow, comfortless strip of a room was Dick's armoury, den, and refuge. It was furnished with extreme simplicity. At the farther end two rusty leather arm-chairs flanked a cast-iron stove in the corner, and were balanced in the other and darker corner by a knee-hole writing-desk littered with seeds and bulbs and spurs and bits of fishing tackle, and equipped for its real purpose with a forbidding-looking pen and inkpot, and a torn piece of weather-beaten blotting-paper. At about a third of the way down from the terrace door a great screen, covered with American cloth, cut the room almost in two. Against this screen stood two suits of beautifully finished fifteenth-century Italian armour. Between them and the farther end of the room ran a long deal table, with a green baize cover. An odd, dilapidated chair or two stood lonely and disconsolate against the opposite wall. The floor was covered with old matting and a few faded rugs. The walls, however, and the cases ranged along them, gave an air of distinction to the room. There hung trophies of arms of all sorts—a bewildering array of spiky stars like the monstrous decorations on the breast of a Brobdingnagian diplomatist, of guns and pistols of all ages and nationalities, of halberds, pikes, and partisans, of curved scimitars, great two-handed swords, and long, glittering rapiers, with precious hilts. There, too, were coats of chain-mail and great iron gauntlets, and rows of dinted helmets formed a cornice round the gallery.

It was Dick's sanctuary, where, according to family tradition, he was supposed to be immune from domestic attacks. Anyone, it is true, could open the door and worry him from the threshold, but no one entered without his invitation. Here he was master. Here

258

he spent solitary hours dreaming dreams, wrestling with devils, tying trout-flies, making up medicines for his dogs, and polishing and arranging and rearranging his armour and weapons. Until the furies got hold of him he was a simple soul, content with simple things. The happiest times of his life had been passed here among the inanimate objects which he loved, and here he was now spending the hours of his greatest agony.

The words he had just heard from Austin rang like a crazy, deafening chime through his ears. He sat in one of the old leather chairs, gripping his coarse hair. It was unthinkable, and yet it was true. Viviette had told Austin the thing that glowed sacred at the bottom of his soul. The scene danced vividly before his eyes : the two bright creatures making a mock of him and his love, laughing merrily at the trick they had played him, pitying him contemptuously. There was a flame at his heart, a burning lump in his throat. Mechanically he drew from a little cupboard near by a bottle of whisky, a syphon, and a glass. The drink he mixed and swallowed contained little soda. It increased the fire in his heart and throat. He paced the long room in crazy indignation. Every nerve in his body quivered with a sense of unforgivable insult and deadly outrage. Austin's face loomed before him like that of a mocking devil. He had hell in his throat, and again he tossed down a dose of whisky, and threw himself into the arm-chair. The daily paper lay on a stool at his hand. He took it up and tried to read, but the print swam into thin, black smudges. He dashed the paper to the ground, and gave himself up to his madness.

After a while he remembered his appointment with Katherine at three o'clock. He glanced at his watch.

It was a quarter to the hour, and, beyond a cleaning yesterday afternoon, no preparations were made. In an automatic way he unlocked some cases and drew out his treasures, wiped the sword-blades tenderly with chamois leather, and laid them on the long, baize-covered table. Here and there from the cornice he selected a helmet. The great mace used by his ecclesiastical ancestor he unhooked from the wall. Soon the table was covered with weapons, selected in a dazed way, he knew not why. A helmet fell from his hands on the floor with a ring of steel. Its visor grinned at him—the fool, the tricked, the supplanted. He kicked it, with a silly laugh. Then he pulled himself together, picked it up, and examined it in great fear lest harm should have happened to it. He put it on the table, and in order to steady his nerves drank another large whisky and small soda.

He scanned the table, perplexed. Some accustomed and important exhibit was not in its place. What was it? He clasped his head in his hands and strove to clear his mind for a moment from obsession. It was something historical, something unique, something he had but lately mentioned to Katherine. Something intimately connected with this very room. At last memory responded. He placed a chair between the two suits of armour that stood against the screen and the end of the long table, and, mounting, took a mahogany case from a shelf. Then he sat on the chair, put the case on the table, and opened it by means of a small, ornamental key. It contained a brace of old-fashioned duelling pistols, such as were used at the beginning of the nineteenth century. They were long-barrelled, ivory-handled, business-like weapons, provided with miniature ramrods. The velvet-lined

260

interior of the case was divided into various compart-
ments, two for the pistols, one for powder-flask, one for
bullets, one for percussion-caps, and one for wads.   In
his dull, automatic way, his mind whirling madly in
other spheres, he cleaned the pistols, shook the powder-
flask to make certain that powder was still there—he
loved to pour out a few grains into his hand and show
the powder that had remained in the flask for generations, ever since the pistols were last used—counted
the caps, which he had counted many times before,
looked stupidly into the one empty compartment, only
to remember that there never had been any wads, and,
finally, grasping one of the pistols, took aim at a bulb
on his writing-desk at the end of the room.

He had been tricked, and robbed, and mocked.   He
could see the scene when she had told Austin.   He
could hear Austin's pitiless laughter.   He could picture
her mimicking his rough speech.   He could picture
them, faithless, heartless, looking into each other's
eyes. . . . Suddenly he passed his hand over his forehead.   Was he going mad?   Hitherto he had heard
their voices in the dimness of imagination.   Now he
heard them loud in vibrating sound.   Was it real or
imaginary?   He drew deep, panting breaths.

" Dick's not here," said Viviette's voice from the
terrace.   " He has forgotten."

" Really, my dear, I don't very much care," Austin
replied.   " Where you are, I am happy."

" I wish that telegram would come.   It's quite
time.   Don't you think we had better tell Dick to-
day ? "

" No, no.   To-morrow."

" After all, what is the good of hiding it from
him ? "

A laugh from Austin. "You think we ought to put him out of his misery at once?"

It was real! Those two were talking in flesh and blood on the terrace. They were talking of him. His misery! That had but one meaning. And the devil laughed! Unconsciously his grip tightened on the butt of the pistol. He listened.

"Yes," said Viviette. "It would be kinder."

"I stick to the birthday idea. It would be more dramatic."

"The damned villain!" Dick muttered.

"I want to-day," said Viviette.

"And I want to-morrow."

"You speak as if you were my lord and master," said Viviette, in the mocking tones Dick knew so well.

"No other man shall be if I can help it."

The clear, young masterful voice rang down the gallery. Dick slid his chair noiselessly to the side of the screen which hid him from the terrace-window, and, bending down low, peered round the edge. He saw them laughing, flushed, silhouetted against the distant trees. Austin was looking at her with the light of passion in his eyes. She looked up at him, radiant, elusive, triumphant, with parted lips.

"Please to remember we were talking of Dick."

"Confound Dick! In this he doesn't count. I matter. And I'll show you."

He showed her in the one and only way. She struggled for a second in his arms, and received his kiss with a little laugh. They had moved to the far lintel of the door. Dick's world reeled red before his eyes. He stood up and held the pistol pointed. Damn him! Damn him! He would kill him. Kill him like a dog.

Some reflex motion of the brain prompted action. Feverishly he rammed a charge of powder down the pistol. Wads ? A bit of the newspaper lying on the floor. Then a bullet. Then a wad rammed home. Then the cap. It was done at lightning speed. Murder, red, horrible murder blazed in his soul. Damn him ! He would kill him. He started into the middle of the room, just as they walked away, and he sprang to the door and levelled the pistol.

Then reaction came. No. Not like a dog. He couldn't shoot his brother like a dog. His arm fell helplessly at his side. He turned back again into the room, staggering and knocking himself against the cases by the walls, like a drunken man. The sweat rolled down his face. He put the pistol beside the other on the table. For some moments he stood a hulking statue, shaken as though stricken with earthquake, white-faced, white-lipped, staring, with crossed, blue eyes, at nothing. At last he recovered power of motion, drank another whisky, and replaced bottle, syphon, and glass in the cupboard.

He found himself suddenly clear-headed, able to think. He was not in the least degree drunk. To test himself he took up a sword from the table, and, getting the right spot, balanced it on his finger. He could speak, too, as well as anybody. He turned to a long Moorish musket inlaid with gems and mother-of-pearl, and began to describe it. He was quite fluent and sensible, although his voice sounded remote in his own ears. He was satisfied. He had his nerves under control. He would go through the next hour without anyone suspecting the madness that was in his mind. He was absolutely sober and self-collected. He walked along a seam of the matting that ran the whole length of the gallery, and did not deviate from it one hair's-breadth. Now he was ready. Perfectly prepared to deliver his lecture. He sat down and picked up the newspaper, and the print was clear. "The weather still continues to be fine over the British Islands. The anti-cyclone has not yet passed away from the Bay of Biscay. . . ." He read the jargon through to the end. But it seemed as if it were not he who was reading, but some one else—a quiet, placid gentleman, deeply versed in the harmless science of meteorology. Where his real self was he did not know, so he toyed with the illusion.

A voice broke on his ear, coming, it seemed, from another world.

"Dick, may we come in ?"

He rose, saw Katherine, Austin, and Viviette on the threshold. He invited them to enter, and shook Katherine by the hand, as if he had not met her for a long time.

Viviette danced down to the table. "Now, Dick, we're all here. Put on your most learned and anti-quarian manner. Ladies and gentlemen, I call on Mr. Richard Ware to deliver his interesting lecture on the ingenious instruments men have devised for butchering each other."

Dick put his hand to his head in a confused way. His real self was beginning to merge itself into that of the quiet gentleman, and there was a curious red mist before his eyes.

"Come on," cried Viviette. "Look at Katherine. Her mouth is watering for tales of bloodshed."

Dick could not remember his usual starting-point. He stared stupidly at the table for a moment ; then picked up a weapon at random, and made a great effort.

"This is a Toledo sixteenth-century sword—reported to have belonged to Cosmo de Medici. You see here the '*palle*,' the Medici emblem. The one next to it is a sword of the same period, only used by a meaner person. I should prefer it, if there were any killing to be done."

He described one or two other weapons. Then, glancing over his shoulder at Austin and Viviette, who were talking in low, confidential tones a little way off, he stood stock-still, and the beads of sweat gathered on his forehead. Katherine's voice recalled his wandering wits.

"This is a cross-bow, isn't it? The thing the Ancient Mariner shot the albatross with."

"A cross-bow," said Dick. "The iron loop at the end was to put one's foot into when one wanted to load it."

"And this," said Katherine, pointing to a long steel thing with a great knob adorned with cruel spikes, "is the family mace, I suppose. I've seen it before, I remember."

"Yes, that's the mace."

"What a bloodthirsty set of people you must have been!"

Austin came up with a laugh. "There's a legend among us that once mother was left alone in the house and insisted on having this mace near her bed so as to defend herself against burglars. But why do you leave me to tell the story, Dick?"

Dick clenched his fists, and, muttering something, turned and ascended the gallery above the screen. Viviette followed him.

"You're not doing it at all nicely. I don't think you want to."

265

"Can you wonder at that ? " he said hoarse y.

Viviette played deliciously with the fire.

"Why, aren't we intelligent enough for you ? " she asked with childish innocence.

"You know what I mean."

"I haven't the faintest idea. All I know is that you may as well be polite, at any rate."

He laughed. Ordinarily he had little sense of humour ; but now he had flames in his heart and hell in his throat, and red mist before his eyes.

"Oh, I'll be polite," he growled. "By God, I'll be polite ! One may be suffering the tortures of the damned, but one must smirk and be polite ! "

He snatched up the first thing to hand, a helmet that stood on a case, and brought it down below the screen.

"Katherine, Viviette says I'm not delivering my lecture properly. I beg your pardon. I'm rather shy at first, but I get warmed up to my subject. What would you like to hear about ? "

Katherine exchanged a glance with Austin.

"Don't you think we might put off the rest till another day ? "

"Yes, old chap. Put it off till to-morrow. It's your birthday, you know."

"Birthday ? What's that got to do with it ? Who knows what may happen between then and now ? No —no. I'm all right," he cried wildly. "You're here, and you've got to listen. I'll get into fine form presently. Look ! " he said, pointing to the helmet he was holding. "Here is a Cromwellian morion. It was picked up by an ancestor at Naseby. It has a clean cut in it. That's where an honest gentleman's sword found its way into the knave's skull—the puritanical, priggish, canting knave."

He threw the helmet with a clatter on to the table as if it had been the knave's canting head. He caught up a weapon.

"This is a partisan. All you had to do when you got it inside a man was to turn it round a bit, and the wound gaped and tore. This tassel is for catching the blood and preventing it from greasing the handle. Here's a beauty," he went on, taking a sword from the row he had laid out for display, and holding it out for Katherine's inspection. "One of the pets of the collection. A French duelling sword of the middle of the eighteenth century." He gave a fencer's flourish. "Responsive to the hilts, eh? Ah! It must have been good to live in those days, when you could whip this from your side at a wrong done and have the life of the man that wronged you. The sweet morning air, the patch of green turf, shoes off—in shirt and breeches —with the eyes of the man you hate in front of you, and this glittering, beautiful, snaky thing thirsting for his heart's blood. And then——"—he stood in tierce, left hand curved, holding in tense fierceness the eyes of an imaginary opponent—" and then a little clitter-clatter of steel, and, suddenly—ha!—the blade disappears up to the hilt, and a great red stain comes on the shirt, and the man throws up his arms, and falls, and you've killed him. He's dead! dead! dead! Ha! what a time to live in!"

Katherine uttered a little cry of fear, and grew pale. Viviette clapped her hands.

"Bravo, Dick!"

"Bravo, Dick!" cried Austin. "Most dramatically done."

"I never knew you were such an actor," said Viviette.

267

Dick stood panting, his hand on the hilt of the sword, the point on the floor.

"I really do think I've had enough," said Katherine.

"No, not yet," he said in a thick voice. "I've not shown you half yet. I've something much more interesting."

"But, Dick——"

Viviette interrupted her. "You must stay. It's only beginning to be exciting. If you only do the rest as beautifully as you did that, Dick, I'll stay here all day."

Dick, with a curious outward calm, contrasting with the fury of his mock encounter, put down the sword and went to the end of the table, where the case of pistols lay.

"At any rate, I must show you," said he, "the famous duelling pistols."

"They were the very pistols in the duel between his great-grandfather and Lord Estcombe," said Viviette.

"They've not been used from that day—he killed Lord Estcombe, by the by—till this. The case is just as it was left. I was going to tell you the story yesterday."

"I remember," said Katherine, by way of civility. "But Mrs. Ware stopped you."

She was a mild-natured woman, and the realistic conjuring up of gore-dripping tassels and bloody shirts upset her, and she desired to get away. She also saw that Dick was abnormally excited, and suspected that he had been drinking. Her delicate senses shrank from drunkenness.

"You must tell the story," cried Viviette. "It's so romantic. You like romantic things, Katherine. The great-grandfather was a Dick Ware too—Wild

Dick Ware they used to call him. Go on, Dick."

Dick paused for a moment. He had a curious, dull, befogged sensation of being compelled to do things independently of volition. Presently he spoke.

"It happened in this very room, a hundred years ago. Lord Estcombe and my great-grandfather were friends—intimate friends from boyhood. Wild Dick Ware was madly in love with a girl who had more or less become engaged to him. Now, it came to his knowledge that Lord Estcombe had been using black-guard means to win away the girl's affections. And one day they were here "—he moved a pace or two to one side—"just as Austin and I are now. And the girl over there——"

Viviette, with a gay laugh, took up her position on the spot to which he pointed.

"Just in this identical place. I know the story—it's lovely ! "

"An old Peninsula comrade of Wild Dick Ware's was here too—a man called Hawkins——"

"Katherine shall be Hawkins," cried Viviette.

"And in his presence," Dick continued, "Wild Dick Ware told the girl that he was mad for love of her, but that he would not force her choice ; yet one of those two, himself or Lord Estcombe, she must choose, for good and all. She could not speak for shame or confusion. He said, 'Throw your handkerchief to whichever of us you love.' And they stood side by side—like this "—he ranged himself by Austin's side—"opposite the girl."

"And she threw the handkerchief ! " cried Viviette.

"Throw yours ! " said Dick. He looked at her with fierce intensity beneath rugged brows ; Austin with laughing challenge. She knew that she was the object of each man's desire, and her sex's triumph thrilled through her from head to foot. She knew that this jesting choice would have serious import. For some seconds the three remained stock-still. She glanced flutteringly from one man to the other. Which should she choose? Her heart beat wildly. Choose one or the other she must. Outside that room no man lived whom she would marry. Each second strained the situation further. At last her spirit rose in feminine revolt against the trap which Dick had set for her, and, with a malicious look, she threw the handkerchief at Austin's feet. He picked it up and gallantly put it to his lips.

"In the story," exclaimed Viviette, "she threw it to Lord Estcombe. Austin is Lord Estcombe."

"And I'm Dick Ware," cried Dick, in a strangled voice. "Wild Dick Ware. And this is what he did. He dragged the girl out of the room first."

He took Viviette by the arm and roughly thrust her past the screen.

"Then—that case was on the table. And without a word Wild Dick Ware comes up to Lord Estcombe so—and says, 'Choose.'"

He gripped the pistols by the barrels, crossed them, and presented the butts to Austin. Austin waved them away with a deprecatory gesture and a smile.

"Really, old man, I can't enter into the spirit of it, like that. You're splendid. But if I took a hand, it would be tomfoolery."

"Oh, do, do," cried Viviette. "Let us go through with it and see just how the duel was fought. It will be thrilling. You'll have to fall dead like Lord Estcombe, and I'll burst into the room and tear my hair over your poor corpse. Do, Austin, for my sake."

270

He yielded. Any foolishness for her sake. He took a pistol.

" You'll have to be Major Hawkins, Katherine," he said lightly, as if inviting her to condescend to some child's game.

But Katherine put her hands before her face and shrank back. "No, no, no. I couldn't. I don't like it."

" Then I'll be Major Hawkins," said Viviette.

" You will ? " Dick laughed harshly. " Then be it so."

" I know just what they did."

She placed the men back to back, so that Austin faced the farther end of the room and Dick the open French window. They were to take three paces, count one, two, three, and, at the end of the third pace, they were to turn and fire.

Dick felt the touch of Austin's shoulder against his, and the flame at his heart grew fiercer and the hell in his throat more burning, and the universe whirled round in a red mist. Viviette moved to the weapon-laden table.

" Now. One—two—three ! "

They paced and turned. Dick levelled his pistol instantly at Austin, with murderous hate in his eyes, and drew the trigger. The pistol clicked harmlessly. Austin, self-conscious, did not raise his pistol. But Dick, broadening his chest, glared at him and shouted, wildly, madly :

" Fire, damn you ! Fire ! Why the hell don't you fire ? "

The cry was real, vibrant with fury and despair. Austin looked at him for an amazed moment ; then, throwing his pistol on one of the arm-chairs, he came up to him.

"What fool's game are you playing, Dick? Are you drunk?"

Katherine, with a low cry, flung herself between them, and, clinging to Dick's arm, took the pistol from his hand.

"No more of this—no more. The duel has been too much like reality already."

Dick staggered to a straight-backed chair by the wall, and, sitting down, wiped his forehead. He had grown deadly white. The flames had been suddenly quenched within him, and he felt cold and sick. Viviette, in alarm, ran to his side. What was the matter? Was he faint? Let her take him into the fresh air. Austin came up. But at his approach Dick rose and shrank away, glancing at him furtively out of bloodshot eyes.

"Yes. The heat has oppressed me. I'm not well. I'll go out."

He stumbled blindly towards the French window. Viviette followed him, but he turned on her rudely and thrust her back.

"I'm not well, I tell you. I don't want your help. Let me alone."

He passed through the French window on to the terrace. The sky had clouded over, and a drizzle had begun to fall.

Viviette felt curiously frightened, but she put on an air of bravado as she came down the gallery.

"Have you all been rehearsing this little comedy?"

No mirthful response lit either face. She read condemnation in both pairs of eyes. For the first time in her life she felt daunted, humiliated. She knew nothing more beyond the fact that in deliberate coquetry she had pitted brother against brother, and that something cruel and tragical had happened for which she was being judged. Neither spoke. She summoned her outer dignity, tossed her pretty head, and went out by the end door which Austin in cold politeness held open for her. Then she mounted to her bedroom, and, throwing herself on her bed, burst into a passion of meaningless weeping.

Katherine handed Austin the pistol which she had taken from Dick's hand.

"Now you'll believe what I told you."

"I believe it," said Austin gravely.

"That duel was not all play-acting."

"That," said he, "was absurd. Dick has been drinking. It was a silly farce. Viviette egged him on until he seemed to take it seriously."

"He did take it seriously, Austin. He's in a dangerous mood. If I were you I should be careful. Take a woman's warning."

He stood for a moment in deep thought, his gaze absently fixed on the weapon he held in his hand. Suddenly a glint of something strange caught his eye. He started, but recovered himself quickly.

"I'll take your warning, Katherine. Here's my hand upon it."

A moment later, when he was alone, he uncocked the pistol—Dick's pistol. The glint had not been imaginary. It was a percussion cap. With trembling fingers he picked it off the nipple. He passed his hand across his damp forehead, for he felt faint with dread. But the task had to be accomplished. He unscrewed the ramrod and picked out the wad, a piece of white paper, which dropped on the floor. From the barrel held downward a bullet dropped with a dead, fateful thud on the floor. More paper wad—a slithering shower of gunpowder. He put the pistol down, and took up the one he himself had used from the chair where he had thrown it. It was unloaded. His eye fell on the bits of white paper. He picked them up and unfolded them. The daily newspaper lay by the stove, with the corner torn accusingly.

Then he understood. He sank into a chair, paralysed with horror. It was Dick's pistol that was loaded. Dick had meant to murder him. By the grace of God the pistol had missed fire. But Dick, his own brother, had meant to murder him. An hour later he walked out of the room, the case of pistols under his arm, with the drawn face of an old man.

It was not until Dick had stumbled five or six miles through the drenching downpour that the thought reached his dulled brain that he had left the pistols loose for anyone to examine. The thought was like a great stone hitting him on the side of the head. He turned and began to run homewards, like a hunted man in desperate flight.

v

Viviette, having repaired the disorder caused by her tears, went down to tea. Mrs. Ware, Katherine, and a curate deliberately calling or taking shelter from the rain, were in the drawing-room. Austin, to his mother's mild astonishment, had sent down a message to the effect that he was busy. On ordinary occasions Viviette would have flirted monstrously with the clerical youth, and sent him away undecided whether to offer to share his lodgings and hundred pounds a year with her, or to turn Catholic and become a monk. But now she had no mind to flirtation. She left him to the undisturbing wiles of Mrs. Ware, and petted and surreptitiously fed Dick's Irish terrier, whose brown eyes looked pathetic inquiry as to his master's whereabouts. She was sobered by the uncomprehended scene in the armoury—sobered by Dick's violence and by Austin's final coldness. A choice had been put before her in deadly earnest ; she had refused to make one. But the choice would have to be made very soon, unless she sent both her lovers packing, a step which she did not for a moment contemplate.

"You must promise to marry one or the other and end this tension," said Katherine, a little later, after the curate had gone with Mrs. Ware to look at her greenhouses.

"I wish to goodness I could marry them both," said Viviette. "Have a month with each, turn and turn about. It would be ideal."

"It would be altogether horrid !" exclaimed Katherine. "How could such a thought enter your head ?"

"I suppose it must have entered every woman's head who has two men she's fond of in love with her at once. I said yesterday that it was great fun being a woman. I find it's a d.d.d.d. imposition !"

"For heaven's sake, child, make up your mind quickly," said Katherine.

Viviette sighed. Which should it be ? Dick, with his great love and rough tenderness and big, protecting arms, or Austin with his conquering ways, his wit, his charm, his perception ? Austin could give her the luxury that her sensuous nature delighted in, social position, the brilliant life of London. What could Dick give her ? It would always be a joy to dress herself for Austin. Dick would be content if she went about in raiment made of dusters and bath towels. In return, what could she give each of these men ? She put the question to herself. She was not mercenary or heartless. She gave of herself freely and loved the giving. What could she give to Austin ? What could she give to Dick ? These questions, in her sober mood, weighed the others down.

When the rain ceased and a pale sun had dried the gravel, she went out into the grounds by herself and faced the problem. She sighed again—many times. If only they would let her have her fun out and give her answer six months hence !

Her meditations were cut short by the arrival of a telegraph boy on his bicycle at the front gate. He gave her the telegram. It was for Austin. Her heart beat. She went into the house with the yellow envelope containing Dick's destiny and mounted to the little room off the first landing which had been Austin's private study since his boyhood. She knocked. Austin's voice bade her enter. He rose from the desk where, pen in hand, he had been sitting before a blank sheet of paper, and without a word took the telegram. She noticed with a shock that he had curiously changed. The quick, brisk manner had gone. His face was grey.

"It is *the* telegram, isn't it ? " she asked eagerly.

"Yes," said he, handing it to her. "It's from Lord Overton."

She read : "The very man. Send him along to me early to-morrow. Hope he can start immediately."

"Oh, how splendid ! " she exclaimed with a little gasp of happiness. "How utterly splendid ! Thank heaven ! "

"Yes. Thank heaven," Austin acquiesced gravely. "I forgot to mention to you that Lord Overton knows Dick personally," he added, after a pause. "They met at my house the last time Dick was in London."

"This *is* good news," said Viviette. "At last I can give him a birthday present worth having."

"He will not be here for his birthday," said Austin, in cold, even tones. "He must catch the mail to-night."

Viviette echoed : "To-night ? "

" And in all probability he will sail for Vancouver in a day or two. It won't be worth his while to come back here."

She laid a hand on her heart, which fluttered painfully.

" Then—then—we'll never see him again ? "

" Probably not."

" I didn't think it would be so sudden," she said, a little wildly.

" Neither did I. But it's for the best."

" But supposing he wants some time to look about him ? "

" I'll see to everything," said Austin.

" Anyhow, I must be the first to tell him," said Viviette.

" You will do me a very great favour if you will let me have that privilege," said Austin. " I make a particular point of it. I have some serious business to discuss with him before dinner, and that will be the time for me to break the news."

He was no longer the fairy godmother's devoted and humble factotum. He spoke with a cold air of authority that chilled the fairy godmotherdom in Viviette's bosom. Her pretty little scheme dwindled into childishness before the dark, uncomprehended thing that had happened. She assented with unusual meekness.

" But I'm desperately disappointed," she said.

"My dear Viviette," he answered more kindly, and looking at her with some wistfulness, "the pleasures and even the joy of life have to give way to the sober, business side of existence. It isn't very gay, I know, but we can't alter it."

He held out his hand. Instinctively she gave him hers. He raised it to his lips and held the door open for her. She went out scarcely knowing that she had been dismissed. Austin closed the door, stood unsteadily for a moment like a man stricken with great pain, and then, sitting down at his desk again, put his elbows on the table, rested his head in his hands, and stared at the white piece of paper. When would Dick come home? He had given orders that Dick should be asked to go to him as soon as he arrived. Would Dick ever come home again? It was quite possible that some misfortune might have happened. Tragedy is apt to engender tragedy. He shuddered, hearing in his fancy the tramp of men, and seeing a shrouded thing they carried across the hall. He bitterly accused himself for not having sought Dick far and wide as soon as he had made his ghastly discovery. But he had required time to recover his balance. The horrible suddenness had stunned him. Attempted fratricide is not a common happening in gentle families. He had to accustom himself to the atmosphere of the abnormal, so as to state the psychological case in its numberless ramifications. This he had done. His head was clear. His unalterable decision made. Now the minutes dragged with leaden feet until Dick should come.

Viviette was the first to see him. She had dressed early for dinner, and, as the late June afternoon had turned out fine, was taking her problem out to air on the terrace when she came upon him standing at the

278

door of his armoury. His hair was wet and matted, his eyes bloodshot, his clothes dripping, and he himself splashed with mud from head to foot. He trembled all over, shaken by a great terror. The case of pistols had gone. Who had taken them ? Had the loaded pistol been discovered ?

As Viviette appeared, robed in deep blue chiffon that seemed torn from the deep blue evening sky, and looking, in the man's maddened eyes, magically beautiful, he held out imploring hands.

"Come in for a moment. For the love of God come in for a moment."

He stepped back invitingly. She hesitated for a second on the threshold, and then followed him down the dim gallery, past the screen where all the swords and helmets lay scattered on the table. He looked at her haggardly, and she met his gaze with kind eyes in which there was no mockery. No. Nothing had happened, he told himself ; otherwise she would shrink from him as from something accursed.

"My God, if you knew how I love you !" he said hoarsely. "My God, if you only knew !"

His suffering racked her heart. All her pity melted over him. She laid her caressing fingers on his arm.

"Oh, my poor Dick !" she said.

The touch, the choke in her voice, brought about Viviette's downfall. Perhaps she meant it to do so. Who can tell ? What woman ever knows ? In a flash his arms were around her and his kisses, a wild, primitive man's kisses, were on her lips, her eyes, her cheeks. Her face was crushed against the rough wet tweed of his coat, and its odour, raw and coarse, was in her nostrils. She drooped, intoxicated, gasping for breath in his unheeding giant's grip, but she made no effort to escape. As he held her a thrill, agonizing and delicious, swept through her, and she raised her lips involuntarily to his and closed her eyes. At last he released her, mangled, tousled, her very self a draggled piece of chiffon like the night-blue frock, soiled with wet and mud.

"Forgive me," he said, "I had no right. Least of all now. God knows what is to become of me. But whatever happens, you know that I love you."

She had her hands clasped before her face. She could not look at him.

"Yes, I know," she murmured.

In another moment he had gone, leaving Viviette, who had entered the room a girl, transformed into a woman with the first shiver of passion in her veins.

Dick, vaguely conscious of damp and dirt, went up to his bedroom. The sight of his evening things spread out on the bed reminded him that it was nearly dinner-time. Mechanically he washed and dressed. As he was buckling on his ready-made white tie—his clumsy fingers, in spite of many lessons from Viviette, had never learned the trick of tying a bow—a maid brought him a message. Mr. Austin's compliments and would he see Mr. Austin for a few moments in Mr. Austin's room. The words were like the dreaded tap on the shoulder of the hunted criminal.

"I'll come at once," he said.

He found Austin sitting on the chair by his desk, resting his chin on his elbow. He did not stir as Dick entered.

"You want to speak to me?"

"Yes," said Austin. "Will you sit down?"

"I'll stand," said Dick impatiently. "What have you to say to me?"

"I believe you have expressed your desire to leave England and earn your living in a new country. Is that so?"

The brothers' eyes met. Dick saw that the loaded pistol had been discovered, and read no love, no pity, only condemnation in the hard gaze. Austin was pronouncing sentence.

"Yes," he replied sullenly.

"I happen," said Austin, "to know of an excellent opportunity. Lord Overton, whom you have met, wants a man to take charge of his timber forests in Vancouver. The salary is £700 a year. I wired to Lord Overton asking for the appointment on your behalf. This is his answer."

Dick took the telegram and read it with muddled head. Austin had lost no time.

"You see, it fits in admirably. You can start by the night mail. Your sudden departure needs no other explanation to the household than this telegram. I hope you understand."

"I understand," said Dick bitterly. A sudden memory of words that Viviette had used the day before occurred to him. "I understand. This is to get me out of the way. 'David put Uriah in the forefront of the battle.' Vancouver is the forefront."

"Don't you think we had better avoid all unprofitable discussion?" Austin rose and confronted him. "I expect you to accept this offer and my conditions."

"And if I refuse?" asked Dick, with rising anger. "What dare you threaten me with?"

Austin raised a deprecatory hand.

"Do you suppose I'm going to threaten you? I simply expect you not to refuse. Your conscience must tell you that I have the right to do so. Doesn't it?"

Dick glowered sullenly at the wall and tugged his great moustache.

"You force me to touch on things I should have liked to keep hidden," said Austin. "Very well." He took a scrap of crumpled paper from the desk. "Do you recognize this? It formed the wad of the pistol that was in your hand."

Dick started back a pace. "You're wrong," he gasped. "It was *your* pistol that was loaded."

"No. Yours. The cap missed fire, or I should have been a dead man—murdered by my brother."

"Stop," cried Dick. "Not murdered. No, no, not murdered. It was in fair fight. I gave you the choice. When I thought I had the unloaded one I called on you to fire. Why the devil didn't you? I wanted you to fire. I was mad for you to fire. I wanted to be killed there and then. No one can say I shirked it. I gave you your chance."

"That's nothing to do with it," said Austin sternly. "When you fired you meant murder. Your face meant killing. And supposing I had fired—and killed you! Good God! I would sooner you had killed me than burdened my soul with your death. It would have been less cowardly. Yes, cowardly. The conditions were not even. To me it was trivial fooling. To you, deadly earnest. Are you not man enough to see that I have the right to exact some penalty?"

Dick remained silent for a few moments, while the powers of light and darkness struggled together in his soul. At last he said in a low voice, hanging his head:

"I'll accept your terms."

"You leave by the night mail for Witherby."

"Very well."

"There's another point," said Austin. "The most

important point of all. You will not speak alone to Viviette before you start."

Dick turned with an angry flash.

"What ? "

"You will not speak to Viviette alone. When you are gone—for there is no need for you to come back here before you sail—you will not write to her. You will go absolutely and utterly out of her life."

Dick broke into harsh, furious laughter.

"And leave her to you ? I might have known that the lawyer would have had me in the trap. But this time you've overreached yourself. I'll never give her up. Do you hear me ? Never—never—never ! I would go through the horror of to-day a thousand times—day by day until I die, rather than give her up to you. You shall not take this last thing from me— this hope of winning her—as you have taken every- thing else. You have supplanted me since first you learned to speak. It has been Esau and Jacob——"

"Or Cain and Abel," said Austin.

"You can taunt me if you like," cried Dick, goaded to fury, and the whole bitterness of a lifetime surging up in passionate speech. "I have got past feeling it. Your life has been one continual taunt of me. You have thought me a dull, good-natured boor, delighted to have a word thrown at him now and again by the elegant gentleman, and rather honoured than other- wise to be ridden over roughshod, or kicked into the mud when it pleased the elegant gentleman to ride by. No, listen to me," he thundered, as Austin was about to protest. "By God, you shall listen this time. You've made me your butt, your fool, your sort of tame handy-man. I've wondered sometimes why you haven't addressed me as ' my good fellow,' and asked

283

me to touch my cap to you. I've borne it all these years without complaining—but do you know what it is to eat your heart out and remain silent? I have borne it for my mother's sake—in spite of her dislike of me—and for your sake, because I loved you. Yes. If ever one man has loved another I've loved you. But you took no heed. What was my affection worth? I was only the good, stupid ass . . . but I suffered it all till you came between me and her. I had spent the whole passion of my life upon her. She was the only thing left in the world for which I felt fiercely. I hungered for her, thirsted for her, my brain throbbed at the thought of her, the blood rushed through my veins at the sight of her. And you came between us. And if I have damned my soul, by God! the damnation is your doing. Do you think, while I live, that I'll give her up to you? I'll get my soul's worth, anyhow."

He smote his palm with his clenched fist and strode about the little room. Austin sat for a while dumb with astonishment and dismay. His cherished, lifelong conception of "dear old Dick" lay shattered. A new Dick appeared to him, a personality stronger, deeper than he could have imagined. A new respect for him, also a new pity that was generous and not contemptuous, crept into his heart.

"Listen, Dick," said he, using the familiar name for the first time. "Do I understand that you accuse me of sending you out to Vancouver and hastening your departure so as to gain my own ends with Viviette?"

"Yes," returned Dick. "I do. You have laid this trap for me."

"Have you ever heard me lie to you?"

"No," said Dick.

"Then I tell you, as man to man, that until this afternoon I had no suspicion that your feelings towards Viviette were deeper than those of an elder brother."

Dick laughed bitterly. "You couldn't conceive a clod like me falling in love. Well?"

"That's beside the question," said Austin. "I did not behave dishonourably towards you. I came down. I fell in love with Viviette. How could I help it? How could I help loving her? How could I help telling her so? But she is young and innocent, and her heart is her own yet. Tell me—man to man—dare you say that you have won it or that I have won it?"

"What's the good of talking?" said Dick, relapsing into his sullen mood. "If I go she is yours. But I won't go."

Austin rose again and laid his hand on his brother's arm.

"Dick. If I give her up, will you obey my conditions?"

"You give her up voluntarily? Why should you?"

"A damnable thing was done this afternoon," said Austin. "I see I had my share in it, and I as well as you have to make reparation. Man alive! You are my brother," he cried with an outburst of feeling. "The nearest thing in the world to me. Do you think I could rest happy with the knowledge that a murderous devil is always in your heart, and that it's in my power to—to exorcise it? Do you think the cost matters? Come. Shall we make this bargain? Yes or no?"

"It's easy for you to promise," said Dick. "But when I am gone, how can you resist?"

Austin hesitated for a moment, biting his lips. Then,

with the air of a man who makes an irrevocable step in life, he crossed the room and rang the bell.

"Ask Mrs. Holroyd if she will have the kindness to come here for a minute," he said to the servant.

Dick regarded him wonderingly. "What has Mrs. Holroyd to do with our affairs?"

"You'll see," said Austin, and there was silence between them till Katherine came.

She looked from one joyless face to the other, and sat without a word on the chair that Austin placed for her. Her woman's intuition divined a sequel to the afternoon's drama. Some of it she had already learned. For, going earlier into Viviette's room, she had found her white and shaken, still disordered in hair and dress as Dick had left her; and Viviette had sobbed on her bosom and told her with some incoherence that the monkey had at last hit the lyddite shell in the wrong place, and that it was all over with the monkey. So, before Austin spoke, she half divined why he had summoned her.

Her heart throbbed painfully.

"Dick and I," said Austin, "have been talking of serious matters, and we need your help."

She smiled wanly. "I'll do whatever I can, Austin."

"You said this afternoon you would do anything I asked you. Do you remember?"

"Yes, I said so—and I meant it."

"You said it in reply to my question whether you would accept me if I asked you to marry me."

Dick started from the sullen stupor into which he had fallen and listened with perplexed interest.

"You are not quite right in your tenses, Austin," she remarked. "You said: Would I have accepted you if you had asked me?"

286

"I want to change the tense into the present," he replied.

She met his glance calmly. "You ask me to marry you in spite of what you told me this afternoon?"

"In spite of it and because of it," he said, drawing up a chair near to her. "A great crisis has arisen in our lives that must make you forget other words I spoke this afternoon. Those other words and everything connected with them I blot out of my memory for ever. I want you to do me an infinite service. If there had been no deep affection between us I should not dare to ask you. I want you to be my wife, to take me into your keeping, to trust me as an upright man to devote my life to your happiness. I swear I'll never give you a moment's cause for regret."

She plucked for a while at her gown. It was a strange wooing. But in her sweet way she had given him her woman's aftermath of love. It was a gentle, mellow gift, far removed from the summer blaze of passion, and it had suffered little harm from the sadness of the day. She saw that he was in great stress. She knew him to be a loyal gentleman.

"Is this the result of that scene in the armoury?" she asked quietly.

"Yes," said Austin.

"I was right then. It was a matter of life and death."

"It was," said he. "So is this."

She looked again from one face to the other, rose, hesitated for a moment—and then held out her hand. "I am willing to trust you, Austin," she said.

He touched her hand with his lips and said gravely: "I will not fail your trust."

As soon as she had gone he went to the chair where
Dick sat in gloomy remorse and laid a hand on his
shoulder.

"Well?" said he.

"I agree," Dick groaned, without looking up. "I
have no alternative. I appreciate your generosity."

Then Austin spoke of the appointment in Vancouver.
He explained how the idea had occurred to him; how
Viviette had come late the night before to tell him of
what he had never before suspected—Dick's desire to
go abroad; how they had conspired to give him a
birthday surprise; how they had driven over to
Witherby to send the telegram to Lord Overton. And
as he spoke, Dick looked at him with a new ghastli-
ness on his face.

"This afternoon—in the dining-room—when you
said that Viviette had told you everything——?"

"About your wish to go to the Colonies. What
else?"

"And what I overheard in the armoury—about a
telegram—telling me—putting me out of my misery?"

"Only whether we should tell you to-night or to-
morrow about the appointment. Dick—Dick," said
Austin, deeply moved by the great fellow's collapse,
"if I have wronged you all these years, it was through
want of insight, not want of affection. If I have
taunted you, as you say, it was merely a lifelong habit
of jesting which you never seemed to resent. I was
unconscious of hurting you. For my blindness and
carelessness I beg your forgiveness. With regard to
Viviette—I ought to have seen, but I didn't. I don't
say you had no cause for jealousy—but as God hears
me—all the little conspiracy to-day was lovingly meant
—all to give you pleasure. I swear it."

Dick rose and stumbled about the among furniture. The setting sun fell just below the top of the casement window, and its direct rays flooded the little room and showed Dick in a strange, unearthly light.

" I wronged you," he said bitterly. " Even in my passions I'm a dull fool. I thought you a damned cad, and I got more and more furious, and I drank —I was drunk all this afternoon—and madness came, and when I saw you kiss her—yes, I saw you, I was peeping from behind the screen—the things went red before my eyes, and it was then that I loaded the pistol to shoot you on the spot. God forgive me ! May God have mercy upon me."

He leant his arms on the sill and buried his face.

" I can't ask your forgiveness," he went on, after a moment. " It would be a mockery." He laughed mirthlessly. " How can I say, ' I'm sorry I meant to murder you—please don't think anything about it' ? " He turned with a fierce gesture. " Oh, you must take it all as said, man ! Now, have you finished with me ? I can't stand it much longer. I agree to all your terms. I'll drive over to Witherby now and wait for the train —and you'll be free of me."

He turned again and moodily looked out of the window in the full flood of the sunset.

" We must play the game, Dick," said Austin gently, " and go through the horrible farce of dinner—for mother's sake."

Dick heard him vaguely. Below, on the terrace, Viviette was walking, and she filled his universe. She had changed the bedraggled frock for the green one she had worn the night before. Presently she raised her eyes and saw him leaning out of the window.

" Have they told you that dinner is not till a quarter

289

past eight ? " she cried, looking deliciously upwards, with a dainty hand to her cheek. " Lord Banstead sent a message to mother that he was unexpectedly detained, and mother has put back dinner. Isn't it impudence ? "

But Dick was far too crushed with misery to respond. He nodded dejectedly. She remained staring up at him for a while and then ran into the house.

Dick listlessly mentioned the postponement of dinner.

" I'm sorry I asked the little brute, but I couldn't avoid it."

" What does it matter ? " said Austin. He was silent for a moment. Then he came close to Dick.

" Dick," said he. " Let us end this awful scene as friends and brothers. As Heaven hears me there is no bitterness in my heart. Only deep sorrow—and love, Dick. Shake hands."

Dick took his hand and broke down utterly, and said such things of himself as other men do not like to hear. Presently there was a light rap of knuckles at the door. Austin opened it and beheld Viviette.

" I won't disturb you," she said. " I only want to give this note to Dick."

" I will hand it to him," said Austin.

She thanked him and departed. He closed the door and gave Dick the note. Dick opened it, read, and with a great cry of " Viviette ! " rushed to the door. Austin interposed, grasped him by the wrist :

" What are you doing ? "

" I'm going to her," shouted Dick wildly, wrenching himself free. " Read this." He held up the note before Austin's eyes, with shaking fingers. Austin read :

"I can't bear to see the misery on your face, when I can make you happy. I love you, dear, better than anything on earth. I know it now, and I'll go out with you to Vancouver."

"She loves me. She'll marry me. She'll go out to Vancouver!" cried Dick. "It changes everything. I must go to her."

"You shall not go," said Austin.

"Shall not? Who dares prevent me?"

"I do. I hold you to your word."

"But, man alive! she loves me—don't you see? The bargain is dissolved. This is none of my seeking. She comes of her own free will. I am going to her."

Austin put both his hands affectionately on the big man's shoulders and forced him into a chair.

"Listen to me just for one minute, Dick. Dick, you dare not marry. Don't drive me to tell you the reason. Can't you see for yourself why I've imposed this condition on you all along?"

"I know no reason," said Dick. "She loves me, and that is enough."

The greyness deepened over Austin's face and the pain in his eyes.

"I must speak, then, in plain terms. That horrible murder impulse is the reason. To-day, in a fit of frenzied jealousy, you would have killed me, your brother. Is there any guarantee that, in another fit of frenzied jealousy, you might not——?"

A shudder ran through Dick's great frame. He stretched out his hand. "For God's sake—don't."

"I must—until you see this ghastly business in its true aspect. Look at the lighter side of Viviette's character. She is gay, fond of admiration, childishly fond of teasing, a bright creature of bewildering moods. Would she be safe in your hands ? Might you not one day again see things red before your eyes and again go mad ? ''

" Don't say any more," Dick said in a choking voice. " I can't stand it."

" Heaven knows, I didn't want to say as much."

Dick shuddered again. " Yes, you are right. I am a man with a curse. I can't marry her. I daren't."

VI

Presently Dick raised the face of Cain when he told the Lord that his punishment was greater than he could bear. Tears leaped to Austin's eyes, but he turned his head away lest Dick should see them. He would have given years of his life to spare Dick—everything he had in the world—save his deep convictions of right and wrong. He was responsible for Viviette. That risk of horror he could not let her run. He had hoped, with a great agony of hope, that Dick would have seen it for himself. To formulate it had been torture. But he could not weaken. The barrier between Dick and Viviette was not of his making. It was composed of the grim psychological laws that govern the abnormal. To have disregarded it would have been a crime from which his soul shrank. All the despair in Dick's face, though it wrung his heart, could not move him. It was terrible to be chosen in this way to be the arbiter of Destiny. But there was the decree, written in letters of blood and flame. And Dick had bowed to it.

" What's to become of her ? " he groaned.

" This will be her home, as it always has been," said Austin.

" I don't mean that—but between us we shall break her heart. She has given it to me just in time for me to do it. My luck ! "

Austin tried to comfort him. A girl's heart was not easily broken. Her pride would suffer most. Pain was inevitable. But Time healed many wounds. In this uncertain world nothing was ever so good as we hoped, and nothing ever so bad as we feared. Dick paid little heed to the platitudes.

" She must be told."

" Not what happened this afternoon," cried Austin quickly. " That we bury for ever from all human knowledge."

" Yes," said Dick, staring in front of him and speaking in a dull, even voice. " We must hide that. It's not a pretty thing to spread before a girl's eyes. It will be always before my own—until I die. But she must be told that I can't marry her. I can't ride away and leave her in doubt and wonder for ever and ever."

" Let us face this horrible night as best we can," said Austin. " Avoid seeing her alone. You'll be with mother or packing most of the evening. Slip away to Witherby an hour or so before your time. When you're gone I'll arrange matters. Leave it to me."

He made one of his old, self-confident gestures. But now Dick felt no resentment. His spirit in its deep abasement saw in Austin the better, wiser, stronger man.

At a quarter-past eight they went slowly downstairs to what promised to be a nightmare kind of meal. There would be four persons, Viviette, Katherine, and themselves, in a state of suppressed eruption, and two, Mrs. Ware and the unspeakable Banstead, complacently unaware of volcanic forces around them, who might by any chance word bring about disaster. There was danger, too—and the greatest—from Viviette, ignorant of Destiny. Austin dreaded the ordeal; but despair and remorse had benumbed Dick's faculties; he had passed the stage at which men fear. With his hand on the knob of the drawing-room door Austin paused and looked at him.

"Pull yourself together, man. Play your part. For God's sake, try to look cheerful."

Dick tried. Austin shivered.

"For God's sake, don't," he said.

They entered the drawing-room, expecting to find the three ladies, and possibly Lord Banstead, assembled for dinner. To Austin's discomfiture, Viviette was alone in the room. She rose, made a step or two to meet them, then stopped.

"What a pair of faces! One would think it were the eve of Dick's execution, and you were the hangman measuring him for the noose."

"Dick," said Austin, "is leaving us to-night—possibly for many years."

"I don't see that he is so very greatly to be pitied," said Viviette, trying in vain to meet Dick's eyes. She drew him a pace or two aside.

"Did you read my note—or did you tear it up like the other one?"

"I read it," he said, looking askance at the floor.

"Then why are you so woe-begone?"

He replied in a helpless way that he was not woe-begone. Viviette was puzzled, hurt, somewhat humiliated. She had made woman's great surrender which is usually followed by a flourish of trumpets very gratifying to hear. In fact, to most women the surrender is worth the flourish. But the recognition of this

surrender appeared to find its celebration in a funeral
march with muffled drums. A condemned man being
fitted for the noose, as she had suggested, a mute con-
scientiously mourning at his own funeral, a man who
had lost a stately demesne in Paradise and had been
ironically compensated by the gift of a bit of foreshore
of the Styx could not have worn a less joyous expression than he on whom she had conferred the boon of
his heart's desire.

"You're not only woe-begone," she said, with spirit,
"but you're utterly miserable. I think I have a right
to know the reason. Tell me, what is it?"

She tapped a small, impatient foot.

"We haven't told my mother yet," Austin explained,
"and Dick is rather nervous as to the way in which
she will take the news."

"Yes," said Dick, with lame huskiness. "It's on
mother's account."

Viviette laughed somewhat scornfully.

"I'm not a child, my dear Austin. No man wears
a face like that on account of his mother—least of all
when he meets the woman who has promised to be his
wife."

She flashed a challenging glance at Austin, but not
a muscle of his grey face responded. Her natural
expectations were baffled. There was no start of
amazement, no fierce movement of anger, no indignant
look of reproach. She was thrown back on herself.
She said:

"I don't think you quite understand. Dick had
two aims in life—one to obtain a colonial appointment,
the other—so he led me to suppose—to marry me.
He has the appointment, and I have promised to marry
him."

"I know," said Austin, "but you must make allowances."

"If that's all you can say on behalf of your client," retorted Viviette, "I rather wonder at your success as a barrister."

"Don't you think, my dear," said Austin gently, "that we are treading on delicate ground?"

"Delicate ground!" she scoffed. "We seem to have been treading on a volcano all the afternoon. I'm tired of it." She faced the two men with uplifted head. "I want an explanation."

"Of what?" Austin asked.

"Of Dick's attitude. What has he got to be miserable about? Tell me."

"But I'm not miserable, my dear Viviette," said poor Dick, vainly forcing a smile. "I'm really quite happy."

Her woman's intuition rejected the protest with contumely. All the afternoon he had been mad with jealousy of Austin. An hour ago he had whirled her out of her senses in savage passion. But a few minutes before she had promised him all a woman has to give. Now he met her with hang-dog visage, apologies from Austin, and milk-and-water asseveration of a lover's rapture. The most closely-folded rosebud miss of Early Victorian times could not have faced the situation without showing something of the Eve that lurked in the heart of the petals. So much the less could Viviette, child of a freer, franker day, hide her just indignation under the rose-leaves of maidenly modesty.

"Happy!" she echoed. "I've known you since I was a child of three. I know the meaning of every light and every shadow that passes over your face—

except this shadow now. What does it mean?"

She asked the question imperiously, no longer the elfin changeling, the fairy of bewildering moods of Austin's imagination, no longer the laughing coquette of Katherine's less picturesque fancy, but a modern young woman of character, considerably angered and very much in earnest. Austin bit his lip in perplexity. Dick looked around like a hunted animal seeking a bolting-hole.

" Dick is anxious," said Austin, at length, seeing that some explanation must be given, " that there should be no engagement between you before he goes out to Vancouver."

" Indeed?" said Viviette. " May I ask why? As this concerns Dick and myself, perhaps you will leave us alone for a moment so that Dick may tell me."

"No, no," Dick muttered hurriedly. "Don't leave us, Austin. We can't talk of such a thing now."

Again she tapped her foot impatiently.

"Yes, now. I'm going to hear the reason now, whatever it is."

The brothers exchanged glances. Dick turned to the window, and stared at the mellow evening sky.

Austin again was spokesman.

" Dick finds he has made a terrible and cruel mistake. One that concerns you intimately."

" Whatever Dick may have done with regard to me," replied Viviette, " I forgave him for it beforehand. When once I give a thing I don't take it back. I have given him my love and my promise."

" My dear," said Austin, gravely and kindly. " Here are two men who have loved you all your life. Don't think hardly of us. You must be brave and bear a great shock. Dick can't marry you."

297

She looked at him incredulously.

"Can't marry me? Why not?"

"It would be better not to ask."

She moved swiftly to Dick, and with her light touch swung him round to face the room.

"I don't understand. Is it because you're going out into the wilds? That doesn't matter. I told you I would go to Vancouver with you. I want to go. My happiness is with you."

Dick groaned. "Don't make it harder for me."

"What are you keeping from me?" she asked. "Is it anything you don't think fit for my ears? If so, speak. I'm no longer a child. Is there another woman in the case?"

She met Austin's eyes full. He said: "No, thank God! Nothing of that sort." And as her eyes did not waver, he made the bold stroke. "He finds that he doesn't love you as much as he thought. There's the whole tragedy in a few words."

She reeled back as if struck. "Dick doesn't love me?" Then the announcement seemed so grotesque in its improbability that she began to laugh, a trifle hysterically.

"Is this true?"

"It's quite true," said poor Dick.

"You see, my dear," said Austin, "what it costs him—what it costs us both—to tell you this."

"But I don't understand. I don't understand!" she cried, with sudden piteousness. "What did you mean, then—a little while ago—in the armoury?"

Austin, who did not see the allusion, had to allow Dick to speak for himself.

"I was drunk," said Dick desperately. "I've been

drinking heavily of late—and not accountable for my actions. I oughtn't to have done what I did."

"And so, you see," continued Austin, with some eagerness, "when he became confronted with the great change in his life—Vancouver—he looked at things soberly. He found that his feelings towards you were not of the order that would warrant his making you his wife."

Before Viviette could reply the door opened, and Mrs. Ware and Katherine entered the room.   Mrs. Ware, ignorant of tension, went smilingly to Austin, and, drawing down his shapely head with both hands, kissed him.

"My dear, dear boy, I'm so glad, so truly glad. Katherine has just told me."

"Told you what, mother?" asked Viviette quickly, with a new sharpness in her voice.

Mrs. Ware turned a beaming face. "Can't you guess, darling? Oh, Austin, there's no living woman whom I would sooner call my daughter. You've made me so happy."

The facile tears came, and she sat down and dried them on her little whisp of handkerchief.

"I thought it for the best to tell your mother, Austin," said Katherine, somewhat apologetically. "We were speaking of you—and—I couldn't keep it back."

Viviette, white-lipped and dazed, looked at Austin, Katherine, and Dick in turns.   She said, in the high-pitched voice, to Austin :

"Have you asked Katherine to marry you?"

"Yes," he replied, not quite so confidently, and avoiding her glance—"and she has done me the honour of accepting me."

Katherine held out a conciliatory hand to Viviette. "Won't you congratulate me, dear?"

"And Austin, too," said Mrs. Ware.

But Viviette lost control of herself. "I'll congratulate nobody," she cried shrilly. She burned with a sense of intolerable outrage. Only a few hours before she had been befooled into believing herself to be the mistress of the destinies of two men. Both had offered her their love. Both had kissed her. The memory lashed her into fury. Now one of them avowed that she had been merely the object of a drunken passion, and the other came before her as the affianced husband of the woman who called herself her dearest friend.

Katherine, in deep distress, laid her hand on the girl's arm. "Why not, dear? I thought that you and Dick—in fact—I understood——"

Viviette freed herself from Katherine's touch.

"Oh, no, you didn't. You didn't understand anything. You didn't try to. You are all lying. The three of you. You have all lied, and lied, and lied to me. I tell you to your faces you have lied to me." She swung passionately to each in turn. "'Austin can never be anything to me but a friend'—how often have you said that to me? Ah—Saint Nitouche! And you"—to Austin—"how dared you insult me this morning? And you—how have you dared to insult me all the time. You've lied—the whole lot of you—and I hate you all!"

Mrs. Ware had risen, scared and trembling.

"What does the girl mean? I've never heard such unladylike words in a drawing-room in my life."

Dick blundered in: "It's all my fault, mother ——"

"I've not the slightest doubt of that," returned the

old lady with asperity. " But what Austin and Katherine have to do with it I can't imagine."

The servant opened the door.

" Lord Banstead."

He entered a cold, strange silence. Every one had forgotten him. He must have attributed the ungenial atmosphere to his own lateness—it was half-past eight —for he made penitent apology to Mrs. Ware. Austin greeted him coldly. Dick nodded absently from the other side of the room. Viviette, with a sweeping glance of defiance at the assembled family, held herself very erect, and with hard eyes and quivering lips came straight to the young fellow.

" Lord Banstead," she said. " You have asked me four times to marry you. Did you mean it, or were you lying too ? "

Banstead's pallid cheeks flushed. He was overcome with confusion.

" Of course I meant it—meant to ask you again to-day—ask you now."

" Then I will marry you."

Dick strode forward, and, catching her by the wrist, swung her away from Banstead, his face aflame with sudden passion.

" No, by God, you shan't ! "

Banstead retreated a few paces, scared out of his life. Mrs. Ware sought Austin's protecting arm.

" What does all this mean ? I don't understand it."

Austin led her to the door. " I'll see nothing un-pleasant happens, dear. You had better go and tell them to keep back dinner yet a few minutes."

His voice and authority soothed her, and she left the room, casting a terrified glance at Dick standing threateningly over Lord Banstead, who had muttered something about Viviette being free to do as she liked.

"She can do what she likes, but, by God! she shan't marry you."

"I'm of age," declared Viviette fiercely. "I marry whom I choose."

"Of course she can," said Banstead. "Are you taking leave of your senses?"

"How dare you ask a pure girl to marry you?" cried Dick furiously. "You, who have come straight here from——"

Banstead found some spirit. "Shut up, Ware," he interrupted. "Play the game. You've no right to say that."

"I have the right," cried Dick.

"Hush!" said Austin, interposing. "There's no need to prolong this painful discussion. To-morrow—as Viviette's guardian——"

"To-morrow?" Dick shouted. "Where shall I be to-morrow? Away from here—unable to defend her—unable to say a word."

"If you said a thousand words," said Viviette, "they wouldn't make an atom of difference. Lord Banstead has asked me to marry him. I have accepted him openly. What dare you say to it?"

"Yes," said Banstead. "She has made no bones about it. I've asked her five times. Now she accepts me. What have you to say to it?"

"I say she shan't marry you," said Dick, glaring at the other.

"Steady, steady, Dick," said Austin warningly. But Dick shook his warning angrily aside, and Austin saw that, once again that day, Dick was desperate.

"Not while I live shall she marry you. Don't I know your infernal beastly life?"

"Now, look here," said Banstead, at bay. "What the deuce have you got to do with my affairs ? "

"Everything. Do you think she loves you, cares for you, honours you, respects you ? "

Viviette faced him with blazing eyes.

"I do," she said defiantly.

"It's a lie," cried Dick. "It's you that are lying now. Heaven and earth ! I've suffered enough to-day—I thought I had been through hell—but it's nothing to this. She loves me—do you hear me ?—me—me—me—and I can't marry her—and I don't care a damn who knows the reason."

"Stop, man," said Austin.

"Let me be. She shall know the truth. Every one shall know the truth. At any rate, it will save her from this."

"I will do it quietly, later, Dick."

"Let me be, I tell you," said Dick, with great clumsy, passionate gesture. "Let's have no more lies." He turned to Viviette. "You wrote me a letter. You said you loved me—would marry me—come out to Vancouver—the words made me drunk with happiness—at first. You saw me. I refused your love and your offer. I said I didn't love you. I lied. I said I couldn't marry you. It was the truth. I can't. But love you ! Oh, my God ! My God ! There were flames of hell in my heart—but couldn't you see the love shining through ? "

"Don't, Dick, don't," cried Katherine.

"I will," he exclaimed wildly. "I'll tell her why I can't marry any woman. I tried to murder Austin this afternoon ! "

Katherine closed her eyes. She had guessed it.

303

But Viviette, with parted lips and white cheeks, groped her way backwards to a chair, without shifting her terror-stricken gaze from Dick; and sitting, she gripped the arms of the chair.

There was a moment of tense silence. Banstead at last relieved his feelings with a gasping, " Well, I'm damned ! "

Dick continued :

" It was jealousy—mad jealousy—this afternoon—in the armoury—the mock duel—one of the pistols was loaded. I loaded it—first, in order to kill him out of hand—then I thought of the duel—he would have his chance—either he would kill me or I would kill him. Mine happened to be loaded. It missed fire. It was only the infinite mercy of God that I didn't kill him. He found it out. He has forgiven me. He's worth fifty millions of me. But my hands are red with his blood, and I can't touch your pure garments. They would stain them red—and I should see red again before my eyes some day. A man like me is not fit to marry any woman. A murderer is beyond the pale. So I said I didn't love her to save her from the know-ledge of this horror. And now I'm going to the other side of the world to work out my salvation—but she shall know that a man loves her with all his soul, and would go through any torment and renunciation for her sake—and, knowing that, she can't go and throw herself away on a man unworthy of her. After what I've told you, will you marry this man ? "

Still looking at him, motionless, she whispered, " No."

" I say ! " exclaimed Banstead. " I think——"

Austin checked further speech. Dick looked haggardly round the room.

"There. Now you all know. I'm not fit to be under the same roof with you. Good-bye."

He slouched in his heavy way to the door, but Viviette sprang from her chair and planted herself in his path.

"No. You shan't go. Do you think I have nothing to say?"

"Say what you like," said Dick sadly. "Nothing is too black for me. Curse me, if you will."

She laughed, and shook her head. "Do you think a woman curses the man who would commit murder for the love of her?" she cried, with a strange exultation in her voice. "If I loved you before—don't you think I love you now a million times more?"

Dick fell back, thrilled with amazement.

"You love me still?" he gasped. "You don't shrink——"

"Excuse me," interrupted Banstead, crossing the room. "Does this mean that you chuck me, Miss Hastings?"

"You must release me from my promise, Lord Banstead," she said gently. "I scarcely knew what I was doing. I'm very sorry. I've not behaved well to you."

"You've treated me damned badly," said Banstead, turning on his heel. "Good-bye, everybody."

Austin, moved by compunction, tried to conciliate the angry youth, but he refused comfort. He had been made a fool of, and would stand that from nobody. He would not stay for dinner, and would not put his foot inside the house again.

"At any rate," said Austin, bidding him good-bye, "I can rely on you not to breathe a word to anyone of what you've heard this evening?"

Banstead fingered his underfed moustache.

"I may be pretty rotten, but I'm not that kind of cad," said he. And he went, not without a certain dignity.

Dick took Viviette's hand and kissed it tenderly.

"God bless you, dear. I'll remember what you've said all my life. I can go away almost happy."

"You can go away quite happy, if you like," said Viviette. "Take me with you."

"To Vancouver?"

Austin joined them. "It is impossible, dear," said he.

"I go with him to Vancouver," she said.

Dick wrung his hands. "But I daren't marry you, Viviette, I daren't, I daren't."

"Don't you see that it's impossible, Viviette?" said Austin.

"Why?"

"I've explained it to Dick. He has hinted it to you. You're scarcely old enough to understand, my dear. It is the risk you run."

"Such men as I can't marry," said Dick loyally. "You don't understand. Austin is right. The risk is too great."

She laughed in superb contempt.

"The risk? Do you think I'm such a fool as not to understand? Do you think, after what I've said, that I'm a child? Risk? What is life or love worth without risk? When a woman loves a fierce man she takes the risk of his fierceness. It's her joy. I'll take the risk, and it will be a bond between us."

Austin implored her to listen to reason. She swept his arguments aside.

"God forbid. I'll listen to love," she cried. "And

306

if ever a man wanted love, it's Dick. Reason! Come, Dick, let us leave this god and goddess of reason alone. I've got something to say which only you can hear."

She dragged him in a bewildered state of mind to the door which she held open. She was absolute mistress of the situation. She motioned to Dick to precede her, and he obeyed, like a man in a dream. On the threshold she paused, and flashed defiance at Austin, who appeared to her splendid scorn but a small, narrow-natured man.

"You can say and think what you like, you two. You are civilized people—and I suppose you love in a civilized way according to reason. I'm a primitive woman, and Dick's a primitive man—and, thank God! we understand each other, and love each other as primitive people do."

She slammed the door, and in another moment was caught in Dick's great arms.

"What do you want to say that only I can hear?" he asked after a while.

"This," she said. "I want you to love me strongly and fiercely for ever and ever—and I'll be a great wife to you—and, if I fail—if I am ever wanton, as I have been to-day—for I have been wanton—and all that has happened has been my fault—if ever I play fast and loose with your love again—I want you to kill me. Promise!"

She looked at him with glowing eyes. All the big man's heart melted into pity. He took her face in both his hands as tenderly as he would have touched a prize rose bloom.

"Thank God, you're still a child, dear," he said.

Printed in the United States
30096LVS00002B/72

9 780766 184565